MW00618160

PENGUIN BOOKS

WHAT REALLY HAPPENED

BANAPHOOL is the pen name of the Bengali author, playwright and poet Balai Chand Mukhopadhyay. Born in Bihar in 1899, he began writing as a teenager and under the pseudonym Banaphool ('wild flower' in Bengali) to hide his work from his tutors. He is most noted for his short vignettes, often just one page long, but his body of work spanned sixty-five years and included numerous poems, short stories, novels, plays and essays. In addition to his literary works, he was also a physician and practised medicine throughout his life. He died in 1979.

ARUNAVA SINHA is an Internet professional by day and a translator of classic and contemporary fiction by late night. His published translations include Sankar's *Chowringhee* (2007) and *The Middleman* (2009), Buddhadeva Bose's *My Kind of Girl* (2009), Moti Nandy's *Striker Stopper* (2010), Dibyendu Palit's *Illicit* (2010) and Sirshendu Mukhopadhyay's *There Was No One at the Bus Stop* (2010). Born and educated in Kolkata, he now lives in New Delhi.

What Really Happened

Stories

BANAPHOOL

Translated from the Bengali by

ARUNAVA SINHA

PENGUIN BOOKS

PENGUIN BOOKS

Published by the Penguin Group

Penguin Books India Pvt. Ltd, 11 Community Centre, Panchsheel Park,
New Delhi 110 017, India

Penguin Group (USA) Inc., 375 Hudson Street, New York, New York
10014, USA

Penguin Group (Canada), 90 Eglinton Avenue East, Suite 700, Toronto,
Ontario, M4P 2Y3, Canada (a division of Pearson Penguin Canada Inc.)

Penguin Books Ltd, 80 Strand, London WC2R 0RL, England

Penguin Ireland, 25 St Stephen's Green, Dublin 2, Ireland (a division of
Penguin Books Ltd)

Penguin Group (Australia), 250 Camberwell Road, Camberwell,
Victoria 3124, Australia (a division of Pearson Australia Group Pty Ltd)

Penguin Group (NZ), 67 Apollo Drive, Rosedale, North Shore 0632,
New Zealand (a division of Pearson New Zealand Ltd)

Penguin Group (South Africa) (Pty) Ltd, 24 Sturdee Avenue, Rosebank,
Johannesburg 2196, South Africa

Penguin Books Ltd, Registered Offices: 80 Strand, London WC2R 0RL, England

First published by Penguin Books India 2010

Typeset in Sabon by Guru Typograph Technology, Dwarka, New Delhi
Printed at Replika Press Pvt. Ltd, Sonipat

Contents

Translator's Note

WHEN HE WASN'T IN HIS DISPENSARY OR AT A PATIENT'S bedside, Dr Balai Chand Mukhopadhyay could have chosen to spend his time with his family, or contemplating nature, or keeping himself abreast of the latest developments in medicine, as physicians and pathologists are expected to do. Instead, he chose to be one of Bengal's most prolific writers, under the pen name 'Banaphool'.

By the time he died in 1979, at the grand old age of eighty, he had written 586 short stories, sixty novels, five plays, numerous essays, several thousand poems and his autobiography. He was also a painter, a skill that is clearly discernible in his writing, where he would distil the unique from the everyday to imbue his characters with compassion and humanity.

Of all his works, Banaphool is best-known for his short stories. They are unique for many reasons, but most of all for their length—or the lack thereof. For Banaphool was the pioneer—and, arguably, the best practitioner—of the 'short short story'. He wrote as many as 125 stories that are less than a page in length, some no more than a couple of paragraphs. Another 161 are only slightly longer, each just shy of two pages. While other writers might barely have started describing the setting or introduced the principal characters or, at best, concluded a dramatic opening statement, Banaphool would have finished and moved on to his next tale.

From the very first sentence his stories cut to the heart of the matter, plunging the reader into the world of his characters without expending paragraphs on background, atmosphere or characterization. In the space of a few paragraphs, he revealed hidden absurdities about human relationships or unlikely connections between situations and people, and even managed to tie up loose ends with nonchalant ease—not for him the open-ended narrative! Only the focused eye of an artist combined with the precision of the scalpel-wielding surgeon could produce such rich stories so economically.

Banaphool is known to have published close to 600 stories—who knows how many more he wrote? The writers he has been compared to—O. Henry, Chekhov and Guy de Maupassant—produced far fewer. It is now accepted that it was Banaphool's scientific temper that enabled him to scrutinize people with the same detached accuracy with which Dr Mukhopadhyay tracked their pulse and fever. But that cannot account for the sheer range of his oeuvre in terms of both content and genre—realistic but also fantastic; naturalistic as well as symbolic; gritty and fabulous; empirical yet surreal. Such was his versatility.

Banaphool didn't write to delight people. He wrote so that people could discover the things that they can be delighted by. His incomparable stories are sure to find readers everywhere, in every generation.

ARUNAVA SINHA

What Really Happened

I WAS ALONE IN MY HOSTEL ROOM IN THE AFTERNOON. Everyone else was in college, but I wasn't. Tapati had promised to visit. I was waiting for her, the door locked. Vidyapati, Jaydev, Chandidas, Rabindranath—none of them made any sense. Only her face and her eyes did.

. . . Footsteps on the staircase. There was a knock on the door. I opened the door with beating heart. A loutish man with a moustache stood outside.

'Are you the one who wrote this letter to Tapu?'

He pulled out my pink letter from his pocket.

'Yes. Who are you . . .?'

'I am Tapu's father. Rascal!'

He slapped me. I fell. He left. I stayed on the floor. Do you know what I did as I lay there? I constructed a second Taj Mahal. I made a mausoleum for the love I had never found, would never find. The artwork on this mausoleum was exquisite too. But alas, no one would ever get to see it, for I was not Emperor Shahjahan, I was the impoverished clerk Haran Bose's son Bijon Bose.

What Always Happens

THE FOUR-YEAR-OLD ABHI WAS SUBSERVIENT TO NO ONE. He drank his milk only after making hundreds of demands and throwing several tantrums. He had to be coaxed and cajoled into putting on his clothes. He needed a lot of entreaties, a lot of baits, a lot of hugs before he agreed. Then his grandmother tried to comb his hair, to which too there was great opposition. He simply refused to let his freedom be encroached on. He insisted on doing things his own way. After it was all done, he climbed on to his rocking horse and said, 'Giddyap! Giddyap! I'm going to be late getting to work.'

Everyone laughed.

Abhi's father had a job. He had been hurrying since morning, asking for his breakfast. He rushed through the semblance of a bath, and then gobbled the piping hot meal of rice and vegetables laid out for him. Getting through that somehow, he proceeded to put on his coat, trousers and tie before the mirror, making all kinds of strange faces. And he kept berating his wife unnecessarily, demanding various things. Then he shouted at the servant, 'Tell Ram Singh to get the car ready, I'm going to be late getting to work.'

He rushed out.

No one laughed.

What Never Happens

PEOPLE REFERRED TO HABU AND GOBU AS TWIN SOULS. Indeed they were. They lived in the same village. They went to the same village school. Even when they moved from their village to a town, they went to the same school. They lived in the same room in the same hostel. Theirs may not have been a blood relationship, but it was one of entwined hearts. They used to eat the same things at the hostel. After classes, both of them went to Rajen-babu's shop for four luchis and two jilipis each. Both had a knack for football, both played as defenders, both were good players. That was when they had earned the epithet of twin souls.

They had such similar tastes that they even wore shirts with the same print. A certain red-striped fabric you could get those days was what both used for their high-neck jackets. Both loved marbles. On holidays, both of them went off to fly kites of identical colours, using identical reels. You didn't see such similarity too often.

When they passed their final school examinations, both turned out to have passed in the third division. They didn't bother to get their mark sheets, or else they would probably have found that they had received identical marks too. After that performance, they weren't excited about going to college. Their town had no colleges—even if it had had any, their marks would not have been good enough. It was beyond their dreams to join a college in another town. Eventually, they had to get jobs.

Their classmate Ramlakshman Dhandhania had a press. Both of them got jobs there. They even got a place to stay

3

behind the press. They did their own cooking. Habu was the cook. Boiled rice and vegetables for lunch, daal and roti for dinner. Life went on. Sporting identical haircuts, wearing identical clothes and shoes, they lived in contentment. They worked side-by-side at the press all day, slept side-by-side in the same bed at night.

One day, the owner of the press—Ramlakshman's father—took Gobu along with him to Calcutta to buy some raw material. Gobu was in Calcutta for seven days. Habu hated it. He didn't have a moment of comfort till Gobu returned. He became very anxious on reading about a bus accident in Calcutta. He ran to Ramlakshman, asking, 'Gobu wasn't on the bus, was he? They had also gone to Burrabazar, after all.' Ramlakshman burst out laughing. Habu was a little dismayed by his response. 'Can't sleep nights?' Ramlakshman asked. Indeed he hadn't been sleeping. But he couldn't possibly admit it. He looked away.

Returning after seven days, Gobu said, 'See what I've got for you. Try it on . . .' It was a cheap ring—imitation jewellery, of course—but the stone on the ring was a lovely blue.

'I got you one too . . . I'll try mine on after you try on yours . . .'

Habu also pulled out a ring with a blue stone. And it fit Gobu perfectly. Their rings on their fingers, they smiled at each other. Suddenly Habu's eyes filled with tears. 'Are you crying? Why?' Gobu tried to laugh, but soon his eyes had tears too.

Really, how alike they were. You hardly ever saw anything like this. Not just their appearances, but their minds were in tune too. Each of them knew what went on in the other's mind—decent, obscene, everything. Neither hid any secrets from the other. At least, Habu was under the impression he knew everything about Gobu.

But about a year later, he realized there was something about Gobu that he did not know. He knew that Gobu was in love with a girl in the neighborhood. That Gobu had contracted gonorrhoea was not unknown to him either. But he would never have got to know that Gobu had bought a lottery ticket when in Calcutta. However, when the newspapers ran the news that Gobindo Sarkar, aka Gobu, had won the first prize in the lottery, becoming the owner of several lakhs of rupees, it no longer remained a secret.

Gobu left for Calcutta as soon as the news came out. Habu was amazed. What was this! 'You must have bought a ticket too,' said Ramlakshman, 'but Gobu was luckier . . .'

'I didn't buy one . . .'

'But the two of you have always been in tune. You do everything together. Why should I believe you if you say you didn't buy a ticket? Just admit that you aren't as lucky as he is . . .'

'I didn't buy a ticket . . .'

'I don't believe you.'

What happened a month or two later was even more incredible. Habu received a letter. From Gobu.

Dear Habu,

Come as soon as you get this letter. I've bought a high-quality press with the winnings. You and I will be joint owners. The deed needs your signature too. Half the money I won is yours. Don't be late. I cannot eat the stuff the restaurants here serve. I'm dying for the meals you cook. We'll have the same boiled rice with vegetables and daal and roti here too. You'll cook. I can't stomach any other kind of food. Come as soon as you get this letter. See the address below.

Yours,
Gobu.

What Could Happen

'MRS MITRA, YOU'RE LATE TODAY AS WELL. IT'S PAST 11.30 . . .' Mrs Mitra looked abashed. Then she smiled her lovely smile, saying, 'I'm really very sorry about this, Mr Lahiri. But my mother-in-law has been ill for some time. The doctor is inevitably late. So . . .'

Mr Lahiri was a stern IAS officer. Pursing his lips, he said, 'Really? I'm sorry to hear that. But still I have to tell you that you cannot be so late. How will anything get done if you're not here on time? So many files piled up . . .'

'I'll finish all the pending work today, I will.'

'Very well. By the way, why do *you* have to wait for the doctor? Isn't there anyone else at home?'

'No. My husband's been transferred to Siliguri, you see. There's just a maid, besides myself. The doctor says my mother-in-law's got typhoid.'

'You really should engage a nurse.'

'We can't afford to, sir. It costs twenty-five rupees a day. As it is, the doctor's fees and medicines already add up to fifteen rupees a day.'

'Get her admitted to a hospital then.'

'It isn't easy to get a hospital bed. Besides, she doesn't want to be hospitalized.'

'I see. Well, do get on with those pending files now.'

As soon as Mrs Mitra sat down at her desk, Manoranjan appeared. He used to be her classmate. They had taken their MA exams together. There was another, far from irrelevant, fact. Manoranjan was also in love with Mrs Mitra. He'd been suffering from this romantic fever from the time they'd been students together. He hadn't been cured yet. The handsome, powerful Manoranjan didn't need to work for a living. He was the only son of a wealthy father. But as soon as he heard that Mrs Mitra had got a job here, he pulled strings to get a job in the same place. He worked as a petty clerk on a paltry salary. The authorities had not expected to be able to hire someone with a first-class MA degree in English Literature on a salary of just a hundred rupees. They had hired him instantly.

Manoranjan had proposed marriage when they were still in university. He met every criterion except one—his caste could not match hers.

Mrs Sushila Mitra belonged to an orthodox family. She didn't want to oppose her parents. It was on their instructions that Miss Ghosh had become Mrs Mitra. Not too long ago—it had been just six months. She had started working even before her marriage, continuing afterwards. Her husband Baldeb Mitra had asked her to give up her job. But Sushila Mitra had not. She had sensed that her husband's income would not be enough for them. Running a household on two hundred and fifty rupees when prices were rising every day would be impossible. So she hadn't resigned. But Baldeb was unhappy. And then he was suddenly transferred. He was even more annoyed at not being able to take Sushila along. His mother said, 'I'll stay with my daughter-in-law. I don't want to leave my home.' But she had been ill for the past few days. Sushila did feel it would be better not to go to work and stay with her mother-in-law instead. But she couldn't get leave of absence. Her boss berated her even for being late.

However, Sushila's biggest problem was Manoranjan. If he'd been the nasty type, she could have told him off. But she knew he was one in a million. Although she hadn't been able to accept his proposal, he hadn't let her go. 'Whatever happens,' he kept saying, 'I'll always be with you.' He hadn't said it in as many words, but that's what his behaviour suggested.

That day he said, 'Let's share those pending files—they'll get done today. That's not a concern. What I'm saying is, go ahead and get a nurse for your mother-in-law. Don't fret about the expenses.'

'I have to. That's why I haven't been able to afford a nurse.'

'I'll pay . . .'

'Why should I take your money?'

'You would have if we'd been married. Just because we're not, do I have to be a stranger? Don't you believe I care for you?'

Sushila lowered her head in an attempt to hide her embarrassment.

Then she said, 'There's another side to it. What will my husband think if I take your money?'

'Why should he think of it badly? Don't friends help one another when in trouble?'

Smiling her lovely smile, Sushila said, 'If the friend in question is a handsome young man like you, people are bound to read more into it.'

There was an extremely stubborn, unrelenting personality lurking within Manoranjan. This personality had made him perform many incredible feats in the past—swimming across a river in full flood, downing huge amounts of dessert after an enormous meal. That personality suddenly asserted itself.

'I *shall* help you,' he said.

'You can't. I simply won't take your money.'

'You have to.'

She was even more late in getting back home that day. The sight that confronted her had her extremely worried.

In the throes of a fever, her mother-in-law had fallen off her bed. She had been unconscious since then. 'Concussion,' said the doctor.

She died the next day.

After the last rites, Baldeb told Sushila, 'While my mother lay dying, you were pen-pushing in office. All that is over and done with. Now I'm telling you clearly—leave the job, or leave me. You can't keep sailing on two boats . . .'

What happened after this?

Here's what could have happened:

1. Sushila said, 'I cannot leave my job, I'd rather leave you . . .'

2. Sushila left her job. They barely survived on one salary. Suddenly something dramatic happened. A letter arrived by registered post. Sushila opened it to find a will. Manoranjan had committed suicide, leaving her his estate of two-and-a-half-lakh rupees. But Sushila didn't accept the money for herself. She used it to set up the Manoranjan School.

3. Sushila didn't give up her job. A few days later, her husband Baldeb was grateful that she hadn't. For both his hands were injured in a bus-accident and had to be amputated.

Actually, none of this happened.

Things went on just as before. Baldeb and Sushila had frequent rows over her decision to continue working. But despite that, Sushila didn't resign. She didn't leave her husband either. Manoranjan didn't leave Sushila. The classic example of Platonic love, he kept hanging around her. This out-of-tune triangular song kept playing. Nothing dramatic happened.

Conjugal Dreams

1

SUDHIR ARRIVED WITH A BOUQUET OF FLOWERS. A SMILE suffused his face. His heart seemed to want to spread its wings and fly.

'Hashi, I have some good news,' he said on entering. 'What'll you give me for it? I won't tell you if you won't.'

Hashi said, 'Tell me.'

'What'll you give me?'

'What can I possibly give you? All right, I'll embroider your handkerchief. I've found a lovely pattern.'

'No, not acceptable.'

'Then what do you want? Chocolate? I have some.'

'Am I a child to be fobbed off with chocolate?'

Hashi smiled. 'I don't want to hear the news, then,' she said. 'I offered to embroider your handkerchief, offered you chocolate, but since you'll have none of it . . .'

'I'm off, then.'

'You simply will not tell me?' Hashi called after him.

'I can tell you if you give me what I had asked for the other day,' he said, smiling meaningfully at Hashi.

Hashi controlled herself in sudden confusion. 'I've told you I can't.'

But when she looked at Sudhir she was afraid. She heard him say, 'I'd meant to laugh about it. But that was not possible. Forgive me. I've heard your wedding's been arranged with that fellow from Santragachhi.'

Sudhir left.

'Just a minute, Sudhir-da!'
Sudhir didn't return.

2

Alaka arrived.

The same Alaka for whose evening visits Ajay would wait all day, hoping to catch a glimpse of her.

'Ajay-da, is "pate" an English word?' Alaka was saying.

'Yes, it refers to the top of the head.'

'Really?'

'Check the dictionary. "Pate" means the head.'

'So Baruna-di was right.'

Ajay said, 'Tell me another word for the brain.'

'Head?' Alaka blinked.

'The head is a part of the body.'

'So's the brain.'

Ajay smiled and said, 'So that's how well you know the language. How can the head and the brain be the same?'

'What's the difference?' Alaka smiled too.

'In that case there's no difference between you and that stupid girl who washes clothes. Both are women, after all,' Ajay dead-panned.

'And who is this stupid girl who washes clothes?' asked Alaka.

'The washerman's daughter at the end of your lane. A young girl—about your age.'

Alaka smiled obliquely. 'Ajay-da seems to be observing things very closely these days. Even the washerman's daughter has not gone unnoticed.'

'Of course! Don't you have to verify the quality of your belongings?'

'Who belongs to you?'

'There *is* someone.'

Alaka suddenly began arranging her desk, distractedly.
Ajay looked out the window for no apparent reason.

3

The two of them dreamt their separate dreams.
The two of them lay intimately entwined.
Hashi's hand was on Ajay's breast.
Ajay and Hashi. Husband and wife.

Sunanda

SUNANDA APPEARED BEFORE THE LIFT AT FIVE TO TEN. Offering a formidable salute, the liftman opened the door for her. In a couple of minutes she stood before her office cabin on the first floor, where the bearer offered another huge salute and parted the curtains for her. Settling down in her chair, Sunanda glanced at the office clock. Entering the cabin, the bearer switched on the fan. The gust blew some papers off the desk. The bearer scrambled to gather them from the floor and put them back on the desk, placing a paperweight to hold them down. Sunanda was astonished at the sight of the paperweight—a beautiful marble-inlaid piece of art. But this wasn't here before—all she had was the standard office-issue disc. Where did this one come from?

'Where did this paperweight come from?'

'Chandar-babu changed it . . .'

Chandrakanta Ghosh was Sunanda's private secretary.

The clock struck ten.

'Tell Chandra-babu I'm looking for him.'

The bearer left.

Returning in a few minutes, he said, 'Chandar-babu isn't here yet.'

Sunanda glanced at the clock once more.

'All right, inform him as soon as he arrives.'

The bearer left. Sunanda sat for a few minutes, biting her lower lip.

Sunanda Debi had a dark complexion, small, brow-less eyes, and a face like a featureless, lumpy fruit. But she was very well educated, with an MA and a PhD. She had done

13

much of her considerable academic research work in London and the US, which was why she had had no trouble securing a job on her return to India. She had made it to a high post strictly on her own merit. She came from a poor family, with ten siblings. If it hadn't been for a scholarship, she wouldn't even have been able to get through school and college. She had gone abroad, too, on a government grant. Majestic in her self-earned glory, she had now taken on the entire responsibility for her family.

Sunanda began clearing the files on her desk. When she was through, she glanced at the clock again. It was almost ten thirty. Chandra-babu was nowhere in sight. Incredible!

Chandrakanta finally walked in with a hangdog expression well after ten thirty.

'Just take a look at the time . . .'

Looking guilty, he said, 'I know I'm late again. My wife's not feeling well. We had to go to the doctor. . .'

'You're lying,' said Sunanda sharply. 'I know perfectly well you're not married. Your father is hunting for a bride for you. He wants the princess *and* half the kingdom for his clerk of a son. I have all the information.'

Chandrakanta seemed to die of shame. His eyes dropped, while his face looked like a lump of soggy bread.

'Where did this paperweight come from?'

'It's my personal paperweight, I got it for your use. The one here was really ugly . . .'

'Please take your paperweight back. The paperweight provided by the office will do just fine for me. What's that you're carrying?'

After a few moments of silence, Chandrakanta's murmur could barely be heard. 'Cashewnuts.'

'Cashewnuts? You plan to munch on cashewnuts during office hours?'

'I got them for you. I believe you love cashewnuts . . .'

Sunanda was speechless for a while. Then her nostrils flared, while flames seemed to emanate from the corners of her eyes.

'What does this mean? Get out! I'm suspending you with immediate effect. How dare you remain—leave now . . .'

Chandrakanta Ghosh burst into tears. Taking a step forward, he prostrated himself at Sunanda's feet melodramatically, saying, 'I'm helpless, forgive me, forgive me this time . . .'

Whether Sunanda forgave him or not remained a mystery, for she woke up almost immediately, stung by a bedbug. Her horrible life suddenly lay fully revealed. The same stinking bed, dirty walls, the sleeping figures of her half-naked brothers and sisters, the horrible stench from the drain outside. Her mother could be heard speaking.

'Wake up quick, Suni! Turn on the stove. Your father has to eat before he goes to office, it's Monday.'

She recalled that Chandrakanta Ghosh had come with an entourage to consider her as a prospective bride. She recalled how her father had fawned on them. She recalled that nearly ten rupees had been spent buying snacks for them. But Chandrakanta had not approved her. She recalled everything.

Her father was speaking.

'Make sure Suni's dressed up for the evening. Ramtaran Mitra from the office is coming over . . .'

Sunanda had been good at her studies, always topping her class. She had passed her matriculation exams in the first class. But her father didn't let her continue.

Sunanda rose. She left through the back door. She didn't return. You may have seen her photograph in the Missing Persons column in the newspaper, or you may not have.

The Master and the Servant

1

THE WIFE IS VISITING HER PARENTS. I SHOULD BE BREATHING a sigh of relief, but cannot. The man Friday is coming in the way. The servant in whose care the wife has deposited me is extremely efficient—not a single slip in his duties, not a thing out of place, all orders being complied with unprotestingly. And yet I am on tenterhooks. I am not at ease. For the manservant is my wife's informer. His name is Arindam. And while he doesn't protest against my behaviour, he observes everything I do. Although he lives close by, he's spending the night at my home these days. Apparently his wife is visiting her parents too.

The wife-deprived servant is keeping an eye on the wife-deprived master. Where I go, when I get back home, what kind of people I meet, how spicy I want my food, how frequently my clothes are being washed, what kind of pictures the books I'm reading have—all of it is under his silent surveillance. It appears he's preparing a clandestine charge sheet, to be presented at the appropriate time as he stands by obsequiously, saying, 'All of this is the truth.'

2

Therefore I live in fear. I have to appease the man in both action and indication. His joy is mine, his sorrow finds an echo within me. I even tip him every now and then, with or without reason. But still he has the air of a CID official—I am unable to feel comfortable. I've been longing to invite someone over for dinner, but I dare not say it. We live in the boondocks—lacking even a restaurant where I could take the person out—so there's no option but to do it at home, and Arindam has to organize it all. At the dinner table, I wonder how to broach the subject. Knowingly or unknowingly, I'm sure I have committed several sins—perhaps the weight is already unbearable. I reflect on whether this too should be added.

It won't be a casual transgression, after all.

Suddenly Arindam says, 'Try the milk, please, sir. Tell me if you like it.'

Taking a sip from the bowl, I look at him. He's staring at the bowl with a severe frown. I realize I dare not praise the taste.

'Not too good,' I say.

Arindam departs to his other duties with a grave 'Hmm.' I seldom meet the moustachioed old milkman who supplies our milk, for I am a late riser. I feel a pang at the thought of the humiliation that Arindam will inevitably heap on him tomorrow morning. There isn't even time to warn him.

3

During dinner two days later, Arindam says again, 'Try the milk, please, sir.'

Sipping, I glance at him.

A delighted expression.

I have to conceal the truth. 'It's good, rather good.'

I drain the bowl. But I decide I have to get hold of the milkman tomorrow. Somehow. I have to accost him on the road when he's leaving and berate him. I cannot do that in Arindam's presence. Who knows what pact the two of them have! But I will die if I have to have such water-laced milk every day.

4

At dawn, I am thunderstruck.

It's not Mr Moustache.

A young girl is measuring out the milk on the porch, while Arindam gazes at her tenderly.

Not in the least put out by my sudden appearance, he says, 'Since you didn't like the old milkman's stuff I sacked him and appointed a new one. She's the one who supplied the milk yesterday, which you enjoyed.'

I look on in silence for a few moments.

For a few moments only.

Then I tell him gravely, 'Get some extra milk. You have to make pudding. Ruby, the hospital nurse, is having dinner here tonight.'

'Yes, sir,' Arindam says deferentially.

The Vigil

RAJEN WAS A COLLEGE STUDENT AT THE TIME, PUTTING UP at a boarding house in Bowbazar. Of all the difficulties of life as a student, the greatest was the lack of money. Because of his generosity, Rajen's father had never succeeded in becoming wealthy, making sure that he spent every penny he earned. Neighbours still remembered the way he had splurged at his daughter's wedding, entertaining the groom's party in the most lavish of ways.

As a result, he wasn't able to provide his son with money for anything other than bare necessities. Near the end of every month Rajen would frequently be penniless, turning to his friends for support. He had several well-off friends, too, who were able to lend him money. Rajen was well liked by most people, one reason being that he had inherited his father's spendthrift ways. When he had the money he spent it recklessly, taking his friends out for meals and movies. He was not a disciple of the bee or the ant—the butterfly was more his role model.

He would be in dire straits at times as a consequence, but that didn't change his nature. His friends—particularly Kumar Alokendra Moulik—would inevitably rescue him. An extremely charitable person, Moulik never demanded repayment in cash. But there was a problem. He wrote long poems, which had to be listened to with rapt attention, with their praises being sung as well. Whenever he ran out of money, Rajen had to perform this penance.

That particular day, Rajen suddenly needed a little more money than usual. His sister's father-in-law's cousin had turned up at his doorstep. The visitor was a rustic gentleman, sticking out like a sore thumb in sophisticated Calcutta. Having located Rajen's hotel after hunting high and low, he asked the doorman, 'Does Netto's son live here, my friend?' The doorman, himself a denizen of rural Bihar, said, 'No idea.' Whereupon he repeated the question to one of the boarders, who responded, 'I don't really know everyone's father's name. If you can tell me the person's own name I can let you know whether he lives here.'

'His name is Rajen. He goes to college.'

'Would that be Rajen Das?'

'Yes, that's right, Das.'

'Go straight up to the third floor in that case. He's in room number three.'

The visitor braved the stairs all the way to the third floor.

It being Sunday, Rajen was in his room. Standing at his door, the rustic relative cleared his throat loudly. Rajen saw a man of medium height, with arms reaching down to his knees, standing outside. The man had a formidable moustache, large, bloodshot eyes and a prominent lower lip.

'Is Rajen here?'

'I am Rajen.'

'Don't you know who I am?'

'I'm afraid not. Who are you?'

'I'm Botuk-Bhoirab Ghosh. Your sister's father-in-law's cousin. How could you have forgotten me? I was part of the groom's party at your sister's wedding—don't you remember me eating seventy mangoes after dinner? Remember now?'

'I do. Please come in.'

Although Rajen couldn't recognize Botuk-Bhoirab, he certainly recollected the story of the seventy mangoes.

Entering the room and settling down on Rajen's bed, Botuk-Bhoirab expressed his unhappiness again. 'Where I live, every single human being knows me. And you didn't recognize me even though we're related . . .'

'I saw you just the one time, that too five years ago. That's why . . . Whom are you visiting?'

'You.'

Rajen was surprised.

'Really? Is there something I can do for you?'

'You certainly can. Do you suppose people visit one another without reason? Those days are long gone. Everyone's got a reason these days for everything they do.'

Taken aback even more at this preamble, Rajen responded with silence.

So did Botuk-Bhoirab for a few minutes, before continuing. 'You may laugh when you hear why I'm here—after all, you young men belong to a new generation that doesn't believe in past lives and rebirth. But I do. I firmly believe that if you have any desires unfulfilled in this life, you will be reborn to fulfil them. Until all your wishes are met, you cannot transcend desire, and until you can transcend desire you will not be released. You may not believe any of this, but I do. Had my son been alive I wouldn't have had to turn to you—nor, for that matter, if I'd been rich. If I had had some money to spare I could have fulfilled my desire without leaving home. But I'm a poor man. My family survives on the earnings from a small restaurant I have outside Purulia station. There's never enough money left over for fancies and desires. But I've been wondering for years now whom to confide in. My son's gone; if he'd been alive he'd have taken care of it, I know, somehow or the other—he was such a good boy . . .'

Botuk-Bhoirab stopped suddenly. Rajen saw his mouth had fallen open, his lips quivering. But recovering soon, he resumed talking.

'I've been thinking about this for quite some time. Trouble is, it's not the kind of thing you can talk to anyone about. If you do, they'll assume the old man's become senile. Then I ran into your sister Durga at a wedding the other day—wonderful girl. She told me you live in Calcutta, gave me your address too. I was convinced you'd solve my problem. You being Netto's son, I'm assuming you're as large-hearted as he was, and since you live in Calcutta, there should be no problem . . .'

'What *is* the problem?'

'It's not a very difficult problem,' said Botuk-Bhoirab after some hesitation. 'All it needs is some cash.'

'Why don't you tell me what it is?'

'I want to eat at a well-known Western resturant. I've had all kinds of Indian food, but never the Western kind. I believe it's exquisite. I want to eat my fill once, just once.'

'I hope your eating habits aren't old-fashioned, then.'

'Not at all. I'm fine with chicken. Everyone is, these days . . .'

'There's something else, though.'

'What?'

'They won't let you in without Western clothes.'

'Fine, buy me some.'

'We have to buy some for me too—I have to go with you, don't I?'

'Of course we do. Fine, buy some clothes for both of us. Here's all the money I have—I'm just keeping enough for my train fare.'

He pulled a soiled ten-rupee note out of his pocket.

'Never mind, let me see what I can do.' The words slipped out before Rajen knew it.

He was worried, however. This was going to be an expensive affair.

'Why don't you have lunch and take a nap? I need to go out for a bit.'

Off he raced to Alokendra Moulik. He was the only hope in this crisis. If necessary Rajen would be the audience to every poem of his, whatever that might bring upon him.

The expenses came to over one hundred and fifty rupees. Botuk-Bhoirab alone ate enough for three people. He gave his suit to Rajen before leaving, saying, 'Get it altered to your size. I'm so happy. Bless you. You've proved yourself a worthy son. What can a poor, ordinary man like me wish for you? May you live long, may you be an emperor. You must visit me at Purulia, you simply must. I will give you the meal of your life. You'll come, won't you?'

'I will.'

'Yes, do. I'm going to be waiting for you.'

'All right. When we have holidays, perhaps.'

Rajen saw Botuk-Bhoirab off at the station. He wept when leaving, repeating his request through his tears, 'You must visit me, you must, you must.' Rajen eventually visited Purulia ten years later, in search of employment. A well-known local lawyer had promised to arrange an audience with the magistrate, who would decide whom to give the job to.

Although Rajen's train was due to arrive at seven in the evening, a five-hour delay because of a derailed engine meant that he arrived only at midnight. He had, however, had his dinner by then. Nor did he have much luggage. He could have spent the night at the waiting room in the station had he not decided to visit the lawyer's home to prove that he wasn't late out of choice. A job was, after all, a serious matter.

As soon as he left the station, he ran into Botuk-Bhoirab, who was elated at his visit.

'Rajen! Finally! Come to my restaurant. Here we are—how late you are, Rajen.'

Rajen spotted a well-stocked, well-done-up restaurant opposite the station.

'Come in now, let me give you dinner.'

'I can't eat a morsel now, I had dinner only a short while ago. I'll be back tomorrow. I need to meet Nilkantha-babu now, it's very urgent . . .'

'One quick visit to the restaurant?'

'Not now, tomorrow.'

But when Rajen returned the next day, Botuk-Bhoirab was nowhere to be found. Instead of the restaurant, all he could see was an empty plot of land. Nothing else.

Walking up to another shop close by, he asked, 'Can you tell me where Botuk-babu's restaurant is?'

'The restaurant wound up five years ago, when Botuk-babu died.'

'What do you mean died? I saw him last night!'

'You were mistaken,' the shopkeeper grinned.

An old man sitting nearby said, 'It may not have been a mistake. Other people have seen him too, standing by the station gate whenever a train arrives. Jatin-babu has seen him twice, Ramen once, Kalu too. You didn't know? This has been going on for five years now!'

'I've seen him too,' said the shopkeeper. 'I didn't want to scare this gentleman.'

'Botuk-Bhoirab hasn't been released,' said the old man. 'Must have some unfulfilled desire.'

Through the Binoculars

IT WAS WINTER. I SAT WITH MY BACK TO THE DECEMBER sun. Suddenly my eye was caught by something on the parapet of the house across the road. I fetched my binoculars from my room. Our winter guest, the redstart, had arrived. Like it did every year. I looked through the binoculars. The bird seemed to nod in greeting, like it did every year. It wagged its tail from side to side, like it did every year. A restless bird. Dark in colour. But as soon as it takes wing the red beneath its wings becomes visible—like a flame streaking out. That explained the name. It didn't stay on the parapet very long, quickly descending to the grass. Grabbing an insect in its beak, it flew off again. I had no idea when it would return.

The next day, a man brought a letter. Large, tentative letters on a ruled page torn out of an exercise book.

Respected sir,
    You gazed at me for a long time through your binoculars yesterday. I was standing at the upstairs window. Would you let me know why?

Parul

On questioning the man, he told me they had moved in a couple of days ago.
'How old is Parul?'
'She's nine . . .'
Needless to add it was the bird I'd been looking at; I hadn't even caught sight of Parul. But how could I possibly

tell her that I hadn't spotted someone as remarkable as her?
I had to think of her self-respect, after all. So I wrote:

> My dear Parul,
>   I was indeed looking at you. You reminded me of my
> granddaughter Tultul. She doesn't live here, but she visits us
> sometimes. I saw her in you yesterday. You must come over.
>
> Your new dadu

Dispatching the letter, it occurred to me that my
granddaughter was just like that redstart. A momentary
visitor. She came for a brief while, moved around restlessly,
charming us with a display of colours. And then she
flew back home. I gazed at her through binoculars too.
Binoculars of age.

I put the binoculars to my eyes again. I saw Parul
standing at the window. She was dressed in a shiny red
frock. She chuckled at me. So sweetly. She had a dimple
in her cheek.

Side by Side

1

I WAS FED UP OF SITTING, SLEEPING, PLAYING CARDS, MEETING friends, gossiping and so on. I had no peace. The real reason was penury. I had done everything I should have. I had passed my exams, applied for jobs everywhere, even sold insurance—all to no avail. Of course, there were still a lot of things to try out. Sometimes I wondered if I should set up a grocery shop, or a general store, or at the very least a corner shop for cigarettes, but . . . oh, these flies would drive me crazy! The instant I lay down, they settled on my eye. All these flies, and how hot it was, too! I couldn't even think peacefully for a moment. I sat up. It was very difficult to keep sitting and thinking in the middle of the afternoon. And as soon as I lay down, the flies appeared! If only I had some money, I could have sprayed some insecticide and got some peace to think things over. You must be laughing at me, thinking of me as a very analytical person.

There is no thought as simple—and yet as complicated—as the one about your livelihood. That's all I thought of, morning, noon and night. I was not thoughtful, I was thought-struck.

I made up my mind. I'd go to Calcutta. In Calcutta I'd try my very best. There was no point being stuck here in the village. If it was a store I was going to open, Calcutta was the best place for it. I might even get a job. You never know. All this time I'd only posted my applications.

27

It wasn't entirely impossible to get a job by doing the rounds of companies.

Going to Calcutta was the correct decision.

The next morning I got hold of my father's silver hookah and went out. I'd have to pawn it for some money. There was no sense in going to Calcutta without any. Don't let the silver hookah fool you into believing I'm a rich man's son. My father was a man of fine tastes, which probably explained why he hadn't left anything for me when he died. Pawning the hookah yielded about ten rupees. I had another ten already. So I got going.

2

I moved into a distant relative's home. The relationship was so complex that it was impossible to determine just what kind of relative Bikash-babu was of mine. He was my mother's niece's father-in-law's sister-in-law's nephew's brother-in-law's brother-in-law. Only some serious mathematics could bring out the precise relationship. Without getting into all that, I simply said when we met, 'Well, you know who I am, don't you?' He obviously didn't, but nevertheless said, 'It's been a long time! So, er... do you live near Bamboo Villa?'

I realized the symbolic significance. 'No, I see you don't know who I am,' I said. 'I didn't really expect you to. I live in Bankura. Actually, deep in Bankura. I am your...' I repeated the formula I had memorized from my mother and ended, '... and you are our Hemanta's brother-in-law. So many of our near and dear ones live in the bylanes of Calcutta, one never gets to meet them. So I thought of paying you a visit.'

Spotting my discoloured trunk and tattered mattress

on the porter's head, Bikash-babu asked, 'Are you planning to stay here?'

'Not too long—a couple of days only.'

'I see.'

The porter dropped his load, took his money and left.

A little later, Bikash-babu, too, got dressed, had his breakfast and left. I sat by myself. The stasis didn't last too long, however. A bunch of boys and girls of different shapes and sizes clustered around, some demanding lozenges, some asking for kites, some simply inserting their hands into my pockets without a word. Some were inordinately pleased by the mole on my ear. Only children can get so friendly in such a short time.

I was forced to leave too.

3

The last time I had come to Calcutta was ten years ago—to study. Now I couldn't find a single one among the people I knew back then. My fellow-students had all dispersed. The professors were new. The mess I used to live in had been converted into a laundry. Nobody recognized me, nor did I recognize anyone. Eventually I had to return to Bikash-babu's residence.

Three days passed this way, one after another. I met Bikash-babu briefly every morning. He was always in a rush, so as not to be late at work. He went shopping for food every morning, proceeding directly to rub oil into his body before his bath once he had handed over the provisions. Rushing through that, he kept haranguing his wife to get his food ready even as he had his bath. 'Is it ready? I'll get late. Quarter to nine already. It'll take some time to get there.' Bolting his food at lightning speed, he left. He never returned before ten o'clock, sometimes eleven o'clock, at night. So I hardly got an opportunity to strike up a friendship with him. He was a busy man. I envied him. How nice it was to go to office every morning, be busy with work all day, sleep peacefully at night. Why not take his help? Surely he could find me a job if he tried hard enough!

4

I joined him the next day.

Just as he was about to leave, I said, 'I'm coming with you too.'

'With me? Why?'

'Something to discuss. I mean . . .'

'Come along, then. Don't dawdle, I'm getting late. That bugger will turn up if I take too much time.'

I left with him immediately.

As we walked along, he asked, 'What's it about?'

'Actually . . .' I didn't know how to bring this up.

'I can't lend you any money, I'd better let you know that right away.'

'No, I don't want to borrow anything. I'll tell you in the tram.'

'I'm not taking the tram. I shall walk.'

'That's fine. So will I. How far is it?'

'Eden Gardens.'

'Your office is in Eden Gardens? What kind of office is it?'

'Who said it's an office?' Bikash-babu looked at me with a smile.

'It isn't?'

'Oh god! Do you suppose I go to office every morning?'

'Where do you go then?'

After a little hesitation, Bikash-babu said, 'I run away.'

I stared at him, speechless. He continued, 'My father had left a fixed deposit. The forty rupees I get as interest on it pays for food and clothing. I haven't got a job even after three years of constant attempts. But I have a first-class MA degree. Let's hurry, we're getting late. If that bugger turns up before me we won't get the bench.'

We walked in silence for a while. 'Don't let the cat out of the bag at home, will you?' said Bikash-babu. 'My wife thinks I'm an unpaid apprentice at some big company. I'll start earning soon. That's why she cooks for me early in the morning.'

We kept walking side by side, silently. Again he spoke. 'I run away, don't you see? Staying home with that bunch of children is intolerable. They can't stop demanding—buy me a whistle, buy me lozenges, buy me a doll! The boy next door has a new red shirt, buy me one too! My wife has her demands as well. So I simply have to get away. You see, don't you?'

Once again, a few minutes of silence followed.

Chuckling, Bikash-babu said, 'Stay at home and there's nothing but trouble, don't you see? The other night my youngest son fell down and bruised his head. He bled a lot through the nose. If I'd been at home, I'd have been forced to make a fuss and call the doctor, even if it meant borrowing money. Thank goodness I wasn't. Come on, let's walk faster. There's just the one bench in the shade of a tree at Eden Gardens—you can spend the entire day on it . . . don't you see? . . . If we're late this other bugger will occupy it . . . don't you see?'

We walked side by side at a furious pace.

That bench had better not slip out of our grasp!

The Missed Moment

1

I SAT IN SILENCE.

My wife lay at my feet. Her dishevelled hair gathered at my feet like dense darkness, her body shook with stifled sobs.

What could I say? I had no words.

Images from the past came to mind.

I remembered those days when I was in school—when my childhood hadn't ended, when the gulf between dreams and reality wasn't so vast.

My best friend at school was Toku—Trailakya. There was a history to the friendship, too. I used to live in the hostel, while Toku lived at home. Winning a scholarship at a minor village school, I joined the high school in town in Class V. That same year, Toku came to Class V after coming first in Class IV of the same school. A shy, fair boy. The teachers egged both of us on with the diligence of spectators at a bullfight.

The Second Master—at whose initiative I had joined the school—called me one day to ask, 'You have to beat that Toku somehow. Can you do it?'

I remember nodding.

I didn't know then what material Toku was made of.

Apparently, the Third Master had told Toku in private, 'You have to beat that boy. I've heard he's clever, but however clever he might be, he's a village yokel, he's bound to be

32

weak in English. If you try, he will never be able to catch up with you.'

That Toku could have whipped me if he'd tried is something I was certain of even today. But Toku did not try. It had helped me save face with the Second Master. Toku was a poet—he started writing poetry—he didn't become one of those 'good' boys who knew their algebra and their textbooks backwards. His poetry, too, was of the kind that put in the shade the glory of my coming first. The dazzle of the newly-risen sun outshone the electric light. After burning the candle at both ends I remained the boy who came first at Manpur School, while Toku went on to become a rising star of Bengali poetry. There is no need to explain the difference, or how big it was.

2

The friendship reached a level where it could no longer be confined to school limits. Toku invited me home one day. His mother's tender affection touched my heart, but it was someone else who charmed me. Toku's sister. She was extraordinarily beautiful. I say 'extraordinarily beautiful' because I am unable to think of a suitably shining, intense, lovely term. I really have not seen anyone as beautiful. Slender of build. Incredible eyes, nose and face. Naturally wavy hair. Her complexion—that was exquisite too. Like jasmine tinged with pink. It seemed as though the imagination of a painter in a trance had suddenly come to life.

I was even more surprised by her behaviour.

She was barely ten—but her gravity astounded me. She barely spoke to me. In every gesture, action and expression she made it clear that I had absolutely nothing to do in her scheme of things. She was completely indifferent to me.

It was a definite blow to my self-esteem. I was silent. What could I have said? I remembered the day very clearly.

I was invited to Toku's quite often. Almost every Sunday. So a few exchanges were inevitable.

I remembered very well what she asked me the first day. 'So you're the one who comes first in my brother's class.'

'Yes,' I admitted.

Would you like to know her response?

'Anyone can come first by memorizing textbooks. Can you write poetry as beautiful as my brother's?'

I remembered clearing my throat in embarrassment. 'I'm not like your brother. I never wanted to be, either...'

'You never can.'

A girl of ten!

3

Four years passed in the twinkling of an eye.

I had visited Toku's place many times during those four years, but exchanged very few words with Malati, his sister. Whenever I visited, I saw her looking at herself in the mirror, or arranging her sari, or doing her hair—some such activity. She loved to keep herself well-groomed in different ways at all times. When she looked into the mirror, she seemed to be looking at her lover. She was in love with her own face. She was fully aware of her extraordinary beauty and never forgot this truth for even a moment.

As she grew older, her magnetic attraction grew in proportion. Given my freshly-aroused instincts—I don't want to waste time sermonizing—what you apprehend is just what did happen. I fell in love for the first time in my life, and that too with a girl who had not even spoken to me properly, whose behaviour and conversation constantly reflected nothing but disregard for me. Strange are the ways of love! I belonged to a compatible family, I had a bit of a reputation as a 'good boy'. Had Malati offered the slightest of assurance, we could have been married. But she didn't offer any. One day, I remembered, we found ourselves alone—I was stammering as a prelude to telling her what was in my heart. Seeing the state I had worked myself into, she smiled. 'I know what you're going to say. But don't. Have you ever seen yourself in the mirror?'

She went out with those words. I remember pacing around the playing field at school for hours that evening. I also remember that despite that harsh blow, I felt no disgust for Malati. On the contrary, I actually took her side when arguing with myself. A woman whose own beauty she could be proud of was bound to be proud of it. Pride was an ornament for beauty. Only dedicated pursuit and sacrifice could get one within reach of a woman's heart . . . And so many more similar arguments!

I didn't get any more time, however. That was the year of my final school examination—after taking my exam I went home. There was no pretext for going back to Manpur in hurry.

4

Four more years went by.

Many a storm swept over my life—both my parents died. I didn't have anyone to call my own any more. I was living a lonely life in a mess in Calcutta. I hadn't forgotten Malati. I hadn't because I couldn't. I had, however, long given up any hope of getting her.

Toku wrote to me sometimes.

He was so absorbed in literature that he hadn't even bothered to pass his final school examination. And yet how easy it would have been for him. Toku's father died too.

They weren't very well off to begin with, but things became worse. One day I got a letter from Toku, asking me to look for a suitable match for Malati. Whatever else he lacked, the groom should be handsome, for Malati had steadfastly rejected two suitable matches because of their dark complexions. 'I'll look for a suitable match,' I replied. 'I do have someone in mind, but he's not particularly handsome. Malati won't approve. I can approach them if you like.'

I waited expectantly.

There was no reply.

5

Some more time went by.

I was studying for my MA. Strange are the ways of the heart. One day, I suddenly discovered that Malati had, at some point unknown to me, moved away from my heart. Her place had been taken by another—Miss Mitra of the soft smile and soft words. My fellow-student. We had met in the library. Miss Mitra had approached me for help on a particular segment of Ethics. That was the beginning. The relationship became intimate gradually, just as such relationships are wont to. It wasn't as though Miss Mitra was beautiful. But I perceived such a cultured attractiveness to her, such a reserved but graceful and intelligent personality, that my heart took on bright colours. Soon I noticed I was thinking of her even in her absence, gazing at her without even realizing it, analysing which saris she looked her best in, looking at the door in anticipation of seeing her.

6

Just when my wedding with Miss Mitra had been finalized— with only a few days to go—Toku arrived at my mess.

I was stunned at what he had to say.

'How is that possible?' I asked.

'I don't know what is and what isn't, I've told you all,' he said. 'Who else will marry her now? Not taking care when lighting the stove—what an awful thing to happen. Ma asked me to see you. I don't even dare make this request to anyone else, you see!' He burst into tears suddenly.

I became very upset at seeing him cry. I tried to explain, 'How can I? I've gone a long way somewhere else. I'll explain to your mother . . .'

I went to Manpur with Toku.

7

I could hear my wife talking as she lay at my feet. 'Not for a moment do you love me—not even for a moment. You never did, you can't have. You've only given me your charity. Who wanted your charity? Why have you given me your charity? Why—why—why—why . . .?'

She kept ranting.

'Listen . . . listen to me . . . look at me now . . .'

She raised her tear-drenched face.

Anyone who had seen Malati's flawlessly beautiful face before would quake at the sight. She was grotesquely burnt. Her face had been virtually roasted when trying to light the stove.

The letter from Miss Mitra, opened, lay close by.

Inside–Outside

OUR MINDS ARE USUALLY SPLIT INTO TWO. ONE PART external, the other internal. The part that's external is polite, social, civilized. But the internal one is not always civilized and social—its habits and thinking processes are strange. The activities of the external mind make the internal one laugh at times, cry at times, and concur only occasionally. The quarrel between them is a daily affair.

Ramkishore-babu's internal mind had long been comatose. The external mind had bullied it into submission. Ramkishore-babu was a lawyer. Whether it was to fabricate witnesses for murder cases, or to destroy poor subjects of rich landowners, or to give advice for forging wills, he had made use of his external, applied mind. The internal mind had initially protested loudly, creating a lot of trouble; these days it lay dormant.

That morning, Ramkishore-babu was walking around his garden, running his hand through the sparse hair on his head. A case concerning the property of a widow had been bothering him for some time. It was due to be heard in court that day, which was making him anxious and distracted.

At this time another middle-aged man appeared, greeting the lawyer and requesting his counsel. Ramkishore-babu did not know him. So he said without any diffidence, 'You do know I charge for advice on legal issues?'

'Yes, I do. How much do I have to pay?'

'Thirty-two rupees.'

'No problem.'

Entering the drawing room, they sat down.

'I have a relative, whose only son was married ten years ago,' the stranger said. 'They haven't had a child, and the chances are not bright either.'

'The husband is healthy, isn't he?'

'Oh yes, there's nothing wrong with him.'

Ramkishore-babu took a pinch of snuff. 'What would you like to consult me about?'

'What we want to know is, if there are no children, who gets the property?'

'Since the man is healthy, he can easily get re-married. There's nothing in Hindu law to prevent that,' Ramkishore-babu replied, drawing the snuff deep into his nostrils.

'True, there isn't. But can you do anything you want to just because the law doesn't forbid it?'

Ramkishore-babu smiled. 'You can't go by sentiments alone. It's our stupid sentiments that are leading us to failure.'

He delivered a short sermon on the evil effects of sentiments. The external mind provided the logic and the words to go with it. The internal mind was silent.

The stranger asked, 'But what if they don't get him married to anyone else? Who inherits the property in that case?'

Ramkishore-babu reeled off the names of relatives who, according to the law, could be the inheritors.

In conclusion, he did not give up the opportunity to add his own opinion. 'Get the boy to marry again. How can an infertile wife bring happiness? A family without children is a crematorium. Look, I'm just telling you what I think is right—forgive me if it hurts your sentiments.'

'Not at all,' protested the stranger. 'You're a plain speaker and a genuine well-wisher of the client's—it's because we've heard as much that we've come to you.'

Paying the fee of thirty-two rupees, he left.

Four or five days later, a carriage drew up before Ramkishore-babu's residence. A young woman got off and went inside.

Ramkishore-babu was a widower. His household was run by the cook and the servants. In the middle of the afternoon there weren't too many people home, besides a young servant. Ramkishore-babu was at the courts. The young servant took the luggage in. On the trunk was emblazoned a name—Sarojini Debi.

From his behaviour, it was obvious the servant didn't know who Sarojini Debi was. On his part, he was astonished by the young woman's behaviour.

Getting her luggage placed in the veranda inside the house, Sarojini asked the servant, 'Where's sir?'

'At the courts.'

'When will he be back?'

'I don't know.'

She sat down on the trunk. An embodiment of misery.

Ramkishore-babu was astonished on his return. 'Sori! You here? Not a word in advance!'

'I can't stay there any longer.'

'Why? What's the matter?'

Ramkishore-babu was increasingly surprised by his daughter's behaviour.

'They're getting him to marry again. You've agreed too.'

'What do you mean, I've agreed?'

'They sent a stranger to gauge what you really think. Apparently you said it was best to get the man married again.'

From the background, his internal mind had grabbed Ramkishore-babu's external mind by the throat.

Robbed of the power of speech, he looked helplessly at his only daughter.

'Did you really say that, Baba?' she asked.

Gratitude

1

THE HOUSE ON WHOSE FIRST FLOOR MR ADHAR AICH LIVED was rather dilapidated. The hardware store he owned was in Burrabazar. The house was in no way proportionate to his financial muscle. Had he wanted, he could have rented a flat on Chowringhee. He had inherited a fortune from his father. And yet he chose to live in a room whose doors and windows couldn't even be shut properly. Adhar Aich was living in such austerity because of Ms Bose. Ms Bose worked with the telephone department.

He had become acquainted with Ms Bose during the mayhem over the release of a new film. Upset at being unable to buy a low-priced ticket, she was on her way back from the theatre when Adhar Aich literally fell for her.

'I'm so sorry, please forgive me. Such a rush today... Do come this way, out of the way of this mob.'

When both of them had extricated themselves, he asked, 'Did you manage to get a ticket?'

'No, all but the best tickets are sold out, they said ...'

'Wait a minute then. Let me get you a ticket.'

'Here, let me pay you for it ...'

'Later. Let me see if I can even get a ticket.'

Adhar Aich left, reappearing a short while later with two expensive tickets. 'Let's go.'

'You got the tickets?'

' I did. This way ...'

They sat next to each other on comfortable padded chairs, a fan whirring overhead, and watched the film.

Adhar Aich had skilfully extracted Ms Bose's address that very evening. After paying her a few visits, he moved into the same building. He had hesitated initially on seeing the weather-beaten, ramshackle structure, but love won out eventually, and he moved in.

Mr Adhar Aich was a Brahmo, while Ms Juthika Bose was a Christian. But in the records that are maintained by the god of love, religion is not included. They fell in love with each other, but in secret, without disclosing anything. Ms Bose met Mr Aich every single day, but he wasted every one of such opportunities with trite questions about her health, or politics, or other issues. The one thing that shone within him like a diamond in the darkness was just what he could not get himself to reveal. Ms Bose was in the same situation.

2

But one day the ice broke in an amazing manner.

Unable to wait any more, Adhar Aich decided to pour his heart out through a letter. On pale blue notepaper, he wrote:

Dear Ms Bose

By God's infinite grace we met at the theatre some time ago. The moment I saw you, I felt, here at last is the person I have been looking for all this time, in expectation of whom I have been living a lonely life . . .

Having got thus far, Mr Aich felt he wasn't doing the right thing. Tearing out the sheet, he scrunched it into a ball and flung it into the corner of the room.

The next day, however, he reflected, why not write it, after all? Why be embarrassed about proposing marriage? To find out what he had written the day before, he looked for the rolled-up ball of paper in the corner. To his utter surprise, he discovered not a blue but a pink paper pellet. He hadn't used pink notepaper! Unrolling the pellet, he read:

Dear Mr Aich

I am embarrassing myself by telling you what I am about to. But I'm going to say it anyway. You bought me a ticket to the film the other day, refusing payment. You moved into the same building as myself, despite the pains of living here. You're perpetually looking for ways to do the smallest thing for me. I understand what all this means. Any woman would. But have you not understood what lies in my heart? Do I have to spell it out? I don't mind doing that, but I'm embarrassed . . .

That was the end of the letter.

3

The next day, at his hardware store, he gave an important instruction to his clerk.

'Don't sell mousetraps any more. And buy out every mousetrap from every store nearby that sells them and put them in the godown.'

'Is the price likely to rise?' asked the clerk.

'No. I won't sell mousetraps any more. I won't let anyone else sell them either. Buy each and every mousetrap out there.'

'Yes sir.'

Then he telephoned his Hindu friend Hariprasad.

'Hello, Hari? Is that Hari? You have to do something for me. I want you to organize a puja for Ganesha. Not just any old puja either, but a lavish one. I'll pay for everything. Please order the idol immediately. They should take special care of the rat—make it nice and big. Yes, the rat. It's thanks to the rat that we're getting married. A rat ensured our letters got to each other. Ha ha ha, you're right, the cupid's arrow is now the rat's teeth. She lives in the next flat. And the house is infested with rats. Please ensure the Ganesha puja is done properly. I could have done it myself, but I'm a Brahmo, she's a Christian. Wouldn't it look odd? So we need you as a shield. There is such a thing as gratitude, after all. Order the idol rightaway—I'm sending two hundred rupees immediately. Of course you must accept the money. All right, all right . . .'

Transition

1

THE KHEJUR GUR SHONDESH TURNED TO ASHES IN MY MOUTH. Not that they weren't perfectly good.

Let me tell you the story from the beginning.

Harimohan was a wealthy man. He didn't lack for money. So I knew he wasn't going to simply die without medical attention. The finest treatment that money could buy would be available—and so it was. Two well-known, highly qualified doctors came twice a day to take care of him. Two nurses could have been engaged too—but Sarama, Harimohan's wife, refused. She took on the responsibility of nursing him herself, and her competence compelled the doctors to acknowledge that there was no negligence whatsoever. It was doubtful whether even a salaried nurse could have done as much.

The illness was a deadly one, though—tuberculosis. Harimohan kept coughing up blood, and had fever every day. Tests had revealed tuberculosis germs—there was not the slightest scope for doubt. Money would probably ensure excellent treatment, but it was unlikely to yield results. On the contrary, our recurring thought was that the final act of the play of his life was close at hand.

Harimohan was my childhood friend. We used to sit side by side in class and the intimacy that had been converted to friendship was, for some reason, still intact. It would have been natural for it not to have been so. Love between the rich and the poor is very fragile. Why it had persisted for us, I have no idea. Anyway, I used to visit him every day to inquire after his health. I had to specially go for another reason—besides his wealth and his wife, there was no one in the world Harimohan could call his own. Of course, wherever there's sugar there are ants. Plenty of ants used to circle around him too, but as soon as it was established beyond doubt that Harimohan was suffering from tuberculosis, the ants vanished—possibly in search of a different mound of sugar. I was the only one to remain. The formal relationship I had had with Sarama as a friend's wife now deepened through this route. Now I feel it would have been better if it hadn't.

2

Harimohan was coughing.

The gut-wrenching cough of tuberculosis.

When the coughing fit stopped, he said, 'The throat's a lot worse. I'm going mad with the ointment and the gargling. Why won't this cough let up?'

'It will, it will, don't panic,' I said.

'I'm not one to panic. But you know what? This continuous coughing is very annoying.' Just a few words and he was back to coughing.

Both of us remained silent for some time.

'Have you heard? They found nothing in the sputum,' said Harimohan. 'I knew they wouldn't. It's just the flu, that's all.'

Sarama entered with a cup of milk.

When his coughing fit ended, Harimohan said, 'What's that you've brought now?'

'Milk.'

'Milk! At this hour!'

'The doctors recommended it.'

'You people have to give me some respite. Didn't I just . . . ' the coughing fit began again.

Recovering, he continued. 'I had the medicine a short while ago, then the gargle, then the spray, then the fruit juice—and now milk!'

'But the doctors said if you eat well you'll recover quickly. It's only a little milk. Here you are.'

Sarama held the cup for him.

After two sips, Harimohan said, 'No more, I beg of you, I'm stuffed . . .'

'No, you must finish it. Please tell him he must.'

I requested him too.

'All right, another sip for your sake.'

He refused to have more than half a cup.

Sarama took the cup into the next room. I rose too. It was late in the evening. I had to tell Sarama something before I left. The doctors had warned me not to let Harimohan know of the fever. 'It's past nine,' I told Harimohan. 'I must be on my way. I'll come again tomorrow.'

'All right.'

Harimohan turned over on his side.

3

I went into the next room. I was transfixed at what I saw. Sarama was drinking up the remainder of the milk from Harimohan's cup. 'What are you doing?' I said.

Sarama was embarrassed at being caught. 'Nothing,' she said, red-faced.

Then, controlling herself, she said firmly, 'Since you *have* seen it, there's no point trying to pretend. Please don't tell anyone.'

'That's fine, I won't. But why're you drinking his leftover milk?'

'What's wrong with having your husband's leftovers?'

'What's wrong!'

I told her as much as I knew about how contagious tuberculosis could be. After hearing me out, she cast a pair of glittering eyes on me. 'That's all very well. But can you explain to me what use it would be for me to live on if he were to die? It would have been another matter if there were children!'

I gave her much advice, all of which she listened to with a smile, her face lowered. She didn't even bother to protest.

4

Harimohan got worse. It could no longer be kept from him that he had tuberculosis. He got to know and became alarmed. The two doctors who were looking after him became alarmed too, and called in two more doctors for consultation. The four of them decided that X-rays were needed. That, too, was done. The X-rays revealed that only one lung had been affected—the other one was still clear. Hence, treatment at a sanatorium was likely to yield results.

There was no lack of money. So Harimohan left for Dharampur immediately. Sarama went with him.

5

I didn't hear from Harimohan for a long time after that. I got some news initially through letters, but nothing more. My interest dwindled; Harimohan did not try to be in touch either. Suddenly I heard one day that Harimohan had gone to Switzerland. But no details were available. Why shouldn't he go, given how rich he was, I surmised.

I continued my clerk's life. My daily grind offered me neither the right, nor the opportunity, to aim for the stars. Harimohan had not even left an address.

6

Ten years had passed by.

I had all but forgotten Harimohan when, out of the blue, a letter arrived one day. Just two lines:

Dear Naresh,

I'm reaching Calcutta next Tuesday. Do meet me if you can.

Harimohan.

The letter had been posted in India. When had he returned? I knew nothing.

On Tuesday, I went to his house on my way back from the office. He was at home. Welcoming me elaborately, he ushered me inside. I was amazed at the way he was looking. Healthy, strong, hale and hearty—who'd have said he had ever had tuberculosis!

'You're completely recovered, aren't you?' I said.

'Yes, completely.'

He became effusive in his praise of the doctors whose medical skills had made it possible.

'You went to Switzerland, didn't you?'

'Yes.'

'What was it like?'

'Beautiful! Far prettier than you read of in books. Come on, let's go upstairs.'

We did. Harimohan started bustling about, 'Sarama, where are you, Naresh is here—get some tea and things— sit down, sit down.'

I sat down a little gingerly on the expensive sofa.

Harimohan continued, 'What have you been up to? You've changed a lot. Look at your hair—there, behind your ears! Completely grey! How can you look so old at this age! Over there youth starts at fifty, you know.'

He stressed the word 'start'.

I didn't tell him that I had developed a daily bout of fever and that the doctor was suspecting I had tuberculosis too—there was no point. All I said was, 'There's a lot of difference between them and us. And why do you forget? I've been working as a clerk since I was twenty—haven't had a moment to catch my breath.'

'So what? Do people lose weight because of working hard?' Harimohan laughed uproariously. This earth-shaking laughter was his speciality. Its force hadn't weakened at all—on the contrary, it was stronger now. I began to envy him the flowering of his health and the youthfulness of his mind. He didn't seem to have aged after turning twenty-five.

Sarama came in, bearing a plate of snacks.

I was even more amazed to see her. Could ten years change a person so much!

Sarama probably got a little uncomfortable because I was staring at her with a frown.

'Let me get the tea.'

Putting the plate of snacks on a low table in front of me, she departed. Who was this?

'I can't recognize Sarama at all!' I told Harimohan. 'She's changed so much in these ten years.'

Harimohan looked at me for a few moments. 'Yes, she's changed,' he said. 'This is a different Sarama you're seeing—not the one you knew. That Sarama died a long time ago. She had tuberculosis too. In both lungs.' After a pause, he continued, 'Eventually her intestines gave way too. I spent a lot of money, but couldn't save her.'

Both of us were silent. Finally, it was he who spoke.

'I couldn't do it—had to get married again. I searched for a girl with the same name. I'd become used to that name. The original person won't come back, but the name . . .'

He stopped. Sarama was entering with the tea. When she handed Harimohan a plate laden with food, he said, 'I can't eat all that. There's much too much there.'

Sarama said, 'The doctors said you must eat well. You're not eating at all these days. Tell your friend, will you?'

'Did you get khejur gur shondesh for Naresh?' asked Harimohan. 'He loves them.'

'Yes, I did.'

Smiling, she handed me a plate.

A Love Story, 1964

IT WAS RAINING TORRENTIALLY, THE SKY GREY. I WAS THINKING of sitting in the empty room upstairs and writing some poetry. The tree in front of the house was being serenaded by flowers in full bloom. The window offered a view of black clouds amassed on the horizon, just as described in *Meghdoot*. My entire heart . . . Suddenly the peon entered. The editor had written a letter. He wanted a short story. Preferably a love story. The poem I'd have written in that empty room upstairs wouldn't have lacked for love. Maybe I'd have written a nice love poem to my wife who cooked, washed clothes, ground the spices, brought the children up . . . But alas, the editor did not want a poem, he wanted a story. I felt a story wouldn't emerge until I had conquered the poetic itch. I shut the window. I thought I'd go upstairs and shut the windows there too to keep this rain away, or else it would be impossible to write a story. Suddenly three figures appeared in the doorway—one of them female, the other two male. The woman was young, but had no signs of being married. Of the two men, one was undoubtedly young too, while the other was older, though I couldn't quite guess how old. I don't know why, but I imagined there was an invisible love triangle here, and if I could find out its details in some way, I might get a good plot for a story.

It was the woman who spoke first.

'We heard you have a room free to rent out upstairs.'

'Well, it's not free exactly. I use it to write and read in . . .'

The older man came forward, saying politely, 'Can't you rent it out for about a week?'

'What do you need it for?'

'This is my daughter and this, my son-in-law. They've just been married legally by the marriage registrar. But since we're Hindu, it doesn't seem complete without the traditional ceremonies, especially the wedding night, you know. I do have a house, but it's packed to the rafters—refugees all over the place. Even the terrace, which has no roof, is choc-a-bloc with people. Since you're a writer, I know you'll understand. That's why we came to you. I do hope you'll agree.'

I had to agree. That was the end of the short story.

People started streaming into the house soon after.

They did leave a week later. I wasn't home when they went. I found a letter in a sealed envelope on my desk. When I opened it, I found not a letter but a cheque for a hundred rupees. I wouldn't have earned more for the story. Still, I was saddened. I hadn't given them the room for the money. I had given it . . . Sheela's face kept appearing before my eyes. My daughter Sheela had got herself an MA degree. No one would marry her because of her complexion. Nor did she get a job as there was no one to lobby with. The only thing that *was* easily available in the country was what she eventually got. She got herself a lover. One day, she left with him, without saying anything to anyone. I'd heard they'd got married. Sheela was a Brahmin's daughter, while her lover was the son of a barber. Modern law didn't come in the way of their getting married. Did they have their ritual wedding night? Where? Suddenly tears sprang to my eyes. I got up quickly and lit a cigarette.

By Jove

SUNILA WOULD HAVE BEEN BETTER NAMED SOMETHING WITH the word 'dark' in it. But in contemporary society, we try to make the unpalatable truth palatable by layering it in cream and powder. And so the girl with the burnished black complexion had a name that referred to fair-skinned people. But though she was very dark, Sunila had lovely features, and could be called beautiful. Moreover, she was well educated, her eyes radiating intelligence. She was definitely attractive. Sunila as well as her parents had been hoping for a fair-skinned, handsome, wonderful husband for her who would come into their grasp after eluding film producers, setting off sparks of envy among neighbours. And if he happened to have a high-paying job in England or Germany, that would truly be the icing on the cake.

But that didn't happen. All one's wishes never come true, do they?

Sunila married a person who was neither handsome, nor endowed with any spectacular qualities. A college graduate, all he did was pursue literature in his village home. Plump and lard-covered, he resembled a dried cow-dung cake. Tiny eyes, squat nose, potholed cheeks, swarthy complexion. However, they did possess a great deal of land—enough to feed a large joint family. They owned cows, buffaloes, ponds . . . But no car. Their home was twenty kilometres from the station. You had to take a bus and then a bullock-cart to get there. The husband's name was old-fashioned, too: Gobordhan.

Gobordhan was visiting his in-laws at Ballygunge in

Calcutta for the first time. Everyone was taken aback at the figure he cut. His dhoti ended at his knees, he had on a buttoned-up canvas coat and discoloured derby shoes. His hair was cropped close. He used neither soap nor fragrant oil or powder. He preferred toothpowder to toothpaste. He put oil on his body for half an hour every day. People were amazed by the sight of this creature.

'I'm going for a walk,' said Gobordhan.

'You can't go out dressed like that. Dress properly if you want to go out.'

'In that case, why don't you pick out the clothes I should wear. I'll dress just as you want me to.'

That was the day Sunila discovered Gobordhan used a loincloth instead of proper undergarments. Just like a wrestler.

'Oh my god! A loincloth is so vulgar. Don't put that on.'

'I don't feel comfortable using anything else.'

'Why not regular underwear?'

'No, I prefer my loincloth. No one can see it, can they?'

Gobordhon put on a stylish dhoti over his loincloth, a silk vest, a silk kurta, a state-of-the-art gold wristwatch. A diamond ring, too.

Everyone was worried when Gobordhon wasn't back even that night. Mr Goha, Mr Chukkravaarty, Major Gaga, Dr Taarafdaar and several others had come to welcome the new addition to the family. All of them were ultra-modern gentlemen in suits. There were several modern women too. Gobordhan finally returned after 10 p.m.

Dressed in nothing but his loincloth.

'What on earth!'

'They took everything. Lucky I was in a loincloth, or they'd have taken that too.'

'By Jove!' exclaimed Major Gaga in astonishment.

Wanted

THE BOUT OF MALARIA LASTED TWO MONTHS. THE LIVER expanded to fill the entire stomach—my body had wasted away. I heard the doctor had warned that I could contract a serious illness any moment, putting my life at risk. My liver would never get better.

I'd taken my matriculation exams before falling ill—after recovery I heard I'd failed. I used to secretly love a girl in the neighbourhood. She got married the other day. Her husband was far healthier than I, healthier as well as better educated. So my life was a failure in every respect. I even wondered sometimes whether it wouldn't be best to end it all. But I was always the cowardly type, so suicide wasn't possible either.

I'd heard that there is nothing completely useless on this planet. But what about me? Could I ever prove useful?

Despite my ill-health, I'd been to Calcutta to look for a job. I took my meals at a roadside restaurant. That afternoon I was on my way to meet a senior officer at a merchant firm, when I was run over by a car. I don't remember very well what happened after that.

Now I see medical students are acquiring knowledge about human physiognomy from me. They're checking all over my frail body to learn more. At least I have proved useful in some way. I'm so happy.

Needless to add, I'm dead now.

The Travelling Salesman

THE MAIN REASON FOR THE QUARREL, HOWEVER, WAS
Katyayani.

Had Bhoirob not met Hiralal the salesman at the
precise moment when Katyayani's verbal sparks fired the
gunpowder in his soul, triggering an internal war, none of
this would have happened.

Katyayani had long nurtured a desire for buying a
fancy sari.

Being jobless as he was, Bhoirob had not been able to
fulfil that economically powered desire. He attempted
to convince his wife with the conciliatory argument
that he disliked anything ostentatious and that the
country was going to the dogs because of the lust for
luxury. Therefore . . .

Although she was devoted to her husband, Katyayani
was not one to be taken in by conciliatory arguments.

She said, colourfully and incoherently, 'When you get
lockjaw from yawning, why go hunting with a gun?
If there's nothing you're capable of, why did you have to
get married?'

Potent words.

All hot and bothered, Bhoirob quickly dabbed some
hair-oil on his scalp and stormed out. The afternoon
sun was scorching. The first thing he saw was a neem
tree. Not having cleaned his teeth since morning, Bhoirob
broke off a twig.

'Toothpowder for sale—toothpowder, anyone?'

Turning round, Bhoirob saw a complete stranger with a small suitcase in his hand.

And a gentle smile on his face.

Hiralal, the travelling salesman.

Hiralal was not meant to be at this village. He was supposed to be on his way to the town, which he had been. But having nodded off in the train, he'd overshot his destination and been forced to get off at this village.

There was no train to return by before evening. So he had wandered out, despite the heat, in the hope of soliciting some business.

'Where did you spring from?' asked Bhoirob, amazed.

'I sell toothpowder, I have some very good toothpowder to offer you. It can fix anything—tooth decay, bad gums, bleeding, pus, bad breath . . . everything. Excellent toothpowder . . .'

'That's all very well, but where did you spring from? We live peaceful lives here in this village, people like you only—'

'Try it! Excellent toothpowder . . .'

Chewing on his neem twig, Bhoirob said, 'Rubbish!'

'Oh no, very good toothpowder. Do try it out,' said Hiralal, flashing a smile.

Looking at his gleaming white teeth, Bhoirob said, 'You have splendid teeth. Do you use this toothpowder?'

'Yes,' said Hiralal, widening his smile.

Spitting, Bhoirob continued to clean his teeth with the neem twig.

Needless to say, it wasn't a pleasant sight.

'Would you like a tin of this toothpowder?'

With a distorted face, Bhoirob said, 'Bugger off. You people are enemies of the nation. Peddling all the luxuries of the world and ensuring the country goes to the dogs. Got it?'

He continued to clean his teeth with the twig.

Hiralal smiled once more, displaying his beautiful teeth. 'I didn't quite get it. There's no lack of dental disease in the country, is there?'

Suddenly, an agitated Bhoirob said, 'How is that your business? Get out of this village! Your toothpowder trickery won't work here . . .'

Despite being a salesman, Hiralal was a flesh-and-blood human being. Therefore he asked, 'Are you the owner of this village?'

Although a logical query, this statement struck Bhoirob to the quick. It was a fact that he was unemployed, it was a fact that he was more or less uneducated; but it was also a fact that he was strong. He may not have been the owner of the village, but he could force this man to get out of it. It was frauds like these who were driving the short-sighted young men and women of the country mad.

It was hard enough getting enough to eat—leave alone toothpowder.

Spitting on the ground spiritedly, Bhoirob said, 'Get out of the village, I tell you!'

'Who're you to ask me to get out?'

'Get out!' Bhoirob roared.

'Oh I've seen so many Toms, Dicks and Harrys like you.'

At this, Bhoirob charged up to Hiralal and delivered a tremendous slap on his cheek.

Bhoirob's behaviour was indubitably astounding.

But something even more astounding happened after that. Hiralal lost all his teeth at the slap. His false teeth were ejected from his mouth at high speed.

Seeing an amazed Bhoirob staring at his shiny black

moustache, Hiralal smiled. 'That too. I have excellent hair-dye. Want some? Why do you want to assault me? I'm a poor man, I get by as a peddler. At this ripe old age I've lost my son . . .'

After the speechless Bhoirob could speak again, he said, 'All right, give me a tin of your toothpowder.'

The Solution

DESPITE THE BLUE OF THE SKY, THE FRAGRANCE OF THE breeze, the beauty of the flower and my name being Niharranjan, my marriage took place with a village belle from Pakragram named Khyantomoni. After a year, she gave birth to a daughter, christening her Bunchi. I had objected mildly to the name. At that, neighbours and relatives accosted me with the truth, 'Do you plan to name this dark, ugly daughter of yours Pushpamanjari? All these weird ideas of yours . . .'

She was indeed ugly. Not only was she very dark, but her eyes were also of different sizes—one small and one large. Besides, she looked like a halfwit, drooling all the time. It was true that she couldn't possibly be named Pushpamanjari.

A couple of years later.

Khyantomoni was visiting her parents with Bunchi. It was Sunday, nobody had much to do—various subjects were being discussed at the village temple. Suddenly the conversation turned to my situation.

Nripen said, 'Consider Nihar's fate. Not only a daughter, but such an ugly girl . . .'

'Honestly,' agreed Shyam Bose. 'Getting her married will be a nightmare. You'll need pots of money.'

Drawing on his hookah, Haru uncle said, 'But money isn't enough these days—people want the booty as well as beauty. Those oddly-shaped eyes have added to the problem. How you'll solve it I wish I knew . . .'

Everyone was extremely worried.

The peon arrived with a letter for me.

'Who's it from?' asked Nripen.

Finishing the letter, I said, 'From my wife—Bunchi died yesterday.'

Dependent

AFTER GETTING BERI-BERI, I HAD BEEN ADVISED A CHANGE
of air.

I'd been told that Dibakar-babu was the wise, reliable
doctor in these parts. It was him I had called, and was
listening to closely for advice.

He was saying, 'You mustn't overload yourself, eat small
amounts, eat more often if you like, but never too much
at one go. Your heart is damaged, overeating will create
trouble. One more thing—and this is most important—rest.
Physical and psychological rest. You have to rest. Avoid too
much of moving around, too much of excitement.' 'May
I read?' I asked anxiously. A faint smile appeared within
the doctor's salt-and-pepper moustache. 'It's best not to
read novels that might excite you. Stick to the simple ones.'

Then, in a short speech, he explained that excitement
makes the heart beat faster, and that it was dangerous for
a weak heart to beat fast. Apparently my heart had no
reserves of strength.

'Why bother to read, just open your window and soak in
the scenery,' he said. 'You have such a lovely view from
your house, why not just take it in? You shouldn't have
trouble passing your time.'

I realized arguing was pointless.

'May I smoke?'

'Absolutely not.'

Admonished, I remained silent.

Then I asked, 'What am I allowed to eat?'

'Everything, so long as it's light. Anything heavy will

63

cause discomfort. No oil allowed. And don't eat anything that might lead to gas. A couple of light biscuits, or toast, a little something fried—in ghee, mind you—a little tea, a little milk or an egg if you can take it, a couple of rotis . . . You can have things like these, whatever suits you. You'll have to work it out for yourself. It's difficult to tell offhand what kind of food will suit each person. Someone will be bloated by a slice of cucumber, while someone else will be fine even after an entire cup of milk. Just two things to watch out for—don't overeat, and avoid gas. You'll be fine. Avoid rice.'

'What about medication?'

'Of course there will be medication. Pass me a piece of paper, please.'

Taking a spectacle-case out of his pocket, he put on a thick-rimmed pair of glasses. I passed him the pad on the desk.

The doctor filled two sheets with a list of medicines. Two mixtures—one anti-flatulent and the other to boost the heart. A powder to stimulate the bowels, to be taken every night if required. A patent medicine with Vitamin B, for use twice a day. Besides these, I'd have to take four injections a week—one being 50cc of glucose and the other three, of calcium. Once the calcium injections ended, he would start a course of Vitamin B injections, which were apparently excellent for the beri-beri heart. In addition, he prescribed a third mixture with brandy and other ingredients, one dose of which had to be taken in case the heart seemed to be collapsing at any point of time.

Having listed the medication, the doctor said, 'Your blood pressure needs to be measured twice a day. We'll need to have the diastolic pressure and the pulse pressure checked every morning and evening . . .'

'All right.'

Putting his glasses back in their case, he said, 'One more thing, avoid the east wind. The east wind, I have no idea why, affects the heart.'

'All right, I won't expose myself to the east wind.'

Putting his spectacle case in his pocket, the doctor said, 'All right, I'll be off then. Nothing more to worry about—cheer up.'

Smiling, he clapped me on the back and left.

I was relieved to have found a reliable doctor away from home.

That night, I seemed to be having difficulty breathing.

I realized my heart was creating problems. So was my conscience. I'd probably had too much pudding at dinner, I'd smoked a cigarette, and besides, the novel I was reading was a raw, realistic work of Joyce's, without any punctuation whatsoever.

You couldn't blame the heart.

Since I'd been lying down, I was forced to sit up. I sat quietly for some time, hoping it would go away on its own. But even after some time, it did not. It was the dead of night—suddenly, I began to feel scared. I woke my wife, who was sleeping next to me. Shobha sat up hurriedly and started fanning me. She was convinced that fanning cured all illnesses.

But when there was no improvement even after the fanning went on for some time, I said, 'Tell Bhanu to call Dibakar-babu again.'

Bhanu was my brother—he'd accompanied us. He was in the next room.

He left immediately on his bicycle.

Shobha said, 'Why not have the medicine with the brandy that the doctor prescribed? Shall I get it?'

'All right.'

I downed a dose.

Shobha resumed her fanning.

A little later, for whatever reason, I felt better. I had no more difficulty breathing—I was able to lie down. I began to wonder whether I should send the servant with a message for the doctor, telling him not to come. What was the use of paying his fee twice over? He'd been round only a few hours ago.

Bhanu entered.

'Dibakar-babu just passed away.'

'What! How?'

'The civil surgeon said he had a heart attack.'

I sat up.

Shobha started fanning me again.

The Story of the Postcard

'WHY DID YOU WRITE TO ME ON A POSTCARD? IT'S very embarrassing.'

'Why should it be embarrassing? It's a letter to my own wife, not someone else's.'

'Rani's husband writes to her. Such beautiful envelopes, coloured notepaper, so sweetly scented. Such long letters in green ink—I saw them.'

'So what? You think writing long letters in coloured envelopes is the way to show more love? I hinted at many things on that postcard. Maybe you didn't get them. Read it once more . . .'

The husband and the wife were talking to each other in the dead of night. The young wife took the postcard out of the trunk to read it once more.

'Dearest, you probably think I'm far away from you. It's true Dumka is a long way from home. But the truth is that I'm with you. You just have to look. I have to travel in search of a job, there's no choice. But I haven't found one yet. Even if I don't, I'm getting a tray and a basket for you. They make them here. All my love. Your . . .'

'Did you like the tray and the basket?'

'I did.'

He just couldn't tell her the truth. After paying for the tray and the basket, and putting aside money for the carriage, the bus and food, he hadn't had enough left over for an envelope. With the postcard he had run out of all money. He hadn't even been able to buy himself a smoke.

Juthika

1

THE CONNECTION WAS COMPLETELY UNEXPECTED. IT WAS SHE herself who had let me know two days ago that everyone but her would be going to watch a film. She would stay at home as she did not enjoy films. This was an unbelievable opportunity, impossible to let go of. I had written to her that I would visit her at home after work. I had seen her often, she visited our home every day, but I had never got her alone, never had the opportunity. That slender girl with flirtatious eyes was a friend of my niece's. It was as a friend of my niece's that she had been introduced to me about six months ago. After that . . .

I kept glancing at the office clock, waiting for it to strike five.

2

I entered their drawing room with a beating heart. The room was dark. This was where she was supposed to be. Just as I had suggested, she seemed to have dismissed the servants on some pretext. The room was empty. Where was she? I waited in the darkness, turned to stone. Suddenly hearing the rustle of fabric and the clinking of bangles, I turned to find someone sitting on the sofa, but I couldn't see her face. I went forward.

'Juthi . . .'

Juthi didn't respond. Going a little closer, I whispered ebulliently, 'Juthi, you can't imagine how I felt not seeing you at first . . . How long have you been waiting?'

No reply. She shifted and huddled up a little more.

'Are you angry?'

Juthi was silent.

'Why don't you speak, Juthi?'

Juthi lowered her head a little. I sat down next to her. She shrank even more.

Taking her hands, I said, 'Juthi, are you angry?'

Still, Juthi didn't say anything.

'Juthi . . .'

So much was welling up in my heart, but how could I express it all! My pleas had no words. A sigh emerged. Both of us were silent. But even that seemed unbearable after a while.

'Juthi . . .'

Juthika didn't speak. A shiver seemed to run through her, but still she was silent.

'Juthi . . .'

What was the matter with Juthi? Why didn't she speak? One of her hands was held in mine. I could feel a ring on her finger. I'd never seen her wearing a ring. Turning the ring round and round, I said again in a voice throbbing with emotion, 'Juthi . . .'

Suddenly Juthi rose and left. I remained, bemused.

3

Returning home a little later, I found Juthi at our place. Unmoved on seeing me, she asked casually, 'And what makes you so late today?' Looking at her for a while, I said, 'I was stuck somewhere.' My mother went out to get me something to eat. My sister was putting her son to bed in the next room. Since Juthi was alone, I asked, 'Didn't you get my letter?'

'No, what letter? Whom did you send it through?'

'In the post. I'd asked you to wait for me alone in your drawing room. I had something to tell you. Didn't you get the letter?'

'No,' said Juthi blandly, turning the ring round and round on her finger.

Uncle

WE WERE ALL WORRIED FOR UNCLE.

None of us was actually related to him. But nor was anyone quite as close to us as he. He was much older than us. His hair and moustache had greyed, and he looked rather silly in the process. But Uncle couldn't be bothered.

Everyone in the village loved Uncle.

Except one person.

Aunt.

That morning she had turned him out of the house with a few choice blows of her broom. Beleaguered, Uncle had taken refuge in the village temple.

'What's the matter?' Madhab asked apprehensively.

Uncle was silent.

But a little later his eyes lit up with mirth. 'What can I do if the blankets are tattered?' he laughed. 'Old bedclothes are bound to get that way, aren't they?'

'Why not get new blankets then?'

'Are you boys mad? They'll do just fine this year. Where's the money anyway? Run along home, these things keep happening with us. We'll sort it out soon enough. Run along home now.'

We went away.

But not to our homes.

We went to Aunt instead.

What she said was unpleasant but true.

She had been telling Uncle about the blankets for the

71

past three years, but to no avail. She had not been able to cure his nonchalance about the state of the blankets.

'Take a look, my boys, can blankets such as these be used any more? We're heading for a terrible winter—the old bum doesn't even realize he'll be the first to die of pneumonia. If you tell him, he just smiles and says, "Manage with this for now." To hell with that smile! He's a fraud.'

The blankets were truly in dilapidated condition.

Uncle's finances had worsened considerably after the death of the zamindar of Nawabganj. He used to think very highly of Uncle for his various talents. Uncle's earnings came from the five acres of land that the zamindar had gifted him. As long as he was alive, he used to take care of all of Uncle's needs. But his son was a modern young man. He wasn't in favour of needless expenditure such as this. Full of self-respect, Uncle too had stopped frequenting the new zamindar's house.

But Aunt couldn't be bothered with such subtle issues of self-respect.

Her logic was simple: in winter, you need blankets.

We left.

After discussions, we decided we couldn't let them suffer that winter. A contribution of two rupees each would buy them new blankets.

Back at the temple, we found Uncle playing with the local boys with great gusto.

'What brings you boys back?' he asked.

'We have something to tell you.'

Uncle rose.

'What?'

Handing him twenty rupees, we said, 'Take a bus into town immediately. Buy new blankets.'

'Where'd you get the money?'

'All in good time. Take the eleven o'clock bus, you can get the blankets made and return by the evening bus. Please go.'

'What do you mean?'

'No, you must go. Those blankets will not survive another winter. You must go, do you understand?'

Forcing the notes into his hand, we went away. Looking back, we saw him still standing there—in surprise.

It was past evening.

Uncle must be back by now, we thought. We decided to find out what kind of blankets he'd got. We went towards his home.

As we came nearer, we could hear Aunt shouting. Why on earth?

As soon as we entered, Uncle said, 'Tell me, boys, don't you like it? Would you ever get such a piece for eighteen rupees?'

We found uncle with a sitar in his hands.

The Mother-in-Law

HOW DO YOU EXPLAIN FIXITY OF PURPOSE?

I saw a lovely example of it the other day. But before that, let me explain what lockjaw is. It's a condition in which one's jaw drops and does not return to its original position, keeping the mouth permanently open. This can happen during a yawn. And the victim has to stay open-mouthed till a doctor can return the jawbone to its rightful position. The medical name is dislocation of the mandible—a dire situation once it occurs.

I'd been up late with a patient, and just couldn't rub the sleep out of my eyes in the morning. Despite continuous exhortations from my wife, I was snoozing in bed.

There was a crack of lightning—or was it someone knocking on the door?

Emerging, I discovered a young woman, her head half-covered by her sari, waiting for me with an old woman. I recognized them—Nathuni's wife and mother. I had treated them before. Nathuni worked in the neighbourhood flour mill.

'What's the matter?'

The old woman was silent.

Nathuni's wife said her mother-in-law's mouth had fallen open and couldn't be closed. Looking away, she suppressed a smile.

'Really? Let me see.'

Indeed. The old woman had dislocated her jaw.

'Where's Nathuni?'

'He isn't back from the mill yet.'

'How did this happen? Was she yawning?'

'No,' said the young woman—the older one couldn't speak—'not during a yawn.'

'Well, then?'

'Just . . .'

'How can it be "just"? She must have opened her mouth for something.'

Bowing her head, the young woman made small circles on the floor with her toe. Then she spoke diffidently: 'Ma was abusing me. She had just got as far as "Whatta—" when . . .'

This time she had to cover her face to suppress her laughter.

'How long ago?'

'About half an hour . . .'

'All right, sit down. I'll fix it.'

I decided that the foul-tongued old woman should enjoy some more peace, while I completed my morning ablutions.

Setting them down in the room where I examined patients, I went inside.

I returned about an hour later.

Following standard practice, I inserted my thumbs into the old woman's mouth and, exerting considerable pressure on the lower jawbones, tugged hard. The bones fell into place with a click.

The moment I withdrew my thumbs, the old woman said, '—bitch!'

Applied Astrology

SHATRUGHNA MULLICK WAS A RENOWNED FIGURE IN HIS social circle, a circle where the only object of worship is money. Naturally, he who had this deity ruling in all its accumulated glory in the bank was the most revered of them all. Shatrughna Mullick was just such a man. His bank account was bulging at the seams. Some said millions, others, billions. Not just in Calcutta, he owned palatial homes in several cities of India. He ran several businesses—some public, some secret. Those in envy of him referred to him as a shark, while acolytes had named him Mammon. Of course he had enemies. How many of us go through life without any foes? But none of them had been able to defeat him—on the contrary, it was he who had stymied them every time. He had truly honoured the meaning of his name. Using the brute force of money, he had demolished his opponents. He had converted many rebels into slaves, transformed many dedicated government servants into misguided flatterers, purchased many a virgin's virginity, and used the lure of lucre to turn several upright young men into unscrupulous hoodlums. Hundreds of people had been forced to kowtow to his lust for money. But the one thing he had simply not been able to acquire was facial hair. Shatrughna Mullick could cultivate neither a moustache nor beard. Anyone who ran into him in the morning immediately started muttering prayers. There was even a rumour that he was a eunuch. He had not married, preferring to have his sexual needs met by fallen women. But when he felt the need for marriage in order to have offspring,

76

he heard the rumour too, and discovered that no father was willing to give his daughter's hand to him. Alarm for their daughters' fate had led most fathers to ignore the bait of unlimited wealth. Why, an impoverished relative had rejected his overtures, too. He may have found a bride had he looked beyond his caste, but Mr Mullick was beset by orthodoxy. It was not his intention to have his child born to a womb from a different caste. He was opposed to the idea of falling in love and getting married, too. Moreover, it was too much to expect that a girl from a genealogically compatible family would fall in love with him. The community he belonged to was not particularly enlightened. Women in that community were usually confined to their homes.

Even if they hadn't been confined, Shatrughna Mullick would not have cared for them. He considered such women nothing but streetwalkers. And it was impossible for him to imagine in his wildest dreams that a streetwalker could be his wife, could be the mother of his children. Which was why, for all his wealth, he was unable to find a wife. He wished to squeeze the life out of the throat of the rumour that was floating around him. But it was difficult getting to the throat of the rumour—you couldn't set a hitman to kill a rumour. So Mr Mullick was in a pickle. His friend Toton-babu told him, 'It's your lack of facial hair that's lending fuel to the rumour. Just find a way to grow a moustache. See some good doctors.' Shatrughna Mullick consulted a number of well-known doctors—the money flowing freely. He was made to apply many different medicines on his face, even take several injections. But alas, to no avail. He remained as bereft of facial hair as he ever had been. Back then, the medical sciences had not improved to the point they have now, or else the outcome might have been different.

But suddenly, an event of such magnitude occurred that Mr Mullick could no longer focus his attention on the issue of facial hair. It had to be trained elsewhere. Apparently, one Fakir Daw had threatened to disclose to the government the details of the smuggling enterprises through which Shatrughna Mullick had amassed his millions. Toton-babu had tried to silence Fakir Daw with money, but without success. Fakir had told him—let Mullick meet me in private. I will decide on my course of action thereafter. On Toton-babu's advice, Mullick consulted a renowned astrologer. The astrologer was a taciturn man, but very famous. He charged a hundred rupees for a palmistry consultation. He claimed that applied astrology was like mathematics—always precise. It's just that you had to get the math right.

He listened closely to Shatrughna Mullick's story. He scanned both of Mullick's palms carefully for a long while. He even examined the lines on his client's forehead and the soles of his feet from different angles. Then he spoke. 'Get married. All your problems will be resolved.'

'I am fully prepared to get married. But I am unable to find a match because I lack facial hair.'

'Facial hair will be taken care of.'

'Meaning?'

The astrologer was a taciturn man. 'I cannot reveal any more. Just follow my advice.'

Shatrughna Mullick couldn't have been more surprised when he visited Fakir Daw. He would probably have been less astonished had he got the pot of gold at the end of the rainbow.

'Your family's well matched for marriage with ours,' said Fakir Daw. 'Why don't you marry my daughter? In that case I will obviously not reveal anything I know about your business to anyone. Who could possibly be inclined to have their own son-in-law jailed? But I have a condition . . .'

'What condition?'

'You cannot ask to see the bride before the wedding. My daughter is completely opposed to the notion. That's why we have been unable to get a match for her all this while. Nor can you ask for her horoscope. I will not pay a dowry either, for I am a poor man . . .'

Although he furrowed his brows, Shatrughna Mullick knew he had been trapped. It was his duty to agree.

Agree he did.

When he set eyes on his bride for the first time during the exchange of garlands at the wedding, he trembled. She was endowed with both a moustache and a beard.

A Novel in Brief

1

IT WAS A DECEMBER NIGHT. BITING COLD. THERE WAS A slight drizzle. Sanjay had walked into the lane absent-mindedly. Being late in the night, it was almost deserted. Striding along, he suddenly noticed a young woman in a brightly coloured sari standing before a ramshackle house, looking at him. Her glance was timid but inviting. Sanjay paused.

2

A year later.

Sanjay was being roasted by the flames of remorse. Terrible, terrible—just how much lower could he have dragged himself? Thrown out! True, he had been drunk when he arrived. So what? You went there to get drunk anyway. The scene played itself out before his eyes repeatedly.

A dark, slim woman—the light bouncing off her anklets, her blouse, the sequins on her clothes. With the careless grace of an empress, she was showing him the door with her beautiful arm, telling him, 'If you want to behave like a drunkard, get out!' He seemed to hear the jangle of the golden bangles again—once again the armlet suspended from a ribbon of silk swung before his eyes.

The next day, Sanjay went again, his demeanour this time extremely reserved and stern. It was the deserted hour of the afternoon. The empress had changed her appearance, but still looked beautiful. An everyday blue sari, barely any make-up, a lovely smile on her thin red lips, the promise of loving shelter in her long eyelashes. Her face lit up when she saw him.

'Welcome,' she said. 'I was worried you might be too angry to come.' Sanjay took a seat silently. There was no opportunity for small talk. As soon as he settled down, she went to her sideboard with a smile and brought out a bottle and a glass, setting them on a small table in front of him. 'Here you are.'

Sanjay's lips moved, but no words emerged. Smiling, she chided him gently, 'How could you behave like that? You have to be civil when you drink.'

She poured him a drink herself, the smile still on her lips.

A frothy, clear, orange drink.

'Here you are.'

Sanjay's temples throbbed with rage.

Accepting the glass, he emptied its contents into a bin.

He didn't look back.

3

A letter came, several days later.

From her.

Don't be angry, come back.

Sanjay smiled bitterly. But decided not to go. It was best to stay away from that den of sin.

But he could not keep his vow. He went. And found out when he arrived that she had left a moment ago. She had an appointment at a rich man's farmhouse.

4

He went again the next day.

But he didn't get to see her.

He would have gone the following day too, but had to go to his hometown instead on receiving a telegram. His father had died.

He couldn't return for the next two months. But he visited her house as soon as he returned. He heard she had moved.

No one could tell him the new address.

5

Suddenly he got the address one day.

A huge house.

A huge gate.

Sanjay wasn't allowed in.

'Permission not granted,' said the gateman.

6

Two years later.

Emerging from his office, Sanjay—now a poor clerk on a salary of thirty rupees a month—saw her photo everywhere, on posters stuck on walls.

There was an incredible crowd at the cinema hall.

Multitudes of people.

Sanjay pushed through the crowds with great effort, but couldn't get tickets. The cheapest tickets were sold out.

Chuno–Punti

PUNTI WAS ON HER WAY BACK HOME AFTER FIVE YEARS. Home meaning Mohanpur village. It was from this Mohanpur that she had once been forced to run away. She had neither stolen nor killed—in fact, the reason for her fleeing her village had nothing to do with anything in the penal code. Her crime was her complexion. Moreover, she was poor and her father was dead. She had had more than a hundred would-be grooms, but none of them had felt inspired enough to select her as a bride. Punti's widowed mother had even prostrated herself at the feet of one of them, but without swaying him. It was Saratchandra Chatterjee's story all over again. Here, too, there was a rich man's son—Dhiresh, the son of a rich local moneylender. Because their genealogies were compatible for marriage, Punti's mother had broached the subject with hesitation. Dhiresh was out on a walk with his best friend Kadam, while Punti's mother was on her way to fetch water from the tank. Sensing an opportunity, she brought it up. If Dhiresh gave his consent, she was planning to throw herself at his father's feet as an entreaty. Hearing the proposal, Dhiresh raised his eyebrows. The upstart had a BSc degree.

'Have you heard of Neptune?' he asked suddenly.

'Neptune? No. I've heard of Nepal. Oh, are you talking about that crippled son of Phulu's, Nengchu? They don't live here any more . . .'

'Never mind,' interrupted Kadam. 'Dhiru's marriage has been arranged already . . .'

'Oh, I didn't know that. Can't you boys find someone for my Punti . . .'

'We'll try.'

'What was that Neptune thing all about?' asked Kadam when she had left.

'You've heard of asking for the moon? I was trying to explain that she was asking for Neptune . . .'

'What an imagination . . .'

Kadam looked at Dhiresh in adulation. 'If she'd been a little fairer I might have considered it,' said Dhiresh. 'She's got nice features, don't you think?'

Kadam responded with a wink of his left eye.

After this, local young men started hanging around Punti's home. Some would emit wolf-whistles, some play the flute, some just mill around.

Punti's mother eventually left with her late one night. She didn't inform anyone where they were going.

Five years later, Punti informed her distant cousin Chanchalkumar that she was coming to Mohanpur with her husband. Chanchalkumar should ensure that her house was cleaned and made ready. She sent two hundred rupees through a telegraphic money order for the purpose. Everyone was astonished.

Punti and her husband arrived on the appointed day. The villagers were even more astonished on seeing them. Punti was dressed fit for a queen. She was accompanied by three servants and two maids. Her husband was strikingly handsome, like a prince! Everyone was dazzled. 'Ma died a year ago,' said Punti. 'Her last wish was that we should organize a feast for everyone in the village after the annual rites. That's specially why we came . . .'

She organized a lavish feast, sparing no expense. From old to young, from the highest to the lowest caste, nobody in the village was left out. She distributed clothes and money among the poor, gave fat donations to the school and the temple. Even Dhiresh and Kadam were dumbfounded. The villagers were in raptures.

Those of her neighbours who used to make disparaging jokes about her looks now lined up to praise her beauty and her fortune without the least bit of embarrassment. The young men were ecstatic over Punti's husband. In looks and in ability, in wealth and in generosity, he seemed unparalleled. Even without being asked, he contributed dollops of cash to the football club, the amateur drama society, the religious groups. He even took part in a play with everyone—singing beautifully.

Having enchanted Mohanpur for a fortnight, they took their leave.

Bardhaman station.

'This is where you want to get off, Chuno?' said Punti.

'Yes, can I have my money now?'

'Of course. Full two hundred?'

'That's what we'd agreed to.'

'Yes, of course. Here you are.'

She gave him the money. 'The fortnight passed like a lovely dream, didn't it? If only it were true . . .'

'Can dreams ever come true? See you at the studio . . .'

Chuno, aka Chuni, got off the train.

Chunoon and Punti were both actors. They had acted as husband and wife at the village to fulfil her mother's last wish.

The train chugged along. Punti sat alone at the window of a first-class compartment, gazing at the horizon. Her hair was flying in the wind, her sari dishevelled—but she didn't pay attention, she sat in silence.

She had made a great deal of money. She had a house and a car of her own. She owned lots of clothes and jewellery. A lot of people pursued her. But . . .

A tear escaped her eye.

Second to None

1

EVERYTHING WAS PERFECT.

My boss at work and the goddess at home were favourably disposed towards me. The boss kept increasing the size of my salary, and the goddess, the size of my family. I had no one else to care for. I'd even inherited some money. I was coasting.

Probhobati, my wife, delivered one-and-a-half children a year on an average, making me the owner of six children in four years—on two occasions she had twins.

Despite this swelling in the number of subjects, we lacked for nothing. But I was suddenly made to look like an idiot.

In the fifth year, too, the wife was pregnant in the natural course of things. But it turned out not to be a simple affair this time, despite being natural. For she went and died. She had been at her parents' house in Shantipur. Although both my father-in-law and mother-in-law had passed away long ago, Probha used to go home for childbirth because my brother-in-law Binod is a doctor. Binod wrote:

A sudden attack of eclampsia killed her within three hours. There was no time to inform you. The kidneys were damaged. Shejdi has returned to Sambalpur with the children. You must have received her letter.

I had, indeed. She wrote:

What can you do? You can't fight with fate. Let your children stay with me for some time. I can't have any of my own, as

87

you know. There won't be any problems. They're well. Don't worry.

Stunned, I applied for leave. As luck would have it, my boss had been transferred, too. So my application wasn't granted.

2

I received another letter from my sister-in-law in Sambalpur. After writing about many other things, she wrote:

> Probha was a pious, fortunate woman. Her going was perfect, leaving behind her husband and children in a glowing family. But that doesn't mean your life is over. It isn't good, either, to live this way. Listen to my advice—get married again. There's a nice girl here. If you're willing, I can talk to them. I quite like her.

And so on and so forth.

After seven days of thought—in other words, after finishing off one tin of tea and five packs of cigarettes—the solution I arrived at to this age-old problem was by no means extraordinary. Part of the letter I wrote my sister-in-law read thus:

> I am not inclined to get married again. I keep thinking of Probha all the time. But, you see, the world doesn't run according to my wishes. It moves—and will continue to move—to its own rhythm. Therefore, becoming emotional may be appropriate but not logical—that's quite true. Besides, we belong to the land where they believe you shouldn't claim the fruits of your action. Moreover, since all of you feel that way, maybe I should make another attempt to keep the family together. As for approving

the bride, that's irrelevant for a second marriage. So long as you approve of her . . .

The wedding date was finalized. It would take place in Sambalpur. My sister-in-law was wise. She wrote:

I've dispatched the children to my elder sister in Lahore. It's not right to watch your father getting married.

I heaved a sigh of relief.

At the appropriate juncture, I wheedled my way to a leave of absence for a week and set off. Alone. I couldn't possibly tell anyone of this wedding, could I? On a whim, I shaved off my moustache. My ugly, fat appearance was bad enough—to turn up for my own wedding with a bushy greying moustache seemed rather out of place.

We were at the wedding hall.

So that veiled woman in bridal finery was about to become my companion. Probha had come into my life the same way once upon a time—where was she now! And now someone else was here. Who knew what her kidneys were like? Stray thoughts ran through my mind. Probha's face kept appearing before my eyes. Who knew what the children were doing now? Did the soul really survive death? This woman didn't seem to be a child, but why was she huddled like that, her face pointing at the floor? What if Probha's ghost . . . ? Get a grip now . . .

The marriage rites proceeded mechanically. The bride refused to remove her veil during the traditional exchange of glances. 'She's very shy,' said my sister-in-law. The same thing was said when we went to our room afterwards. Covering herself from head to toe, she turned on her side and went to sleep. So did I. My sister-in-law hadn't allowed a large gathering. Who wanted to celebrate a second marriage, after all? The girl, too, had no one of her own, having been brought up in someone else's family. The wedding was at my sister-in-law's house, she was virtually the groom's party too. So it wasn't much of a ceremony.

The climax came on the first night we were supposed to spend together.

Racked by anticipation as well as apprehension, I entered the room to discover Probha sitting on the bed, surrounded by my six children and a newborn in her lap. Was I dreaming?

'Shame on you. Shejdi was right, after all,' said Probha.

'What do you mean?'

'What do you suppose? Giving birth was a very painful affair this time. My mistake was to say to Shejdi that you'd suffer terribly if I were to die. "My foot!" she said. "He'll get married again in three months." "Never," I said. Then she and Binod took a bet and hatched this conspiracy. I was in Shantipur all along. I only came this evening. To discover Shejdi has won. They'd got some young man from the neighbourhood to pose as the bride to win the bet. Now pay up the hundred rupees. Shame on you! What kind of people are you men? How could you shave off that moustache?'

No words could describe my state.

The next morning I paid off the bet. Now if only the moustache would grow back!

Within and Without

RUSHING FROM THE BEDROOM INTO THE DRAWING ROOM, I sat on a stool and muttered, 'As if we have a mint at home! Making an idiot of me . . .'

Jiggling my knees, I grunted through my nose, as was my wont, and lit a cigarette.

My thoughts were interrupted suddenly.

A dignified-looking man appeared at the door, greeting me obsequiously. A pleasant smile on his lips, a sandalwood mark on his forehead, dressed in a dhoti and shirt, shod in sandals.

'What do you want?'

'I'd like to meet Hari-babu.'

'My name is Hari.'

He greeted me again, entered the room, fished a letter out of his pocket and handed it to me. It was from Jatin. He'd written:

This gentleman is an astrologer. He's asked for an introduction to my friends, which is why I've sent him to you. If you need a prediction, ask him.

I remembered meeting Jatin just the previous evening. 'I'm being hounded by this very stubborn astrologer. I've given him a letter for you simply to get him off my hands. Please don't mind . . .'

'I don't have any requirement,' I said.

He sat down on the chair near the table, and said, smiling, 'You may not, but I do.'

'Meaning?'

'I need to practise the art I've acquired. You needn't pay a penny. May I read your palm?'

I wasn't busy, nor would I have to pay him. So I agreed to try some astrology, drawing up my stool near him.

He proceeded to examine my palm. His frown got deeper and deeper. After a couple of minutes, he emitted a 'hmm'—not through his lips, but through his nose.

So did I. 'Hmmph!'

The servant appeared at the door.

'Madam's asking for you.'

Irritation! Not a moment of peace to be had!

'I'll be there in a bit.'

The astrologer applied pressure on my palm.

The servant returned.

'She wants you right away . . .'

Despite the presence of a stranger, my tongue was loosened.

'She'll drive me mad!'

Letting go of my palm, the astrologer said placidly, with a pleasant smile, 'Find out what she wants. I'll wait.'

I went.

On my return, I found the astrologer still sitting dignifiedly. He did indeed have a certain aura about him. As I was about to stretch out my palm again, he said, 'I've seen all I needed to. Tell me what you want to know.'

'The present.'

'So you're indifferent about the past and the future. All right, let me tell you about the present. About today, in fact.'

Half expecting him to say something about Malati, I was all ears.

'You have a chance of losing money today,' he said.

'Really! Anything else?'

'Want to know more? Your friends could become your enemies . . .'

'Indeed! Hmmph!'

'So it appears.'

The astrologer rose.

'I'll be back tomorrow. If today's predictions come true, we can discuss your past and your future.'

He left after profuse goodbyes.

In a huff, I proceeded to reflect, not on the astrologer, but on Malati. What a Shylock! Maybe I *had* promised in a fit of ardour last night to buy her an expensive sari today; but did that mean I *had* to buy it today! Pouting her rosy lips, she was in a huff herself. Hmmph!

The servant presented himself at the door again.

'Madam has a terrible headache—she's feverish too. She isn't going to eat anything. She's asked you to have your lunch . . .'

I realized she had wielded the ultimate weapon. I went in, returning after a while with the heartfelt realization that, never mind German medicine or the best of poetry, not even the entreaties of her father would relieve Malati of her headache. I would have to buy her her sari. I also realized that there was no point delaying the inevitable. But when I opened my drawer, my eyes popped out—my wallet was missing! The astrologer had been sitting near this very drawer. I didn't say anything to Malati—it would be useless. Being Sunday, the banks were closed—but I went out anyway. Returning in a couple of hours, I realized the astrologer's second prediction had come true, too. Jatin, Biren, Sushil, Bishu, Habul, Nanda, Paresh, Kalo—I was grievously angry with all of them. Not one of them had agreed to lend me a mere ten rupees. I had to buy the sari on credit eventually.

Call them friends! Hmmph!

A Chapter from the Ramayana

1

THE ACT.

Rama had almost lost his mind after ordering his wife Sita to spend fourteen years in the forest. 'I have perpetrated gross injustice,' he kept telling himself.

He told the family sage Vashishtha, 'Gurudev, this is injustice—gross injustice. Sita has committed no crime—she is innocent, a goddess. I have no right to punish her. I have sinned, I . . .'

Vashishtha stopped him. 'It is the Kshatriya's ethic to uphold truth, my son. You are guided by truth. In following the ethic of truth, you have been true to the calling of the Kshatriya.'

'But this is not the truth, this is a lie,' protested Rama. 'This is injustice, gurudev, this is falsification, gurudev . . .'

'Do not get agitated, my son. A king's duties are never lightly borne.'

Ramchandra paid him no heed, getting agitated nevertheless.

'I do not want a kingdom, I do not want riches, I do not care for the viewpoint of citizens—I want Sita. I want my goddess. To hell with my kingdom, to hell with my honour . . .'

Ramchandra went mad.

2

By the time actor Nakur Maiti returned home in the early hours of the morning, having played the role of

Rama, his legs were very unsteady—he was completely inebriated.

After much knocking, when his wife Harimati finally opened the door, Nakur-babu said, 'Bitch! Don't you realize I've been knocking on the door for half an hour?'

'I fell asleep,' said Harimati.

'How dare you argue?' raged Nakur.

An almighty kick followed. Mightier than Rama's.

A Funny Story

VERY CLOSELY CROPPED HAIR, THE SCALP SHOWING IN PLACES. Several layers of twine wound tightly around the head and the brow, making the veins in his temple bulge and the eyes red. The grotesqueness didn't end here. The accumulation of cough and snuff in his hairy nostrils was positively ugly, and the picture it created in combination with several days' stubble was anything but pleasant.

A baby screamed in the veranda. Another, an older girl, lay in bed inside the room—ill.

'Krittibash! Kité!'

The gentleman turned bloodshot eyes towards the door. There was no sign of Krittibash.

' Kité!' he called out again, louder.

Nobody came.

'Kité, damn you . . .' he thundered.

Waking up at his roar, the sick girl in the room started crying. A thin, continuous whine. The baby in the veranda had been crying already. Not faintly, but extremely loudly. The two different kinds of crying seemed to make the gentleman even angrier. Raising his voice to incredible levels, he started screaming furiously, 'Kité! Kité! Kité! Damn you . . .'

It paid off.

Kité didn't turn up, admittedly, but a plump woman with turmeric stains on her sari did. That was good enough. The gentleman suddenly softened, looking abashed. Without softening or looking abashed in the least, she glared at him for a few minutes, enraged. Then, one hand clamped on her waist, she brandished the other in the air, asking angrily, 'What's the matter? Why are you making such a racket?'

'The hot water . . .' the gentleman stammered.

'Hot water! Do I have ten hands!'

'But I didn't want you to work on it. Where's Kité?'

'Kité's gone to the market!'

'Didn't you send him already in the morning?'

'I've sent him again.'

'I see.'

He didn't dare say anything more. Krittibash himself arrived at the door, saying, 'Got the spices, Ma.'

As soon as Krittibash's timid eyes fastened on the gentleman's bloodshot ones, he said, 'I'll get your water right away, sir. I've put it on the stove already, must be done by now . . .'

Krittibash disappeared. The woman left, though not before administering several smacks on the back of the baby crying in the veranda, saying, 'Whine, whine, whine! This damned girl will drive me crazy!'

The crying worsened. The sick girl cried out in her thin voice, 'Terrible headache, Baba.'

Considering the aggressive mood his wife was in, the gentleman did not think it wise to ask her for anything. He checked his daughter's temperature himself. It was very high—105 degrees. Staring at the thermometer, Harihar didn't sigh. 'Turn over, don't scream,' he snarled at her.

The six-year-old girl turned over on her side.

The doorknob rattled. Opening the door, Harihar saw just what he had feared—the grocer with the bill.

'Day after tomorrow,' he said. 'I have no money today.'

The man left with a few choice words.

'Here's your water, sir.'

Turning, Harihar saw Krittibash waiting timidly with the kettle in his hand.

'Bring the bowl.'

Putting the kettle down, Krittibash left, returning with a large bowl and some cold water. Harihar mixed the hot and cold water himself, checking with his fingertips whether the temperature was right. It wasn't. He was about to add some hot water, when the sick girl began to throw up.

'Kité, take care of her . . .'

Krittibash tried to look after her. Harihar got his mix of hot and cold water just right. 'Help her lie down,' he instructed. 'After that, bring me my small table and paper and pen.'

Settling himself into a chair with broken arms, Harihar dipped his feet into the warm water for a footbath. Krittibash brought his pen, ink and a small table.

The bugs in the chair started biting. Two dogs quarrelled in the next lane. The crying in the veranda continued. His head throbbed impossibly. Pressing down on his veins with the fingertips of his left hand, Harirhar shut his eyes and tried to think. He had to write it that very day. The editor was urging him, and his own urges were even stronger. His brows furrowed, Harihar tried to work on a plot for a humorous story. It was for his humorous stories that he was famous.

Moonlight

1

THE MOONLIGHT WAS BEAUTIFUL.

The world looked unreal. My heart roamed a dreamworld like a cloud—touching everything lightly, not pausing anywhere, in no hurry to get anywhere. The current of time flowed slowly; my entire consciousness, absorbed, also floated along unhurriedly. It was late at night. I looked out the window with dreamy eyes. Suddenly the gate opened with a bang, snapping the dreamweb. A man entered, tottering. A bottle under his arm, he spoke in English. 'Excuse me, my name is Khrishthacharan Kharmakhar! I can do magic! I can swing an elephant! You see this elephant? Now watch this . . . round round round round . . .' Holding the bottle in both hands, he tried to twirl it around his head. I had to call the durwan.

Khrishthacharan Kharmakhar was thrown out by the scruff of his neck. But the dream was shattered. I just couldn't put it together again. I couldn't think of the moonlight as anything but moonlight. My mind lost its lightness, becoming dolorous again. Unseen, the Almighty probably chuckled.

2

The next day.

The night was moonlit once more. As beautiful a moonlight as the previous night. Sitting on the first floor,

I looked out the window as before, lost in fervent dreams.
My heart, adrift, seemed to be looking for someone on the
distant horizon. The line between reality and fantasy was
slowly being erased.

'Sir . . .'

Someone was calling. Not Khrishthacharan, I hoped.

If it was him again, he would be taught a lesson.

The moonlight went to hell. I was wracked by irritation
from head to toe.

'Durwan . . .'

Another servant arrived to announce that the durwan
was out shopping.

'Go, find out who's calling,' I instructed him.

Returning in a bit, he said, 'There's a man with a bottle
under his arm.'

'Tottering?'

'Yes sir.'

'Knock the scoundrel to the ground.'

In a minute, my expectations were fulfilled. There was a
sound of something heavy falling to the ground, followed
by a sharp cry. I was at peace, assuming that Khrishthacharan
had been taught a lesson. But my dream was shattered
again. That day, too, the Almighty chuckled.

3

The third night.

That night, too, moonlight flooded the sky, as I noticed
occasionally, rather glumly. The window of my cell was
very small—I couldn't even see through it clearly. There was
a dream too. But that belonged to the lawyer. The moustache-
flaunting Paresh-babu. Paresh-babu was an expert lawyer.
I wondered whether he'd succeed in getting me out. The

person whom my servant had knocked to the ground the previous night was not Khrishthacharan. It was a malaria patient. The bottle under his arm was of Edward's Tonic. A foreigner. He had probably come to seek shelter for the night. Wounded by the blow from the servant, he had died. Now Paresh-babu was my only hope. I was well neither in mind nor in body. I thought I had a fever. The Almighty smiled.

4

I was free.

Investigations had revealed that the bottle of Edward's Tonic had contained not Edward's Tonic but alcohol. Paresh-babu also proved that the man had tumbled to the ground because he was drunk, which had caused his death.

I had always hated alcohol. I was not in the least upset over the man's death. But I was rather ill. Possibly because of my time in gaol. The judge was so stern, he refused me bail.

The doctor who was looking after me entered.

That evening, too, there was moonlight.

'Look, doctor, how beautiful the moonlight is,' I said joyfully.

'There's not much of moonlight,' the doctor said in surprise.

'Enough to make me want to dance,' I said.

'How many doses of the medicine have you had?'

'All of it.'

'All? Why on earth? It had a lot of brandy.'

I didn't answer.

I was busy watching the moonlight brim over.

The Almighty laughed uproariously.

5

Ten years later.

I was bankrupt. My liver had rotted, there was fluid in the stomach.

My senses had acquired amazing perceptiveness.

I still saw moonlight in the daytime.

The Almighty was grave.

The Tailor

1

SO MUCH WORK, NOT A MOMENT'S RESPITE.

I'm irritating myself with the clacking of the sewing machine, but I don't have a choice, as I have to supply two hundred and fifty flags by tomorrow morning. The only consolation is the jingle of silver inaudible under the clacking.

Nirmal came in. I knew him, a local college student. He got all his shirts and kurtas tailored by me.

'Shishir-da, we need fifty tricolour flags for the college union,' he said.

'No time today, my boy, try somewhere else.'

'No one has any time, I've been to everyone.'

'Everyone's making flags?'

'Everyone.'

It wasn't a lie. Every single tailor in town was engaged.

'I really don't have the time. Even with four tailors at work I can't manage . . .'

'But I *have* to have them. I can pay more if you like . . .'

'It'll cost double.'

'All right.'

Nirmal agreed immediately.

I'd have to work through the night—there was no choice.

Mahatma Gandhi was due to pass through this station the next day. The entire town would be present to greet him, waving flags.

2

Two years had passed.

That day, too, there was not a moment's respite. That day, too, the constant clacking of the sewing machines was annoying me, but I was forced to tolerate it helplessly. That day, too, it was the same thing—two hundred and fifty flags to be delivered by the next morning. That day, too, Nirmal came in.

The same requirement.

'Shishir-da, we need fifty flags for the college union.'

I gave the same answer.

'No time today, my boy, try somewhere else.'

Nirmal gave the same answer as he had two years ago. 'No one has any time, I've been to everyone. You *have* to do it for us—we can pay more if you like.'

Sensing the same opportunity as last time, I demanded double the price.

As before, Nirmal agreed.

The occasion was the same as before, too—Mahatma Gandhi was due to pass through this station the next day. The entire town would be present, waving flags. Everything was the same, but with a small difference. This time the flags were not tricolour, they were black.

The Star

MINU, JITU, HARU AND FONTI WERE SLEEPING ON THE terrace that night on a sheet, under a star-studded sky. Everyone gazed at the stars. Suddenly Minu asked, 'What do you suppose they resemble?'

JITU: A bunch of white marbles on a black floor.

HARU: White beads, not marbles.

FONTI: Lousy poetic ideas. Shall I tell you?

MINU: Tell us.

FONTI: They look exactly as that fat dark nanny of ours would look if she had scabs all over her.

MINU: Ugh! Only an ugly mind like yours would have such an ugly thought.

Suren, their eldest brother, came up to the terrace.

MINU: What do the stars resemble, Bor-da?

SUREN: They look like peas scattered all over the place.

HARU: I have another image. They're celebrating Diwali there in the sky, and the daughters of the gods have lit countless lamps.

Suren was a student of science in college.

'Indeed they're lamps,' he said. 'But not tiny. Each of them is huge. Enormous balls of fire swaying in outer space . . .'

Suren explained the science behind the stars. One by one, everyone fell asleep.

Minu dreamt. A girl just her age was sitting by her, smiling.

'None of you could recognize me.'

'Who are you?'

'I'm a star. I live in your eyes.'

She disappeared into the sky like a comet. Minu woke up. She found everyone else asleep. Looking up at the sky she found countless stars there. All of them smiling at her.

The Homecoming

I was on my way home from Shimla, a couple of days before Durga Puja. I'm an insurance agent who has to travel on work. I hadn't succeeded in claiming the 'life' I'd been chasing. Someone else had grabbed it before I could. I was feeling low.

The compartment I boarded turned out to have not one but three exquisitely beautiful women. My eyes were dazzled. A young man was accompanying them. He was extremely handsome too. Being dark and stout as I am, I felt embarrassed to take a seat next to them. Yet I did. After a while, I asked the young man diffidently, 'Where to?' His eyes were glued to a film weekly—the photograph of a half-naked actress seemed to have mesmerized him.

'Where to?'

'I beg your pardon?' he asked, startled.

'I was asking where you're going.'

'Calcutta.'

'Me too. It'll be nice to travel together.'

He immersed himself in his magazine again.

The magazine had an advertisement for our company. In the hope of attracting his attention to it, I said, 'That's an ad for our company, the kind of bonus we offer . . .'

His eyes transfixed on the half-naked actress, the young man said, 'None of this stuff makes any sense to me.'

'Bonus payouts don't make sense to you! You *are* insured, aren't you?'

'Makes no sense to me. I'm looking at what does make

107

sense.' He went back to the photograph. But I wasn't about to let go easily. 'I find it hard to believe that a man of such refined taste does not understand life insurance. If you'd just spend a nominal amount every month, your life would—

'Don't bother me about money,' he interrupted. 'If you do want to discuss finances, do it with my mother.'

I greeted his mother cordially. 'It appears your son does not wish to discuss this,' I said. 'I'm sure you agree with me that life insurance is a must for everyone.'

The glow of a gentle smile spreading across her face, she said, 'I don't know much about it either. If you don't mind, would you care to explain a little more?'

'Certainly!' I began to spout our hypnotic catchwords— but, amazingly, they seemed to make no impression on her. The other two women listened to my sermon with close attention too, but remained unimpressed.

Pausing, I said, 'I hope I've been able to explain everything.'

'Oh yes, you haven't left anything unexplained,' said the first woman. 'It's just that I don't need life insurance.'

'Not you, perhaps. But your husband? Your son?'

'My husband has conquered death. Why would he need life insurance?'

At this point Ganesha poked his trunked head out of the top bunk and said in a stentorian voice, 'You people are talking too much. Do you suppose we'll get any sleep the next four days? Better get some sleep now while you can.'

My eyes popped out of my skull. I realized my error. Durga was travelling to Calcutta, her children Lakshmi, Saraswati, Kartik and Ganesha with her. Prostrating myself, I said, 'I am an imbecile, forgive me.' Smiling, Durga said, 'You have done no wrong, son. Show me your form; let me get the Calcutta pujas insured. Your sermon has charmed me.'

Amala

1

THE GROOM'S FAMILY WAS COMING TO TAKE A LOOK AT Amala. The groom's name was Arun. The very sound of his name made Amala glow. How many pictures she had painted with her imagination! Handsome, comely, young, strong, stylish hair—the perfect man.

Arun's brother Barun represented the family. Peeping at him, she thought, 'My brother-in-law.'

The visit was over. Amala had been approved. Her happiness knew no bounds when she heard. She even dreamt of him that night.

But the wedding didn't take place—the price couldn't be settled upon.

2

Some time later, it was someone else's turn. This time the groom came himself. His name was Hemchandra. Peeping from the background, Amala saw a quiet, gentle, nice-looking man—peaches-and-cream complexion, curly hair, imported glasses, very pleasant appearance.

Once again, Amala's heart went out to the stranger.

She thought—what a lot of things she thought!

This time the price was right, but the bride wasn't.

3

Finally, the bride was approved, the price was right, the wedding took place. The groom's name was Bishsheshwar.

Fat, dark, rotund—a graduate and an employee in a merchant firm.

When they set eyes on each other during the wedding, Amala's breast was suffused with such a tenderness! She was charmed by her quiet, well-mannered, uncomplicated husband.

Amala is happy.

A-B-C: A Geometric Story

1

A AND B WERE INSEPARABLE FRIENDS.

Not just that, both their lives had circular orbits. They borrowed money, they returned the loan, they borrowed again. Although their lives followed circular paths, their evening paths followed straight lines. Both of them had the same evening destination, where they spent the entire night before returning in the morning. When they did have to return the same night, however, their courses did not remain straight lines, they zig-zagged a bit.

Their debts increased.

Life lost its richness, then found it again.

A was materialistic.

B was idealistic.

B got his cash sometimes through sweet-talking, sometimes through tears, sometimes through consummate acting. When he didn't get any despite asking directly, A simply picked pockets. The materialistic A.

2

C.

The sixteen-year-old C. A's daughter. Her mother was dead. But she was yet to be married. The desire burning within her was clearly visible.

The materialistic A saw everything, understood everything, but was unable to do anything about it. No one in Bengal had a pocket deep enough to be picked to cover the dowry.

111

Both A and C sighed.

B came.

A, B and C. Not the eternal triangle. Father, father's friend and daughter.

A and B went out, taking a straight line to the spot where it was possible to be a quadrilateral.

3

The idealistic B.

Sentiments rose within, but no words flowed.

He wanted to write poetry, but no rhymes flowed.

All he could think of to rhyme with 'love' was 'shove'.

No, no, no. Life was only a series of nos.

And yet, rainbows rose—with not seven but seven hundred colours!

B's emotions welled up within him.

The days went by.

4

Two months passed.

The shehnai was being played. A melancholy Puravi Ragini wept in the evening skies. The Mitras' daughter was getting married down the road.

A—the materialistic A—was waiting at home for B. Puravi didn't charm him, the delay irked him. Why was B so late? If they were late then . . .

Half an hour passed. An hour passed.

'Swine . . .'

Angry, A left.

He went alone.

Puravi played on.

C sighed deeply.

5

A returned an hour or so later.

He returned very irritated, for he had had to come back empty-handed—the doors were already closed by the time he had reached. Back home, he was even more annoyed. Why was the door locked here as well?

He banged on the door.

Once, twice, thrice.

A bashful C opened the door.

B was sitting on the bed.

A and B looked at each other for one moment. For one moment only. Then A went out suddenly.

On his way out, he locked the door. Petrified, C told B to escape through the window.

But the iron bars.

A returned an hour later—the materialistic A.

With a priest in tow.

'Marry her, you swine, marry her.'

B agreed.

The shehnai had switched to Raga Iman.

Boy or Girl?

1

THE MATERNITY HOSPITAL.

Annakali and Namita were in the same room, on adjoining beds. Annakali was forty, Namita seventeen. Both would deliver their babies any time now.

Annakali's skin was drawn tightly across her face, making her cheekbones stand out. Her forehead was thickly veined, her eyes yellowish, her teeth jutting out, her belly huge, her limbs rickety. She was half bald. The mother of seven children, with an eighth on the way. The last time she had almost died giving birth, which was why she was in the hospital this time round, on the doctor's advice. Her husband was a clerk.

Namita was beautiful. This would be her first child. She didn't even look pregnant at first glance. She was well nourished, looking even lovelier at the hint of imminent motherhood. Her husband was a doctor. He had had her admitted to the hospital to ensure that the delivery of the child was conducted scientifically.

2

Despite the differences in age, appearance and finances, they had struck up a friendship. Initially, of course, they had started conversing in a reserved, polite and socially acceptable manner. Each of them tried to magnify what they perceived as the brightest qualities of the other person. Gradually, they started discussing their husbands and the original reserve began to disappear. By the time they had hit it off with each other, both turned out to be man-haters. Both became vociferous when it came to singing the litany of male flaws. Why, when in the full flow of things both of them now openly cited their own husbands' shortcomings as examples. Annakali's daily backache seemed to have retreated too.

That afternoon, here's how the conversation went.

ANNAKALI: Don't even talk of men; there isn't another race more selfish.

NAMITA (smiling): How they raise hell if the smallest thing isn't in place.

ANNAKALI: But of course! The head of the family can't wait to rush off to his chess game the moment he's back from office. And of course he won't be back till eleven at night, sometimes even midnight. But if a hot dinner isn't waiting for him, all hell will break lose. Is it possible to keep the food hot that late into the night? How long can the stove stay lit, after all? And if you use extra coal, that'll mean trouble too.

NAMITA: It's no different with me.

ANNAKALI: Does he have a chess addiction too?

NAMITA: No, with him it's billiards. Only after his game of billiards, his films and his friends will he get back home late at night. But how angry he gets if you don't open the door at the first knock. As though we're nothing but maids with our only responsibility being to sit by the door, waiting to open it. One night he came back to find me missing— I'd gone to a neighbour's place. What temper tantrums!

ANNAKALI: That temper is all that God's given them, no other quality. That Baikuntha-babu next door makes such a scene every day, coming back drunk. Slaps and kicks have become ornaments for both his wives.

NAMITA (eagerly): How's that?

ANNAKALI: He beats them up every day. He's built like a demon—fat, big moustache, red eyes, dark as sin. I believe he has pots of money. He'll drink every evening, call his wives into his room and lock the door. And the lock is too high for his wives to reach. Then the beating starts. He won't let up till they pass out.

NAMITA: Two wives?

ANNAKALI: Two. And he just got married again the other day in secret. Do you suppose they have any shame? In the olden days they used to have hundreds of wives, now they just can't afford to.

NAMITA (chuckling): But the longing runs deep. There's this man next door, quite old, but we can't even open the window that side thanks to him.

ANNAKALI (wrinkling her nose): Throw 'em out, I say. I'm sick of the race after all that I've seen and heard.

NAMITA: Some addiction or the other is a must.

ANNAKALI: He didn't use to, but now at this ripe old age he's taken to opium.

NAMITA: The other one's a chain-smoker.

ANNAKALI: Selfish, so selfish, all of them.

NAMITA: Every day the papers have something or the other about some scandal one of them has been involved in. Either the wife has been abducted, or she's killed herself because of her husband's torture, or the husband has murdered the wife. There's bound to be something or the other every single day.

ANNAKALI: I don't know about the papers, but I see something like that happening every day. There isn't another race so ungrateful. Take our sons—we carry them for nine months, give them the milk from our breasts for years, and then once they're married, they won't even spare us a glance. Then the wife grows stale too, after which they start looking out—selfish beasts, the whole lot.

NAMITA: Moreover, they're so full of themselves because they're the ones who earn, they never stop reminding us. But here we are playing cook, maid, attendant—no acknowledgement, no reward. You have to beg for every penny. All you get is an anna or two, but such long lectures— don't overspend, luxuries are sinful! As though they're all monks themselves!

ANNAKALI: Them? They're all turtles. They can live in water or live on land, withdraw their heads at the slightest whiff of trouble, tough shell all over, no botheration if you scream and shout. They'll poke their heads out at their own convenience, and once they've got you, you've had it. Stubborn, cowardly, obstinate—perfect turtles, all of them.

NAMITA (laughing): I'd half expected you to pick a snake—but you've chosen a lovely metaphor.

3

Late that night. It was raining incessantly. Annakali's husband Bhajahari Biswas sat in the waiting room for men, sunk in an opium haze. The continuous rain outside, the handsome young man sitting opposite him, the ticking of the clock on the wall—none of it made any impression on him. He sat with his eyes half-closed, dazed, engrossed. He was present only because of the call of duty.

The handsome young man was Dr B.K. Dutta, Namita's husband. Puffing slowly on a long pipe, he was reading with great attention an illustrated love story from a magazine named *True Love Stories*. He was also lost to the world.

In two adjoining rooms, Annakali and Namita lay on two operating tables. Both were undergoing labour pains. Both were being attended to by an obstetrician and a nurse.

Annakali was saying, 'Oh, doctor, help me, doctor, I beg of you . . .'

The nurse said, 'The pain will stop soon, my dear. When you see your son you'll forget the pain.'

The doctor smiled.

'I can't bear it any more, I can't. Call him. I'm dying. Doctor, call him quick, call him, ohhh . . .'

Namita's nurse said, 'Don't worry, it'll be over soon. Come on now, don't do that . . .'

The doctor started washing his hands with soap and water.

About an hour later, Bhajahari Biswas and Dr Dutta were informed that their babies had been born. Looking very pleased, Dutta stuffed more tobacco into his pipe. Bhajahari stared into the distance for a while, still in a haze. Then a faint smile appeared on his face.

The rain had stopped.

Both of them left for their respective homes.

A little later.

The nurse said to Annakali, 'Here you are, my dear, what a lovely daughter you have!'

Annakali's ashen face became paler still.

Casting her eyes on the newborn baby's face, she suddenly screamed, 'A daughter! I've had a daughter!'

'A daughter—lovely, plump, a headful of hair.'

'What about Namita?'

'She's had a son.'

The nurse was about to put the baby down beside Annakali when she suddenly sat up and pushed her baby daughter away.

'That isn't mine, take her away, you must have swapped the newborns.'

'What do you mean? Why would we do that?' asked the nurse in surprise.

'You must have. I can't have had a daughter; the astrologer said I'd have a son this time . . .'

Annakali's voice shook.

'This *is* your daughter . . .'

'No, she's not! I have seven daughters, I don't want another one! I haven't had a daughter, I've had a son. You've given my son to Namita because she's a doctor's wife.'

'How could we possibly do that? This *is* your daughter, take her.'

'No, I don't want a daughter, don't want, don't want . . . Bring me my son, bring me my son . . . I must have had a son.'

Annakali's screams rent the silence of the night in the hospital.

Her helpless screams.

In the next bed, Namita drew her son to herself in fear.

Dead of Night

THE TRAIN WAS LATE THAT NIGHT. PURANDAR SWITCHED ON his torch to check his watch. It was past midnight. He felt considerably distressed. Not just because of the separation, but also at the thought of the two miles of countryside he would have to tramp through late at night all alone in the dark. His in-laws weren't expecting him. He had not informed them intentionally. There was certainly a thrill to having a secret assignation with your wife. Moreover, his in-laws were rather matter-of-fact and unappreciative. All they were known for was being wealthy, and they were quietly getting wealthier still. None of them was inclined towards culture. His father-in-law was nearly sixty, but still had the appearance of a giant. He consumed a litre of buffalo milk a day, hadn't lost any of his teeth, and had created such a spectacle on his face with his moustache and sideburns that even a lion would be scared. His sons—Purandar's brothers-in-law—were following in his footsteps. All of them had studied as far as the primary school in the village allowed, devoting more of their time to body-building, wrestling and duelling with sticks. Each of them sported a large moustache. They were sizeable householders, being the owners of more than 300 acres of land. However, they didn't flaunt their wealth. They could afford a plane, but hadn't even bought a car, making do with a few bullock carts. No other vehicle could negotiate these roads anyway.

After glancing at his watch again, Purandar looked out. It was pitch dark. They were still two stations away. This was the branch line of the branch line, even the boondocks were civilized in comparison—after a couple of such straggling thoughts, Subhadra returned to the centrestage of his mind. She must be waiting for him. By the window, probably. After their marriage, it was he who had taught her the rudiments of the language in order to be able to read and write letters. How sweet her long letters were. This time Purandar had taken things further. He had written her a poem—in simple language, of course—embedding the information of his arrival, even the date and the time.

The hours just don't pass, O my lovely moon
Coming after midnight on the 28th of June.

He glanced at his watch again. When, oh when, would he be able to take Subhadra away to their own home? Surely his father would be able to get him a job once he had passed his BA exam! After all, his father had a good job himself. It was just that he simply couldn't pass his BA exam. And his father too had vowed not to get Subhadra over until he had started earning a living for himself. How much longer could he go on sneaking out of the hostel to visit his wife?

Getting off the train finally, Purandar saw it was one in the morning. He would now have to traverse two miles through a dark field. There weren't any vehicles outside the station, which meant he had no option but to walk. He had his torch, of course, besides his guiding star Subhadra. He started walking briskly.

Whether it was because he was immersed in thoughts of Subhadra or because of the impenetrability of the darkness, he hadn't an inkling of the fact that his life would soon be in danger. If he had, he would have run or screamed. By the time the stick struck his hand, forcing him to drop his torch, there was nothing to be done. For someone grabbed

him from the back and gagged him with a handkerchief
the very next minute. Then, what four of five of them did
to him was not only economically disastrous, but also
psychologically shattering. They relieved him of his watch,
his gold ring, his silk shirt and even his dhoti. Swift
of purpose and fleet of foot, they finished their task at
lightning speed and disappeared.

It wasn't a nightmare, was it? Flabbergasted and naked,
Purandar tried to console himself by embracing this notion.
Then, suddenly, he felt he was wasting time. Untying the
handkerchief with which he had been gagged, he discovered
that it was actually a rustic towel. Wrapping it round
his loins, he ran pell-mell. Why be embarrassed where
Subhadra was concerned?

She had indeed been waiting by the window, it seemed.
She responded as soon as he whispered her name. Her
eyebrows disappeared into her hairline when she saw her
husband's condition.

'What on earth!'

'I was waylaid by highway robbers. Get me a dhoti,
quick. How embarrassing! You must have fallen asleep.'

Purandar tried to regain his poise. Subhadra fetched
him the dhoti that had been hung on the clothesline in
the veranda.

About to put it on, Purandar was stunned.

'How did this dhoti get here? This is the one I was
wearing. I bought this special dhoti specifically for this visit;
sent it to the laundry just the one time, here's the stamp
of the laundry . . .'

Subhadra's smile disappeared.

'Put it on. And have your dinner. I've kept it ready . . .'

'But tell me first how this dhoti got here.'

Subhadra's expression changed. Looking around furtively,

she said softly, 'Don't make a noise now. They've all become highway robbers. The entire family. I'd only heard rumours before this, now I see it's all true. Eat up and then go to the police station.'

'What!'

'These people are dangerous, if they realize you've come to know their secret, they'll murder you. They won't stop at anything. That man who was killed two days ago— probably their doing. Go to the police station quickly. You know the way, don't you?'

'I do.'

'Then don't delay any more.'

The first thing that caught Purandar's eye at the police station left him transfixed. The watch on the wrist of the officer-in-charge was his! He even spotted the P that he had inscribed on the band. He had an impulse to shout, at the top of his voice, 'You damned thief!' But the only thing that escaped his lips was—'Your Honour.' He trembled, his palms joined in prayer.

The Eyes

MOST PEOPLE PROBABLY DIDN'T CONSIDER HER BEAUTIFUL.

It wasn't as though I considered her particularly beautiful either. But I loved her. What her eyes held I cannot tell. I'd never seen such dreamy, lovely eyes in my life. She was also infamous for being naughty.

The plain and lively Mini had stolen my heart. I was captivated by her eyes.

I remember holding her one day when we were alone. 'I wish I could steal your eyes.'

'Why?'

'I'm mad about them. I love them the most.'

I loved her so much, but I didn't get her.

A stranger came and took her away, with music and ceremony.

It hurt so much.

But the pain might have gone, had a tragic incident not occurred.

When Mini came to visit her parents' home, I discovered she was blind in both eyes. Apparently, instead of rosewater, she had applied some other medicine to her eyes.

I met her in private one day.

'Such beautiful eyes lost to carelessness,' I said.

'If you don't know why they were lost, it's best you don't,' she answered.

Rainswept

THE SKY WAS COMPLETELY OVERCAST.

Black clouds had closed in. Lightning split the heavens. The wind was picking up speed.

My mind shut down. Much of the sky was visible through the window. Lying on my stomach on the bed, I waited for the inevitable deluge, my heart overflowing. How dark it was! I took a look at the newspaper. My unease deepened. Where on earth was Kalidas?

The skies rumbled.

'Keshta! Hey, Keshta!'

Keshta, the servant, appeared. I told him, 'It's going to rain. Get a strong cup of tea, will you? Get some cigarettes too while you're at it.'

Through the window I could see the covering of dark clouds getting even darker. Kalidas was essential. No fun without Kalidas. But it was Bhajahari-babu who turned up instead. His front teeth were permanently visible. Our manager.

'There's a letter for you, Sahayram-babu.'

Giving me the letter, he left.

My sweetheart's letter. After ages. My heart seemed to flutter. The sky closed in. Opening the letter, I read it through. And again. And once more.

I grew sad, distracted. Keshta brought my tea. Sipping it, I read my sweetheart's letter for the fourth time. I became even more distraught.

125

The darkening skies made me more and more restless. The darkness was silent.

A few drops at a time, the rain began.

I glanced at my watch. It was a quarter to ten. I was frantic in body as in mind. If only . . . Never mind. From the gramophone next door, the blind singer Krishnachandra De was adding fuel to the fire: '*Ratan palank par baithal dnuhujan* . . .' They sat down together on the bed . . .

A bolt of lightning lit up the sky.

Crack!

I couldn't take it any more. The emotion welling up within simply had to be expressed in words. 'Where the hell is that rascal Kalidas?'

And immediately Kalidas rushed in, soaked to the bone.

'How hard it's raining!'

'How hard it's raining! Do you have any idea how long I've been waiting? This is why our race is going to the dogs. No sense of time. You cad! How do we get there now? No umbrella, no raincoat!'

'Got stuck in the rain,' said Kalidas defensively.

'Last day?'

'Last day.'

'Imagine missing a Greta Garbo movie.' I clucked. 'It's past ten.'

'What's that in your hand?' asked Kalidas, intent on changing the subject.

'Letter from my wife. She's got fever. So have all five of the boys. Both the girls have dysentery. Never mind. Imagine missing Greta Garbo's love scene! How can you forget that?'

I stared at the downpour in impotent rage. The music went on next door: '*Rasabhare duhnu tanu thara thara kanpayee* . . .' How your body trembles with passion . . .

Fulfilment

WHEN I LOOK BACK ON MY PAST, I AM SADDENED. IT WAS
but a happy dream. That memory of my past—it was
truly nothing but a memory now. Sometimes I feel, where
did that life I led disappear? That elegant, gorgeous,
enchanting life?

Once, my life had beauty, it had fragrance, it had
sweetness. In my days of grace, how numerous were the
honey-lusting bees that sang my praises in my ears. Where
were they now?

How enjoyable this sky, this air, this light was once.
There was a time when I was mad about them—where was
that madness now? That natural insanity, that addiction
to pleasure! Where was all that now?

Today I am ripe, experienced. The liquid senses of my
past seem to have calcified into a hard mass.

All I keep thinking is, I know my past will never come
back—but what of my future? Who knew what that would
be like! That I had put aside my joyous youth to become
ripe and experienced—where would this lead me? Where
did its fulfilment lie?

These were the thoughts of a ripe fruit hanging from a
tree. Suddenly the wind knocked it to the ground. Picking
it up in its beak, a bird flew up to a branch and started
pecking away at it with great satisfaction.

An Extremely Short Story

THE FLAME BURNED STEADILY. AS THOUGH IT WAS WAITING for someone impatiently. As though its extreme eagerness had stopped it from flickering. But it did start flickering soon. It was here—the wind was here. The flickering increased. The flame felt as though the wind was making it lose all control.

FLAME: Let me go, what do you think you're doing?

WIND: Can you live without me? Do you know what scientists have said?

FLAME: What?

WIND: That I hold a gas named oxygen. That it's oxygen which has given you form as a flame. Without me, there would be no you.

FLAME: Oh! What ARE you doing . . .?

The wind increased. The flame trembled helplessly.

Elsewhere in the room.

'What ARE you doing?'

'What a fraud! Weren't you awake just for this?'

'Let me go. The light is on, I'm embarrassed . . .'

'Turn off the light, then.'

A round, lovely face came close to the flame.

One puff—and the flame was gone.

'The wind's too strong. Shall I shut the window?'

'Do.'

The window closed with a bang.

Among Birds

I SUDDENLY NOTICED SOMETHING BLACKISH AMONG THE cluster of green leaves on the mango tree. What was it? Surprised, I discovered on a closer look that it was a cuckoo. Not one, but two. One large, one small. The larger one was an adult, the smaller a child. Both male, though they were perched beak-to-beak. What *was* going on? I was astonished.

Cuck-cuck-cuck, said the large cuckoo.

The small one was silent.

Cuck-cuck, said the large one again.

Still the small one was silent.

This went on for about ten minutes. The older one seemed to be whispering secrets to the younger one. Although the younger one was silent, he seemed to be listening in rapt attention.

Cuck-cuck-cuck, it started again, continuing for some time. The small bird shifted, then flew up to another branch. The large one joined him on it. Snuggling up. Then, again bringing his mouth closer, he said, *cuck-cuck*. It seemed to combine affection, request and entreaty all in one cry.

Eventually the small bird said, *cuck*.

The large one cried out in delight, *cuck-cuck-cuck-cuckoo-cuckoo-cuckoo*!

The sound resonated everywhere. There was a hue and cry.

Several cuckoos cried out from nearby trees. As though cheering, it's come, it's come, it's come, it's come. That's our call.

129

Suddenly I noticed a crow perched at a distance. Looking sadly at the small cuckoo. The child could not ignore the invitation behind that look. He flew up to the crow, perching next to him with its beak parted. The crow began feeding him. After his meal, the small cuckoo flew back to his tribe.

This went on every day. The mother-crow fed the child-cuckoo every day. Neither the cuckoos nor the crows objected. There's no politics among birds.

Feminine Mystique

SUMITA SWITCHED ON THE LIGHT WHEN SHE RETURNED home—only there was no light. The poor thing was distressed. Wasn't the bulb working? She didn't have a penny, and pay day was still five days away. But she couldn't do without light either. If Nabendu were here, she could have borrowed some money from him. But he didn't stay on today either. He had dropped by in the afternoon— if only she had asked him then. She did think of it but was embarrassed to ask. Why? Surely she wouldn't have had this reservation had he been her husband. There, alone in the dark, it occurred to her that she wasn't sure whether Nabendu would indeed marry her. He'd never said anything specifically, had he? Immediately she was reminded of Suren. Suren used to visit her too. His behaviour seemed to suggest he wanted her, though he too hadn't said anything explicitly.

All by herself in the gloom, Sumita felt rather helpless. She had an income, earning sixty rupees a month. But she never quite managed on that paltry salary. Films drew her, and she couldn't resist buying a nice sari when she saw one. That trinket—a piffling stone necklace—set her back by ten rupees the other day. She knew it was wrong but she just couldn't control herself. If only she hadn't bought herself that necklace, she wouldn't have been penniless near the end of the month. A companion would have made their collective income see them through the month comfortably. Sumita continued to just stand in the dark. She didn't have enough for a candle. She ate at a boarding house, paying them at one go at the beginning of the month after getting

131

her salary. The man at the general store knew her well enough to let her have cosmetics on credit occasionally— would the shop have candles? Sumita started. Someone was knocking on the door. Must be Suren. But would it be proper to invite him inside in the dark? She waited silently, without responding. But the knocking continued. Eventually she heard her name being called too.

'Sumita! Sumita! Are you asleep?'

It was Suren's voice. Sumita rose quickly, opening the door.

'Oh, it's you. I was just going out . . .'

'Where?'

'Just out . . .'

'I'll come too. I'd come to see you . . .'

They left.

'I don't have a penny, we have to walk,' said Sumita.

'I do. Let's go to the Maidan . . .'

They got into a tram. Sumita seemed to shrink within herself in embarrassment. Why did she have to take a tram ride with his money? Why couldn't she have said, I'm going to walk, if it's my company you desire, walk with me. Why couldn't she say that? And because she couldn't, she felt inadequate. Without being aware of it herself, she felt as though she had, like a beggar, always depended on the generosity of one man or another. Even the companion she was seeking a short while ago was because of this mentality.

'Let's get off.'

They had arrived at the Maidan. They found a secluded spot to sit down side by side. After a few minutes of silence, Suren cleared his throat.

'There was something I wanted to tell you today . . .'

'What?'

'If you have no objection, I'd like to marry you . . .'

An electric current seemed to charge through Sumita. Yet she managed to stay still. Then she said in an even tone, speaking with utmost self-control, 'I have decided not to get married till I have a reasonable income. I don't wish to be a burden on anyone . . .'

'Can a wife ever be a burden for a husband?'

'She can . . .'

Suren tried to persuade her with different kinds of logic. But Sumita just wouldn't understand. Suren simply couldn't climb the peak of self-respect she had suddenly scaled. This time, Sumita walked back home, and lay down after locking the door. She burst into tears. There was a knocking on the door again a short while later.

'Who is it . . .?'

'It's me, Nabendu . . .'

'The bulb in the room isn't working. I'm in bed . . .'

'Open the door. I've brought a bulb . . .'

Sumita was amazed. How did Nabendu know her bulb wasn't working? Opening the door, she asked him just that.

'This afternoon, when you were gone for your bath, it was I who took out the bulb and put in one that doesn't work . . .'

'What? Why . . .?'

'To fool Suren. I'd expected him to go away when he saw the room was dark.'

Sumita's earlobes reddened.

'What if Suren were to come! What's your problem?'

'I have a huge problem. He's angling to marry you. How can I give him the opportunity to be alone with you? . . . Just a minute, let me fix the bulb . . .'

Nabendu put the working bulb back in place with the help of a torch.

'I went to the Maidan with Suren,' Sumita chuckled.
'He proposed marriage . . .'

'Really? What was your answer? . . .'

'I said I'm not getting married till I have an adequate
income. I don't want to be a burden on my husband . . .'

'Fine answer. But . . .'

Nabendu lapsed into silence, his face pale.

'Will you give me the same answer?'

Sumita couldn't bring herself to say, 'I will . . .' She felt a
sudden sense of disaster in her heart. 'I don't know,' she
said. 'It's late, go home.'

Then she burst out laughing.

The Tyranny of Clogs

1

FRENCH-CUT BEARD, FANCY HAIRCUT, COLOURFUL LUNGI, breath stinking of onion and garlic—imagine such a man being named Radhaballabh. His grandfather had chosen the name. In Russia, I believe you are allowed to change your name. In our country too, some students apparently change their name to preferred ones before their final school examinations. Radhaballabh did get an opportunity to take his final school examinations, but the thought of changing his name had not even occurred to him. It is difficult to say why such mishaps take place. Without getting involved in such complicated details, all I want to say is that a more modern name would have suited Radhaballabh better. For Radhaballabh was truly a modern young man. In terms of his thoughts, clothes, conversation and, specially, his income, he was almost post-modern. He was adept at the card games of bridge and flash. These brought him some money too, because of which his maternal uncle was grateful to Radhaballabh. For he no longer had to finance his nephew's cigarettes and film tickets. That amounted to no small savings in the current economic climate.

2

After failing his final school examinations, Radhaballabh had been practising youth. Today's readers must be aware

135

of what it means to practise youth. Detailed descriptions are unnecessary. His activities continued unhindered. But he suddenly received a blow.

The naughty god of love, assailant of Mahadeva, fired his unerringly targeted arrow directly at Radhaballabh Poddar. It is well known that the lovestruck Mahadeva had turned Kama to a pile of ash. Most people may not know what the lovestruck Radhaballabh Poddar did. I do. Bewildered, the poor fellow ended up buying some cream for his face on credit. Soon the mirror, the cream and Radhaballabh were immersed in one another; but that a frowning grandfather Brahma was taking off his wooden clogs was something that the highly distracted Radhaballabh remained oblivious to.

3

It was a young woman named Punti who had slipped through a tram window to unexpectedly appear on the proscenium of Radhaballabh's heart. It is difficult to say how things happen in this world of ours. Punti did have age on her side. But before he could ascertain what that age was—sixteen or twenty-six—poor Radhaballabh was charmed. Once you are charmed, you cannot be clever. In such circumstances, a man is compelled to remove the bridle of logic from the horse masquerading as the mind. The horse kicks up all four of its legs. That was exactly what happened. The captivated Radhaballabh roamed Harrison Street as a man possessed. Not that this was an unusual event. It had happened so many times, after all. On how many different young women must Radhaballabh's eyes have alighted through the windows of trams he had taken on Harrison Road. But as soon as he glimpsed Punti at a first-floor window, every fibre in his body seemed to cry out in unison: Mona Lisa! Every heroine of every contemporary novel seemed to line up with conchshells in the courtyard of his heart to welcome Punti. This was unprecedented.

Such a disaster had never befallen Radhaballabh. It has been said that falling in love makes one feel warm under a full moon and freeze in sunlight. While Radhaballabh's sensory perceptions admittedly did not undergo a change, the densely populated Harrison Road suddenly seemed rather desolate to him. All the other houses on Harrison Road except that particular two-storeyed one had vanished— or so it seemed to the lovestruck Radhaballabh. It was probably on the strength of this impression that Radhaballabh stood that day in the middle of Harrison Road, his face raised upwards, fearlessly whistling his love for Punti, when suddenly, grandfather Brahma's wooden clogs struck him hard. Before he could identify the point of contact, the poor fellow fell unconscious.

The clogs came in the form of a lorry, however.

4

The respected Vidyasagar, object of our morning prayers, had apparently been discomfited many times over because of his inherent kindness. Now it was the altruistic Ramkinkar Hazra's turn. It was out of sheer humanitarianism that the domesticated father of Habli, Minta, Poltu, Bishu and Khokon accommodated the unconscious Radhaballabh in his drawing room. He even summoned the freshly minted doctor next door. Examining Radhaballabh, the doctor pronounced judgement: 'He mustn't be moved. Movement could kill him.' Accordingly, the kind Ramkinkar Hazra subdued his nascent desire to dispatch Radhaballabh to a hospital and arranged for treatment at home. When kindness is generated within the heart, expenses are inevitable. Spending his own hard-earned cash, Ramkinkar followed the doctor's advice and bought an ice-pack. But despite the milk of human kindness flowing within him, Hazra did say to himself, 'What a pain!'

5

Two days later, Radhaballabh opened his eyes.

When he did, he discovered, standing at his bedside, not Punti but Habli.

He shut his eyes.

Opening them again in a while, he saw not Punti but Habli.

Habli brought him fruit juice.

Habli gave him his medicine. Where was Punti?

'How do you feel?' asked Ramkinkar.

'Better today.'

How sweetly Habli spoke!

Habli sat near his head, fanning him.

Habli arranged his bed-clothes.

Habli comforted him.

It was Habli all the way.

Three more days passed.

Punti was nowhere.

Just Habli.

Again the clogs appeared.

No longer in disguise, but as their real self—in Ramkinkar Hazra's hands.

Out of Stock

YOU CAN'T GET ANYTHING IN THE SHOPS THESE DAYS. NOT even the bare essentials of food. The shopkeeper claims to have run out of everything. Jagadish-babu went in search of a couple of crucial medicines the other day—he suffered from both diabetes and rheumatism—but he could get neither insulin nor colchicum. The shopkeeper said he'd run out of both. He couldn't get saccharine either—the shop had run out of it. It had run out of Horlicks too. Everything seemed to have run out after Independence.

Jagadish-babu's servant Poltu seemed to have run out of everything too. Nothing seemed to be left either of his body or of his mind. A skeletal frame, lustreless eyes, all his front teeth gone, emaciated limbs, almost bald—with the little hair remaining having almost turned grey. He was a refugee from Pakistan. Apparently he used to be a well-off resident of a village in Faridpur district once upon a time, celebrating every festival lavishly. He had a full family, including children and grandchildren. All of them were killed in the communal riots—he was the only one who had managed to escape. Apparently he was a Brahmin. Jagadish-babu didn't believe any such claims, however. A Brahmin! He looked like a cobbler.

'Why did you flee, leaving your family to be slaughtered by the butchers?' he had asked Poltu as much.

Poltu had answered in his dialect. 'I'm not a man, I'm a beast. That's why I ran away, out of fear for my life. I repent my action every single day. Will you do me a favour, sir?'

'What?' asked Jagadish-babu curiously. He was worried Poltu might suddenly ask for money.

'You have a gun, don't you? I saw you killing a mad dog the other day. Kill me. This time I won't run away. I'll stand fast . . .'

He really did strike a pose. Steeped in drama, Jagadish-babu was captivated by this statement. Patting Poltu's back, he said, 'Are you mad? Just stay the way you are. If you can settle down, I'll get you married again. You can have another family . . .'

Had Jagadish-babu correctly interpreted the flash in Poltu's eyes in response to this promise, he would have been very scared.

He'd got Poltu cheap. You didn't get a full-time servant those days in exchange for bread and board alone. Poltu ate very little, too. He couldn't eat much. Although he had never said so in as many words, he wasn't actually accustomed to such coarse rice. And he could barely stomach the inedible vegetables that came with it. He forced himself to eat somehow, out of sheer hunger, but he could never eat much—he felt nauseous.

Jagadish-babu had indeed got him cheap. But he used to suspect Poltu of pocketing some of the shopping money. There was reason too—for he did the same. Although his salary was two-hundred-and-fifty rupees, his income was five hundred rupees, sometimes as much as six or seven hundred. All of it from bribes. It was beyond him to accept that there could be honest people on earth. The only honest people, he felt, were those who had not yet been caught stealing. He kept an eagle eye on Poltu, meticulously checking the prices of every item purchased. But he had never been able to prove that Poltu had stolen any money. Of course, it wasn't easy keeping track where vegetables were concerned. Prices fluctuated every day. What cost eight annas today might go up to twelve annas tomorrow, while today's twelve-anna-product might cost only ten tomorrow. It was difficult to catch someone pilfering in this situation, but Jagadish-babu still wrote up daily accounts. As he did that day.

'How much for the cigarettes today?'

'No cigarettes. They've run out of them, will be available the day after . . .'

'Sugar?'

'No sugar either, they've run out . . .'

'Biscuits?'

'Run out of biscuits too . . .'

'Fish?'

'The large ones are ten rupees a kilo, got some of the smaller stuff . . .'

'How much?'

'Six-and-a-half rupees a kilo.'

'What! What else did you get?'

'They've run out of potato. Got some pumpkin for ten annas . . .'

'Such a small pumpkin and ten annas?'

Poltu was silent.

'Where's the change?'

Jagadish-babu started counting.

As he counted, he frowned.

'Thirty paise short. Why? I gave you five rupees . . .'

Poltu counted too. It was indeed thirty paise short. He was dressed in an old ragged shirt that his employer had given him. Putting his hand into his pocket, he discovered it was torn.

'The pocket is torn, sir. I didn't notice. I'd put the change in here. Must have slipped out . . .'

Jagadish-babu couldn't control himself any more. He stood up, shouting.

'First, you don't get anything that we need. You claim they've run out of everything. Then you steal thirty paise and claim that the pocket's torn—you thief!'

'No sir, I didn't steal . . .'

'Get out of my sight!'

He slapped Poltu.

The emaciated Poltu slumped to the floor. His body had run out of everything, but he managed to sit up, his head bowed.

But there was something he hadn't run out of. Tears. They flowed down his cheeks.

Just Like New

SHE COMES. SHE COMES EVERY DAY. SHE WAITS FOR ME IN silence, but I can never make it. There are far too many obstacles. The river is not far from my home, but I'm unable even to cover this short distance and go to her. Consider the past three days.

Just as I was about to go out at about five in the evening on Friday, dressed for the occasion, an old man turned up.

'Don't you recognize me?'

I looked at him for a while. No luck.

'Not really . . .'

'I was a friend of your uncle's. I'm here to inquire after a young man they're matchmaking for with my granddaughter. He seems to be a decent fellow. His father holds you in high regard. Will you come with me to their place, son?'

I was depressed at the thought. But I had to accompany him. I couldn't go down to the river, as planned.

On Saturday, we ran out of fuel for the stove. By the time I got some and managed to get my cup of tea, it was too late anyway. And as I left, I ran into a bunch of young men and women. In town for a wedding, they'd come to see me. They wanted to discuss the current state of politics and literature in the country. This time, too, I was unhappy. But I couldn't turn them down. The discussions were not worthwhile. What is worth mentioning is that two hours were wasted. So no trip down to the river that day, either. She must have left. There was no point.

On Sunday I'd just got out the door when a bunch of neighbours ran in.

'There's a snake in your garden . . .'

'Snake! Where?'

'Came in over the eastern wall. Probably jumped inside that bush . . .'

Some of them had sticks in their hands. My servant Durga joined them with one of his own. Another young man fetched a spear of some kind. There was a commotion. Their sticks rained blows on that bush. But no snake emerged.

'Are you sure there's a snake in there?'

'Of course, saw him ourselves. An enormous snake . . .'

The blows continued. The bush was in shreds. Then the snake finally emerged. Indeed, a huge snake. A blow from Durga's stick smashed its head. Now, a huge flat snake.

By the time the hunters left with the snake and war-whoops, it was past seven. It would be futile to go down to the river now.

On Monday, too, I was delayed. My wife said we had run out of rice. I had to run to the grocery. I had to sweeten the grocer before he'd part with a couple of kilos of rice for three rupees. By the time I was back darkness had fallen. It seemed I wouldn't get to meet her today either. The appointed hour had gone by. But suddenly I was determined. I *would* go. So I did.

She hadn't left. She was still there. But in a different guise. My assignation was with dusk.

But the one I saw had no luminescence about her. Instead, countless stars twinkled on her dress—with the star named Swati brightest of all, shining on her crown. This wasn't dusk, this was night in all her youthful radiance. It was lovely to see dusk in her new identity—night.

A Play of Colours

MAYA HAD SAID, 'ALL RIGHT, SINCE THAT'S WHAT YOU want, I'll take the red one . . .' A few simple words were all they were. The incident was a simple one, too.

I'd bought two saris for the festival season. One red, one orange. She'd chosen the orange one. 'I'm dark,' she'd said, 'red won't suit me.' But my mother said the orange one should go to my sister. She hadn't chosen a colour, she'd chosen a price. The orange sari was two rupees costlier.

Drawing her aside, I said, 'Take the red one, Ma—'

She didn't let me finish.

'All right, since that's what you want, I'll take the red one,' she'd said. She did. And went everywhere with a smile, dressed in that red sari.

So many things had happened since then.

There had been the earthquake in Bihar, the famine in the fifties, the Second World War, the death of Rabindranath Tagore, the disappearance of Subhash Chandra Bose, our independence, the death of Gandhi by Godse's bullet. Maya had been dead twenty years. I was bed-ridden with paralysis. None of the events I mentioned made any waves within me. The only thing that did were those words—'All right, since that's what you want, I'll take the red one . . .'

An oil painting of Maya hung on the wall. The artist had draped her in an orange sari at my request.

Yesterday morning, I suddenly saw the sari was not orange but red. I called the doctor. Examining my eyes, he said, 'There's something wrong with your eyes. The sari is still orange.'

Tilottama

1

EVERYONE'S LIFE WITNESSES THAT DRAMATIC MOMENT sometimes, when all calculations, all plans, go awry in an instant. The north-flowing river current suddenly flows south; high mountain peaks are suddenly transformed into bottomless canyons. And all this happens to ordinary people—you don't have to be a Rama or a Ravana.

Nakul Nandy was an ordinary man, and his son Gokul wasn't out of the ordinary either. Like many other young men, he too had passed his BA exams and now spent his days with friends, indulging in cards, amateur theatre, or political and literary discussions—in other words, doing nothing useful. As with everyone else, marriage proposals rolled in for him as well. Gokul was a suitable boy in the marriage market. A three-storeyed house in the heart of town, his father's moneylending business, and his mother's family's wealth had ensured that Gokul would never need a job to make a good living for himself. What God had granted him would comfortably allow him to play Riziya on the amateur stage for the rest of his life and improve the excellence of the theatrical arts.

The proposals continued to come in. His father Nakul Nandy was an experienced man. The bride whom he selected after taking into account horoscope, family, pulchritude and quantum of dowry was nicknamed Tilé. Her full name was Tilottama. Being old-fashioned, Mr Nandy did not send his son, but went himself to approve of the bride.

Gokul was charmed by her name. The image he conjured up was of none other than that of the Tilottama of poetry.

2

But at the wedding he was unpleasantly surprised. She was Tilottama all right. As dark and round as the til—the sesame. Small eyes with a fearful, apprehensive look in them. And this was the woman whose hand he had to accept amidst the usual sounds of a wedding. There was no alternative. But he was unpleasantly surprised.

So was his father Nakul Nandy. His son's father-in-law did not turn out to be the straightforward sort of person he had assumed him to be. The man kept wringing his hands and behaving obsequiously, but hadn't honoured any of his promises. He had paid five hundred rupees less than he had promised as dowry, claiming he hadn't been able to get hold of the money yet, that he would pay it later. The trousseau he had provided was of poor quality. The bridal dress was already leaking colour. There was no wristwatch—it had apparently been ordered from Calcutta but hadn't arrived yet. Who knew whether the ring was really a gold one—it looked like brass. Had he actually become involved with a fraud?

When he had made his demands, the fellow had agreed to everything, rubbing his hands. His demands had admittedly been on the higher side, but then why would he have accepted that ugly, pasty-faced, fat girl as his daughter-in-law had it not been for the cash? Everything had a price, after all. But what a turnaround! Who would have expected such behaviour of such a fawning character! He had to take the brunt of it all at home, too. Gokul's mother announced repeatedly at the top of her voice that Nakul had become senile. How else could anyone have knowingly picked such a horrible witch as his daughter-in-law? How awful! Nakul escaped with a lie—'That's not the girl they showed me. The girl I saw was fair, with long hair, lovely features, soft. Liar, thief, fraud! I'll get my son married again.'

Everyone agreed. Even Gokul.

3

Of course, he did get acquainted with Tilottama. He couldn't help observing that Tilé seemed to be a very nice person. Niceness seemed to be part of her face, the way it was of an eggplant. She was very shy too. It had needed a lot of coaxing and cajoling to get to know her. And he was astonished, too. She didn't seem in the least bit perturbed about the fact that everyone had poured abuse on her father. She was never surprised by the fact that the sun rose in the morning or that it rained during the monsoon. She wasn't now, either. These things happened where marriages were concerned—there was nothing to be surprised or upset about.

If she had wanted to, she could have protested against the lie Nakul Nandy had told about her. But she didn't, remaining silent without a second thought. She was gratified at having got Gokul as her husband—why get into unnecessary arguments? Every moment, she felt she was undeserving of him, that she had entered this heaven of happiness simply on the strength of luck despite not being entitled to it; she didn't wish to create trouble and be banished from this joyous existence.

'My parents are saying they'll get me married again,' said Gokul.

Tilé remained silent.

'Don't you have anything to say?'

'Why not? Hindus do marry many times over.'

'You won't mind?'

'Me? No.'

She added after a pause, 'Even if I do, I'll be all right if it makes you happy.'

Pique, thought Gokul. But he didn't say anything.

4

About a year went by.

A year was long enough to be rid of all illusions about Tilé. She was neither educated, nor good at music, nor sophisticated. She had neither beauty nor other qualities. All she could do was work like an ox. She did piles of dishes, washed heaps of clothes—all without demurring. Gokul's mother didn't let her into the kitchen, so she kept herself immersed in all other chores. It was beyond her to keep track of things like whether the moon had risen in the sky, whether the songbird had sung in the woods.

The thespian and poet that he was by nature, Gokul eventually admitted defeat. How long can you go on making love to a maid!

Although his father was still upset with his father-in-law, he hadn't brought up the subject of a second marriage. It was difficult for Gokul to make the suggestion on his own. But God smiled on him.

5

'Chandragupta' was going to be staged. Actors to play Seleucus and Antigonus had been identified, but costumes could not be located. Gokul was on his way to Calcutta to collect Greek costumes. As he was buying his ticket at the station, he spotted an old woman being jostled about in the crowd. She was unable to manage her own luggage and get her ticket. People kept shouldering her aside, so that she couldn't make progress in the queue. Gokul helped her out, buying her a ticket. She was travelling to Calcutta too, and without a male guardian, so Gokul had to take that responsibility as well. They got into the same compartment. Going to a lot of trouble, even quarrelling with a fellow passenger, Gokul managed to secure some space for her to lie down.

The old woman was charmed.

When the compartment became emptier, she pulled out her paan-case and gave Gokul one. She also pulled out some zarda from a shiny silver container. Gokul refused, not being used to it. The old woman directed some into her open mouth, smiling. 'When I became a widow I had to give up almost everything one by one—this is the only thing I haven't been able to give up yet.'

Chuckling, she spat through the open window.

They started chatting.

They went on chatting. As a result, she got to know everything about Gokul. He bared his heart to her, divulging everything. He didn't hide anything, couldn't hide anything, didn't even feel the need to hide anything. In other words, Gokul was charmed, too. After hearing the whole story, the old woman said, 'Now that you're planning to marry a second time, have you found a girl?'

'Not yet.'

Popping some more paan and zarda into her mouth, the old woman said, 'Let me come clean, too. I have a daughter, her father died after she was born. I've been looking for a boy for her. Your caste is right, I like you very much, my daughter's not bad either. If you like . . .'

Gokul hadn't expected this. He didn't know what to say.

'Come and meet Usha. If you like her . . .'

'Your daughter may object when she knows I already have a wife,' Gokul stammered.

'Usha overrule me! She's not that kind of girl. It's true I made sure she went to school and learnt music and everything, but I haven't allowed her to be disobedient like other girls these days. So what if you already have a wife. Besides, if you're about to get married again, you must have decided to abandon her, eh?'

'Of course . . .'

'So what difference does it make whether you have such a wife or not . . . eh?'

'Of course.'

6

Usha, contrary to her name, wasn't dawn. She was mid-afternoon.

A bright golden glow of sunbeams seemed to glitter around her. There was electricity in her eyes, her gestures, her smile, her glances. Gokul had never heard an alaap in Gour-Sareng of such virtuosity on the sitar before. Such subtle musicality in every note of laughter was beyond his wildest imagination.

Gokul could remain indifferent no more.

7

Everything was finalized within a month or so. Usha's mother came along with Usha, renting a house near theirs to complete the negotiations. At the sight of Usha, Gokul's mother was not merely captivated but beside herself with joy. Gokul's father was beside himself with joy, too, when he saw the sum of money on offer. This wedding would bring in ten thousand in cash, plenty of jewellery and a smallish zamindari too. Apparently there was some scandal associated with Usha's mother, which had come in the way of her daughter's marriage all this time. Nakul Nandy was not troubled by that knowledge. He not only ignored it, he also kept it from everyone else at home, lest the wedding be cancelled on those grounds. Everyone misses a step or two when young, there was no sense bothering about it—such was his logic. Usha did set a condition to which Gokul as well as his parents agreed. Once they were married, Tilottama must be sent back to her parents forever.

8

It was two in the morning.

Gokul was sleepless and alone—Usha's mother was due to arrive the next morning for the engagement. But where was Tilottama? So much had happened, but she hadn't said a word—it was his duty, after all, to seek her permission too. Gokul tossed and turned. Tilottama came to bed very late, after completing all her chores, and then left the bed again very early in the morning. It was difficult to get a moment with her. He hadn't met her in private in the last twenty or twenty-five days—they had not discussed things at all. He had to ask her. Gokul waited.

Suddenly he woke up. Tilottama was leaving the bed, stiffly. It was morning.

'Listen.'

'What?'

'It's my engagement today. You remember, don't you?'

'I do.'

'You have no objection, do you?'

'None.'

'They've asked for you to be sent back to your parents after the wedding—you've heard?'

'I have. I'll go. If you deign to visit once or twice, that's all I ask. I'd better go, there's a lot to do.'

She left.

Gokul was lost in thought. He sat up in bed. Then he got out of bed and walked over to the window. He could see Tilottama doing the dishes by the ash-heap.

9

Usha's mother arrived with everything needed for the engagement—lots of things. She brought an enormous garland too. Usha strung it together—working all night, she said with a smile.

Gokul came in, freshly bathed. A mat was laid out for him. Just as he was about to sit on it, the garland round his neck, Gokul's mother said, 'Someone needs to blow the conch, I have a boil on my lips. Tilé, where are you? Blow the conch!'

Tilottama stood at the door stiffly, conch shell in hand.

As soon as she blew on it, an electric current seemed to run through Gokul's body, from head to toe—a sudden bolt of lightning that destroyed everything.

'Pardon me, please.'

Tearing up the garland, he raced upstairs.

A Breeze

WHEN IT HAPPENED, IT SEEMED TO HAPPEN WITHOUT warning. I was astonished. But when I reflected on it later, I realized that's how these things happen. Why, how or why at that precise moment—I have no idea. All I know is that the lotus blooms in the morning and the evening star at dusk—why, I do not know.

It was unbearably humid that day. There was a cloudy atmosphere, no breeze, obviously no rain, either. The evening became truly intolerable. I took my chair out into the open, facing north. Before me was the murky sky with a light cloud cover.

Facing the northern sky, I remembered a small incident from the distant past. There's a tiny star between the Great Bear and the Little Bear, named Thuban. I suddenly remembered the joy of seeing that star for the first time. I used to study astronomy back then, staying up nights to discover new stars. Now I'm a rich trader in sawdust. I no longer rack my brains over the stars in the skies.

I remember nicknaming Thuban, Thebby. Thebby was a childhood friend. I was about ten then, Thebby about five or six. She used to plait her hair, dressed in a colourfully printed frock. Her face was round like a cat's, rather roly-poly in appearance. We played all kinds of games together—hide-and-seek, hopscotch, and so much more. Then Thebby's father was transferred somewhere else. Thebby was lost to me. Still I'd managed to hang on to her for some time, through that star named Thuban. When the stars also disappeared from my life, so did everything else.

Much later, a wind sprang up. Soon afterwards, a rickshaw drew up at the gate. I thought it was Chhedilal, the sawdust dealer. But it was a woman who entered.

'Recognize me?'

'Can't see a thing in the dark.'

'I'm Thebby. I'm a school inspectress now. It's so hot. I was sitting under a fan in the waiting room. Then, when I felt a breeze, I decided to come and see you. Do you remember Thebby?'

A tender round face floated up in my mind's eye, topped by plaits. I couldn't make out the face of the woman who'd come. Suddenly I saw Thuban in the north sky. The wind that had sprung up had parted the clouds too.

Impotent Confessions

SHE HAD BURIED HER FACE IN MY CHEST AND SOBBED THAT day—I haven't forgotten. Burrowing her flawlessly beautiful face into my chest, how she had sobbed! No words, just tears. The room was dark. Impenetrable darkness! Just she and I, alone, late at night. No one else present. My chest was soaked with her tears. The darkness throbbed with her unarticulated agony.

I had no words either.

I remember another night. No darkness that night—the world was flooded in moonlight. The madness she had expressed, her arms around me, had no words either. I could hear the beating of her heart. How wildly her heart beat that night! I did not tell her of the fever that her beating heart sent me into. She wouldn't have understood even if I had. Can people ever understand all you say? And would I even have been able to say it?

Another time.

She lay on her stomach, me next to her. A lonely afternoon. She was reading. I watched her, enchanted. How lovely her body, like a lotus in full bloom. The river seemed to be overflowing its shores. Her clothes did not seem capable of covering her. That ordinary sari had become extraordinary at the touch of her body. Its broad border was red, tragic. Absent-mindedly, she put her hand on me. Did she sense the current that ran through me?

She didn't.

I didn't have the words, either.

I never did tell her. And yet I was her constant companion. Her happiness, her sorrows, her excitement, her exhaustion— I felt them all. I felt them with all my heart. But not for a day, not for a moment did she think of me.

I can swear she did not.

Why should she?

Women are fickle.

Eventually he came.

The one in whose expectation her heart would brim over, the one whose absence made the tears flow down her lashes, the one who had made her swing so long in the suspense of uncertainty—he arrived one day in person as her husband and took possession of her.

I said nothing. I saw their passionate union before my eyes.

That's how the world goes.

I don't know what I look like. Ugly, probably. But believe me, I am alive—I too can feel. Of course I'm ugly. I'm dirty all over. Although my clothes are changed once a week, I have to admit, shamefacedly, that my body is filthy. Greasy. Why? All I can say in answer is that I am impotent. My imagination runs riot, but I am, after all, a pillow. Just a small pillow. I have no hand in things. She soaked me with her tears, thrilled me with her joy, hid her secret love-letters confidently beneath my body, made me the recipient of every unstated message in her heart—and still she discarded me ever so easily, accepting a man instead.

And how little she knows of him.

The Final Instalment

1

I'D JUST RECEIVED MY MEDICAL DEGREE. MY FAITH IN THE medical sciences and in my own capability was unbounded. All I needed was a patient. Renting a room for a chamber, I waited eagerly, all spruced up. But the calls all came for Dr Dinu. You wouldn't find another doctor so old-fashioned. He didn't bother with contemporary techniques of diagnostics. He kept going, quite profitably, with his examination of the pulse and the tongue, the palpitation of the stomach—all kinds of simplistic methods, while we . . . Well, never mind. It was Dr Dinu who called me one day to attend to one of his patients. Two well-known doctors were on the case. My task was to spend the night at the patient's side. Everyone felt the need for a qualified doctor to be present round the clock at the patient's bedside. Dinu-babu entrusted me with the responsibility for the night. Probably because of his friendship with my grandfather.

I arrived to discover it was a huge affair. Every well-known doctor nearby was gathered. Apart from the two chief doctors, a nurse had also arrived from Calcutta. I added myself to the crowd. The boy only had malaria—the malignant variety, admittedly—but still I couldn't understand why so much ceremony was needed to treat malaria. A few grains of quinine would have done the trick, surely.

Having arranged for very complicated techniques of treatment and convalescence, the doctors pocketed their fat fees and left. It was decided that a nurse would remain by the patient's bedside, while I would be in the next room, to be summoned if required. In addition, I had to examine his pulse every two hours by the clock, and check on his respiration too. Before leaving, Dr Dinu said, 'Meet me before you come back here to spend the night . . .'

'All right.'

I left home after dinner, having put all kinds of equipment for administering injections into my bag. Dr Dinu was alone in his drawing room, smoking.

'Come in, sit down. I need to tell you something. Don't even think of doing anything other than checking the pulse and the respiration. Don't you give him any kind of injection . . .'

'If the pulse looks bad, what harm can a strychnine or camphor-in-ether injection do?'

'Don't do anything—you'll just earn yourself a bad name . . .'

Pulling on his hookah for a minute, he said, 'The boy won't survive . . .'

'He's got malaria, he's been given quinine, I don't see any reason he shouldn't . . .'

'He won't. Six of them have died before him. The man's sons don't survive . . .'

'Six dead!'

'Yes. The sons are born one after the other. Each one lives till about seven or eight, then something happens and suddenly they die. The medical treatment is nothing less than excellent every time. Another son is born within a year of the last one dying—and then it's the same story. Six of them have died under my treatment—this one will, too. It's just an expense for him . . .'

Grimly, the old man continued smoking.

I thought he'd gone senile. What kind of scientific logic said that the seventh would die because the previous six had? And if there was nothing to be done, why give me a hundred rupees for nothing? Still, I kept my thoughts to myself. Where was the sense in arguing with the old man?

2

The nurse called me late at night.

I discovered the boy's father—the best-known and richest man in the area, Jagat Sen—sitting quietly by the bed. Looking at him angrily, the boy kept saying, 'Give the doctor his hundred rupees and the nurse his fifty, so I can go. Why're you holding me back, give it to them quickly, I can't stay any more—give it to them quickly—give it to them quickly . . .'

He tried to force himself up. Two of us had to pin him down.

'Give it to them quickly—give it to them quickly . . .'

He didn't sound like an eight-year-old, but like a cantankerous old man. Just as I was wondering whether to give him an injection of hyoscine hydrobromide or of morphine, Jagat-babu suddenly did something very strange. Kneeling on the ground, his palms joined together, he said, 'Nabin-babu, I beg of you . . . I'll return every penny with interest . . . Don't leave, stay, I beg of you . . .'

'No. I won't stay in a swindler's home . . .'

'My son, my son . . .' Jagat-babu cried out pathetically.

The boy tried to force himself up again.

'Give them their fees immediately . . .'

'All right, all right . . .'

Getting to his feet, his clothes dishevelled, Jagat-babu unlocked his safe and handed the nurse and me our fees.

The boy shut his eyes in contentment.

He didn't open them again.

The Suicide

CHANDRAMADHAB WAS AN AMAZING MAN. HE COULD PASS the coldest of winters in a thin cotton shirt, and he had no objection to wearing woollens at the peak of summer. He enjoyed his mutton with bitter vegetables, and writing with a hard pencil. He spoke very little, preferring gravitas most of the time. When he laughed it was in silence, his cheeks puffed out, his eyes almost closing. The tips of his luxuriant moustache poked the corner of his eyebrows. His moustache was astounding. I've never seen anyone with anything like it. It was as though a pair of finches were perched face to face on his upper lip. When Chandramadhab was angry, the parted wings of the finches rose quivering in the air. I'd seen many moustaches with subtly twirled tips, but never such a bifurcated, meaningful, articulate pair. His moustache was extraordinary. He expressed his thoughts through his moustache. When he disagreed with someone, the tips of his moustache seemed to shake their heads and say no.

He turned up one morning. His moustache-tips dropped. I looked at him. My face must have betrayed a question. Taking some money out of his pocket, he said, 'Get a rupee's worth of jilipi for yourself.'

'Whatever for?'

'My mother's died. She used to love jilipi and giving them to people too.'

He asked me about some more of our mutual friends, checking whether they still lived in Calcutta. I heard he had treated all of them to jilipi.

Another day, I saw that the finches seemed delirious, about to take wing. I expected to hear their cry—*mekiki, mekiki*—any moment.

'What's the matter, Chandramadhab?'

Chandramadhab was silent for a while. Then he smiled. His eyes closed, the swaggering tails of the birds had their union with the bushy eyebrows. Almost secretly, he said, 'I'm in love . . .'

'What! With whom?'

'Ramola.'

A month had passed.

One evening, on my return home I found someone sleeping in my bed, covered in a sheet from head to toe.

'Who . . .?'

I got a shock when I removed the sheet. It was Chandramadhab. But sans moustache. Clean-shaven.

'What have you done!'

'Ramola's married someone else.'

The Flu

IT STARTED WITH A HEADACHE. THEN SUCCESSIVE SNEEZES.
The sneezes didn't clear the head. Instead, the pain seemed
to settle down even more firmly on the temples and
between the eyebrows. I felt powerless. Knowing it
wouldn't help, I still took a pinch of snuff. Sneezes again.
Tapati came in. I thought I felt some relief. The sun shone
through the window, glowing on the red border of Tapati's
sari as well as her cheeks. The sky of my heart seemed to
gather some colour, too.

'Why do you keep on sneezing? What's the matter?'

'I don't know. I have a terrible headache.'

I massaged my temples myself.

'Should I?'

'Never mind, let me not bother you.'

'No bother,' smiled Tapati. 'Why don't you lie down?
I do a very good head massage. My brother gets these
headaches too. My massages send him off to sleep. Come
on now, lie down. You have to shut your eyes. Why're you
staring like that?'

I lay down and shut my eyes.

Tapati went to work.

In the afternoon I got fever.

Checking my temperature herself, Tapati said, 'Quite
high. Nearly 103. Do you want to call your doctor?
What's his name?'

I told her the doctor's name and phone number.

163

Tapati went into the next room to make the phone call. I listened avidly. A strange thought suddenly occurred to me. Tapati's voice was like a cockatoo's. I could even visualize the tuft on her head, opening up in excitement every now and then, revealing a pink hue within. What *was* she talking about with the doctor? Did she know him? She was laughing too!

'No, I'm just here for a visit. He's a friend of my brother's. My mother's all right, but she can't see or hear much, you see. Yes, her nurse is back—she was there before I came. Or else it would have been very difficult. Yes, the servant is very helpful.' Without provocation, I had another thought. What did the bird of paradise sound like?

Returning, Tapati said, 'The doctor's coming soon. He seems quite nice. He was asking after my mother. He's promised to do her cataract operation this winter. Tell me, is he married? My friend Runu married a doctor, his name was Amrito Sen too.'

'No, he isn't married.'

I turned over on my side. The veins in my temples throbbed. I felt like someone was chomping on me.

Dr Sen came after a while.

'It's the flu,' he said. 'I'm prescribing a medical mixture. You have to take it every four hours. And three days in bed. Complete rest.' Smiling at Tapati, he said, 'You should put some eucalyptus oil on your handkerchief too. Sniff it at intervals, it's a very contagious disease.'

Dr Sen seemed to be looking at Tapati with a little too much intimacy.

Dear Samar,

I know Tapati's at your place in Darjeeling. What do you think of her? You can understand why I ask, can't you?

I'll be relieved to find a good husband for her. But where are the good husbands. Do think about it.

Sincerely,
Naren

It wasn't a letter, it was a dream. What did such a dream mean?

My head was throbbing again.

'It's time for the medicine.'

Tapati entered, smiling, her head tilted to one side.

Pouring the medicine out with precision, she made me drink it, and carefully wiped my lips with a towel.

I felt rather weak.

In the evening, my throat began to hurt.

'Tapati . . .'

'Yes?'

'Never mind . . .'

'Tell me?'

'Can you check my throat with the torch? It's hurting. But I think—no, never mind, it's contagious.'

'So what? It won't hurt me. But will I be able to make anything out? All right, let me check . . .'

Holding the torch, Tapati inspected my throat for a long time, her face close to mine.

'All I can see is red . . .'

'Red . . .'

I was inspired suddenly.

'Could you put some Mendell's Pigment on it? The bottle's in the other room—a small bottle.'

Tapati fashioned the perfect brush.

'Open wide. At the back of the throat, on the red part?'

'Yes, at the back. Anywhere you like . . .'

My words sounded incoherent to my own ears.

She did put the pigment on with care. My heart began to flutter.

A letter from Naren did arrive the next day.

Dear Samar,

Send Tapati home as soon as you get this. Her marriage has been fixed. She has to be here when the trousseau is bought. She mustn't tarry there at any cost.

Love,
Naren.

The fever went down the very next day.
The head, throat and chest were all clear.
No ache or pain anywhere.
Tapati came to say goodbye before leaving.
'My best wishes,' I said.

The Butterfly

A BUTTERFLY'S BEEN VISITING ME OF LATE, PERCHING ON THE lamp with the blue shade. It sits motionless on it as long as I work at my desk. It has become my evening companion since Asha died.

My friend Someshwar came. He had become a frequent visitor these days. I quaked whenever I saw him. He had stumbled upon the fact that I had developed a weakness for his sister Bela. I was caught between a rock and a hard place. This time Someshwar got down to brass tacks immediately.

'Have you made up your mind about Bela?'

I was silent.

'Please make up your mind one way or the other.' After a pause, he continued. 'You *will* marry eventually, everyone does. If you marry Bela I'll be relieved. Bela loves you, too.'

All true—and yet, I was silent. I had thought I wouldn't get married again. Now it seemed I'd have to—and to no one but Bela at that—but I still couldn't overcome my hesitation.

'Why don't you say something? I won't insist if you don't really want to. Tell me frankly. I'll try with Dwijen in that case. Of course, if you say yes I don't need to talk to anyone else. From what I can make out, Dwijen won't say no, but . . .'

That Dwijen with the toothbrush moustache marry Bela! Was that what he was plotting?

'No need to talk to Dwijen,' I said. 'I'll marry her. But I need some time.'

167

'If you give me your word, of course I'll wait.'
I remained silent.
'You do give me your word?'
'I do.'
'Wonderful! Let me give Bela the good news.'
Someshwar left.
Someone spoke in Asha's voice, 'Then I'm done too. I'm off.'
The butterfly flew out the window.

Love Marriage

KSHANIKA KHASTAGIR WAS STRUCK BY LIGHTNING IN HER head. But she hadn't died yet.

In fact, she was pacing up and down the terrace trying precisely to fathom whether it would be best to die in her situation—and even if it were best, what the easiest and yet most tragic method could be. Kerosene, hanging, drowning, even cyanide—all of these had become rather trite. How about sniffing tuberculosis germs?

Suddenly Ramesh-babu's sandals were heard.

'So this is where you are, Khantu. How childishly you're behaving!'

Kshanika said nothing.

'Why don't you say something?' Ramesh-babu said. 'Do you suppose I'm getting you married off to him right away? What's the matter with just considering it?'

'Baba, I'd never have imagined you'd hand me over to a bigamist,' said Kshanika.

Ramesh-babu said, 'That's fine, you don't *have* to marry him. I liked the young man, which is why I'd suggested it. Well educated, good job, fine health, no children. So what if it's a second marriage? But it's all right. If you don't like the idea, don't marry him. Now go to bed. All that you've developed with all your studies are your tonsils, not your brains.'

The motherly Ramesh-babu escorted his motherless daughter downstairs.

I forgot to mention—I should have right at the beginning—that Kshanika Khastagir had passed her BA examinations with Honours in English. Her photograph had appeared in all the well-known monthly magazines.

The next day, she told her friend Sujata, 'The crisis has been averted. You have to be amazed at his gall. No sooner has his wife died than he's hankering for remarriage. These men have turned us into cigarettes. Light the second one before the first one is out. This man seems to be in even more of a rush. Like he wants to light the holy flames for the next marriage from the funeral pyre of his first wife.'

'What's going on? Who's this man?' asked Sujata.

'His name is Ajay Kumar Bose,' Kshanika answered. 'He's got a government job—writes poetry too. Got too much of the poet in him . . .'

'Really?' was all that Sujata said.

Kshanika hadn't calmed down yet. 'I think there should be a law against such marriages,' she continued.

Sujata said nothing.

But although she didn't, she demonstrated her knowledge of the law on the subject in practical terms. About a month later, invitation cards to Sujata Debi's wedding with Ajay Bose began to be distributed to friends and relatives.

He was now her friend's husband. They were bound to meet. One day, in the course of conversation, Kshanika laughed, 'I see you read that "try, try again" poem very closely in childhood.'

'Of course I did,' said Ajay. 'Besides, you know, after my first wife died, important people urged me day and night—what could I have done? I had my own urgency too, of course . . .'

'Important people? Whatever do you mean?' asked Kshanika in surprise.

'Well, everyone ranging from the bigamous Yajnavalkya to Shelley, Byron, Maupassant, Tagore . . . all of them made such earnest entreaties. Why, even our Satyen Dutta said . . .

Who came, who went
There's no time today
For all that—no, my friend!

'Even that Omar Khayyam—your wedding gift—that gentleman is adamant. Now consider, to honour their requests courteously, what can poor people like us do except get married again?'

Blushing to the tips of her ears, Kshanika said, 'Shut up, shut up. Now I know what you men are like.'

But she couldn't help enjoying Ajay's lively, witty riposte. He had a sense of humour—Sujata would be happy.

Some time later, news came that Sujata had committed suicide. Some more time later, news came that Ajay was getting married again, and this time, it was a 'love marriage' with Kshanika Khastagir!

Shades of Truth

1

DAHLIA, CARNATION, AMARYLLIS, CRIMSON GLORY, HIBISCUS, chrysanthemum—all of them appeared in a rush along with a red scarf. The scarlet rays of the newly risen sun lit them up. The blushing glow on the cheek of the new bride— a hint of her red wedding dress as she sashayed past in a startled moment. Holi festivities seemed to manifest themselves in the vivacity of spring. The mind's sky was painted over with red. The red for the skin, the red for the forehead, the red for the hair all babbled uncontrollably. Flames were lit.

First sight.

2

Then Raag Ashavari was played.

The endless expectation that comes with sky-high hope. The red was transformed into orange by eager anticipation. Orange streaks leapt out of the flames. The orange that's tangled up with the red in the multicoloured monsoon evening sky, that flies around on the fragile featherweight wings of the occasionally straying butterfly, that dreams in the half-bloomed bud of the lascia rose—*that* orange. In the melody of hope resonated the plea of the colour. An orange fog seemed to be descending. Had a flock of orange-breasted birds arrived? Orange waterfalls cascaded everywhere. The Ashavari played on. The red was lost in the orange.

He had come again.

He had paused in front of the house.

3

There was a flood of golden light.

What an exquisite display of molten gold with the autumn sunshine. Daisies laughed, falling over one another in delight. This golden glow in their bodies had never been noticeable before. Oh, they were here too? The golden roses Ophelia and Lonsdale? How radiant their smiles were. They seemed to be people, not roses. What joy, what joy! The gold-hued butterflies sang in unison with the goldfinches. Not just goldfinches, the canaries had arrived too, all of them whistling. Flocks of golden birds descended from the skies, like a golden cloud. Melody permeated everywhere. The gold colour, the gold melody, the gold of the heart filled everything everywhere with a golden glow.

His letter had arrived.

Scented, simple, unadorned.

Reading, she was surprised at first—then overjoyed.

4

Green. Green.

Where had the green been all this while? There was a cavalcade of different shades of green alongside the intricately patterned green ferns. Trees of all kinds—palms, jackfruit, mango, jacaranda, banyan, cactus, jasmine, mahogany . . . The green of their leaves had converged on the eternal green that bears the message of the living, that has a perpetual song on its lips—fearless, enraptured in its dreams of the future, and wanting more all the time. More, more, more . . .

Mynahs and parrots had arrived in the green groves, so

too had robins and nightingales. Waves played over fields of green paddy stretching to the horizon.

Another letter came—she read this one too eagerly.

This one was scented too.

5

The girl in the blue sari came after that.

A sky-blue sari. Her eyes were blue too. Blue flowers in her hair. Such an unusual smile on her lips, a suppressed smile. Was it Cleopatra who had suddenly disembarked from a barge of blue clouds that had travelled upstream on the blue Nile? Laughter glinted in her eyes.

'Hello . . .'

'Hello. I'm afraid I . . .'

'You wouldn't know who I am. We've moved here recently. Just a week ago. Right next door to you.'

'Oh . . .'

'Is your name Mallika Bose too?'

'Yes, why do you ask?'

'I'm Mallika Bose too. The peon has probably delivered two letters meant for me to you. Bikash-da's letters.'

'Oh yes, I was wondering who they were meant for.'

Her voice trembled ever so slightly.

She quickly went inside and fetched the two letters.

'Thank you . . .'

She left with the two letters, raising a wave of blue. Blue, blue, blue . . . A blue ocean all round—blue like poison, blue like pain, blue like unconscious lips.

She sniffed at her hand.

They still smelt of the letters.

6

Ink-blue. Gathering in a mass.

Indigo, eventually.

An indigo ocean seemed to have coagulated, stretching all the way to the horizon. Dark, terribly silent. What were those things in flight? A flock of swallows—flashes of indigo lightning bouncing off their bodies—flying continuously, not stopping. They wouldn't stop.

They drove past her house, together. Both turned to look at her. Both had smiles on their faces.

7

After indigo—violet.

Had a fire been lit at the heart of the indigo? Had its heat turned the indigo to violet? The red, the gold, the green, the orange—where had they all gone? Which part of outer space had they vanished to?

Both of them came that day.

They brought a colourful envelope.

It held their wedding invitation.

'You must come. It's at Violet Villa. Not too far. Quite close by.'

They left.

8

And then?

All black.

The Beggar

SUDDENLY I FOUND A BEARDED MAN KNEELING BEFORE ME, his hands held out in supplication.

'Who are you?' No answer.

I asked again. 'Who are you?' No answer this time either.

This time I almost admonished him, 'Who are you? What do you want?'

He looked at me slowly. He locked his eyes with mine.

I started. The person kneeling before me was nobody but myself. His tattered clothes and unshaven face had camouflaged him. I hadn't been able to recognize him all this while. I stared at him in silent wonder. He spoke slowly. 'I beg of you, don't go around begging like this.'

'Am I begging?'

'Yes you are, all the time, in your head,' he said and vanished.

Death of a Reader

1

ABOUT TEN YEARS AGO.

I was waiting for my train at Asansol station. Someone else was sitting right next to me. He had a book in his hand. Quite a fat novel. After we'd struck up an acquaintance, I learnt he'd have to wait the entire day for his train.

My train was due about three hours later.

Both of us were Bengalis.

Which is why the question I asked him only five minutes later was this: 'May I take a look at your book?'

'Of course, please do . . .'

This was the natural response and precisely what I'd expected.

I took possession of the book immediately.

It was the middle of an unbearably hot afternoon.

But all of it faded.

An astounding novel!

Giving me a sidelong glance, the owner of the book frowned and, taking out a timetable, concentrated on it.

I continued reading breathlessly.

Fabulous book!

Truth to tell, I had never read such a wonderful novel.

Almost like it had whipped me into reading it.

Two hours went by.

Having flipped through the timetable several times, the owner of the book finally looked at me and said, 'It's almost time for your train. Now . . .'

He cleared his throat.

I was entranced.

I glanced at my watch quickly. There was almost an hour to go. But more than half the book was left. I didn't waste my time on conversation. Just devoured the book.

Amazing book!

The rest of the hour seemed to fly.

My train was signalled.

There was still a long way to go.

I was determined.

'I'll take the next train,' I said. 'I'm not going without finishing this book.'

The owner of the book emitted a low cough and lapsed into silence.

The train left. I kept reading.

But I wasn't able to finish it.

I told the owner of the book, 'Oh damn, so many pages missing at the end. Why didn't you tell me all this time? Blast . . .'

In response, he only stared at me without blinking. The veins in his temples looked swollen.

2

Ten years later, I managed to lay my hands again on the aforementioned book.

At my niece's father-in-law's house.

I was escorting her to their house, and was scheduled to return the same day. But I stayed back, lured by the book.

Getting hold of the book at the first opportunity, I began to read it eagerly. Instead of reading the unread portion as a fragment, I decided to start again from the beginning.

I had a funny feeling after a few pages.

Checking, I confirmed that it was the same book.

I proceeded through a few more pages. No, something was wrong.

Still I kept reading.

After a while, I felt I couldn't take it any more.

Was this the same novel that I had read at top speed, completely hypnotized, in the middle of a searing afternoon at Asansol station?

What rubbish people wrote!

This was impossible to read.

I hadn't even realized when that eager reader from ten years ago had died.

This time, too, the book remained unfinished.

The Luxury of Imagination

'DEAR?'

'What?'

'Hasn't the tailor delivered my new suit?'

'No. I've reminded him thrice.'

His wife was answering from her bed. Her tone held a hint of annoyance.

'What a mess. What do I wear now?'

'Wear the old one. No one will know.'

'That's what I do every day. I thought I'd put the new one on today. Why didn't the tailor deliver?'

'No idea. Apparently he's taking part in a protest rally. It seems we don't offer fair pay.'

His wife turned on her side.

'Where's my vest?'

'There on the rack.'

'Uh-oh! Two buttons missing from the coat. Do we have extra buttons?'

No answer.

'Dear?'

'Oh, you'll drive me crazy! Not a wink of sleep all night . . .'

Grumbling, she got out of bed and took two buttons out of a tin, along with a needle and thread.

'But they're different colours.'

'Don't have two of the same kind. Pass me the coat.'

'Won't it look terrible?'

'No one will know. Pass it now, quick!'

He had to.

'Aren't you making any tea?'

'I put some in the thermos last night. I wasn't planning on waking so early. But no chance of that, thanks to you . . .'

'Five fifteen! Quickly now, my tea.'

'Don't rush me. I don't have ten hands like her, do I?'

Eventually the buttons were in place. The Sun put on his old suit, drank his stale tea and rose in Aquarius.

Sanjana, his wife, went back to bed.

A Trivial Incident

RAPT IN THOUGHT, THE LIGHT SWITCHED ON, I WAS DRAFTING the fourth advertisement. There was a slight sound at the door. Turning my head, I discovered she had come. She stood at the door. I was surprised. Her head was uncovered, her hair dishevelled. She didn't seem to have oiled it in days. Or had she shampooed it? I couldn't quite make out. Her neck was stiff, like a stubborn mare's. Her eyes downcast. She was biting her lower lip. Her nostrils trembled. Suddenly I noticed her earrings. The same pattern.

'Hilshi! Where were you all these days?'

Her real name was Sushila. But because I loved hilsa, I'd named her Hilshi.

Entering, Hilshi sat down on a chair. We'd set up home in this very room six months ago.

'Where did you go, Hilshi?'

Her head bowed even lower.

'To Rangpur. My friend Bilu-di works there. She'd gone home on a month's vacation, I was working as her replacement.'

'You bought earrings.'

'Yes, with my own money. You couldn't buy them for me. It was such a small wish but you couldn't fulfil it.'

'I had no money at the time. The publisher paid me a week later. I bought them as soon as he did ... See ...'

I pulled out the box with the earrings from the drawer.

'When I came back with the earrings, you'd left. I thought you may have gone to Biman. He's so rich, he was bound to give you anything you wanted ...'

'How could you think that way?'

'Of course I did. I thought of telephoning him. But I didn't feel like it. I just put three ads in the paper, one after the other . . .'

Suddenly I saw tears brimming in her eyes. And then she began sobbing piteously, her head on the desk.

'Why are you crying?'

'How could you even think that way?'

I thought I should now . . . but that high-powered bulb stood guard like a sentry.

What to do?

The electric company took pity on me. The lights went out.

Horu Is Illiterate

A VILLAGE. THE HOUSE OF ITS CROWN JEWEL, BILASH-BABU.
Renowned in the fields of politics and trade, he even had
an MA degree from the university. His writ ran large
all over the place. Several of his friends were visiting him
that day. They were deep in revelry, the doors locked. A
honey-voiced young woman was singing. Alcohol flowed.

The electric doorbell rang. The doorman opened the
door to discover it was Horu the milkman.

'Bilash-babu is not available today.'

'But he had asked me to come today.'

'No chance today.'

Horu left.

His wife was waiting eagerly.

'Got the money?'

'No, didn't get to meet him today.'

'Three months' payment overdue. How are we supposed
to survive?'

Horu was silent.

'Let's stop the milk,' his wife said.

'Are you mad? How can we do that?' said Horu with a
smile. 'Three children. What will they drink? They don't
get breast-milk.'

'How will we survive without being paid?'

'He'll pay. Don't worry now . . .' Horu smiled at his wife.

Horu was illiterate.

The Corpse

IT ALL STARTED WITH AN ARGUMENT. JIBEN, KANU AND Amal—all third-year students—lived in a Medical College mess. It was winter. They were all dissecting corpses. Each table in the anatomy hall had a corpse on it. The students were busy cutting up the organs and the limbs.

Jiben and Kanu shared a room, while Amal occupied a small room on the second floor, all by himself. Because it was tiny, it was a single-seater.

It was in Jiben and Kanu's room that the argument had begun.

KANU: Quite upset today.

JIBEN: Why on earth? Wife hasn't written?

KANU: She has. It's something else . . .

AMAL: Run out of money?

KANU: Oh no, none of those things. So what if I run out of cash? Nilmani will never refuse a loan.

Nilmani was the owner of the college restaurant. The students had their meals there—on credit.

AMAL: What are you upset about, then?

KANU: The corpse they've given me is a woman's. It has the name Parul tattooed on the arm. I had a thing with a girl named Parul from our village. Haven't met her since then. I kept thinking of her during dissection—almost like she was standing behind me.

Amal burst into laughter.

AMAL: Such a coward! Shame on you! Didn't you see her face?

KANU: What face? The head and neck were dissected

185

already. I was working on the leg, Mohsin on the stomach, Gobindo on the arm. Their partners are Kali, Jatin and Mahabir. They all admitted to a creepy feeling.

AMAL: Rubbish! All bundles of superstition.

JIBEN: Don't you have any?

AMAL: None whatsoever.

JIBEN: Can you eat beef?

AMAL: No problem in theory. I don't because I have no taste for it.

JIBEN: That's nothing but a hidden superstition.

AMAL: Perhaps. But I'll never get goose-pimples like Kanu in broad daylight.

JIBEN: Not even at night?

AMAL: No. I don't believe in ghosts.

JIBEN: What do you mean, you don't believe in ghosts? How can something that people of all classes have believed in since time immemorial be fake? What is the basis of your scepticism?

AMAL: I've never seen one for myself . . .

JIBEN: Have you ever seen Switzerland or Iceland for yourself? Don't they exist? Just because no one had seen bacteria before the microscope was discovered, that doesn't mean they didn't exist, does it?

KANU: Maybe someone will invent a ghostoscope too, and we'll discover them wriggling all over the place.

AMAL: What rubbish!

KANU: But I tell you I felt creepy—that isn't rubbish.

JIBEN: Seen the corpse that came today? Black as sin, built like a ruffian, stubble on his cheeks, bulbous eyes, teeth that look like they're jumping out at you in demonic laughter—even I had goose-pimples at the sight. Wonder which group will get that one to dissect. Looks like it'll jump up and bite if you run a scalpel on it—really scary!

AMAL: I saw it too, I wasn't scared. A corpse is a corpse—what's to be scared of?

JIBEN: Would you dare to enter the anatomy hall alone at midnight and put a red mark on its forehead?

AMAL: Easily.

JIBEN: I'm sure you won't.

AMAL: Of course I will . . .

JIBEN: I can bet you won't. Anyone can make tall claims in broad daylight.

AMAL: Let's make a bet, then. How much?

JIBEN: Ten rupees.

AMAL: Done.

JIBEN: We'll let you out of the mess at midnight tonight. Munna will unlock the anatomy hall for you if we slip him a couple of rupees. I'll let him know, he'll do whatever I ask him to. But you're not allowed to carry a torch or any other light. You must enter the hall in darkness. I hope you'll be able to find your way to the right table. It's directly opposite the prosector's room. Agreed?

AMAL: Agreed.

Jiben couldn't remain at the mess that evening, however. He was invited for dinner to his sister's place. It was decided that Kanu would accompany Amal, waiting at a distance while Amal entered the anatomy hall.

Setting the alarm for a few minutes before midnight, they went to bed, waking up as soon as it rang. Amal had already mixed some red paint in a small bottle. They left with it.

Kanu waited while Amal headed into the anatomy hall. He found the door open—Jiben had arranged everything beforehand. He couldn't see anything when he entered, it was so dark. He waited for a while. There was a small sound, which he put down to a rat scurrying across. When his eyes were adjusted to the darkness, he could make out the shapes of the tables. The table opposite the prosector's room became visible too. He advanced slowly, and then stood for a few moments by the table. Having dipped his finger into the paint, just as he was about to put a mark on the forehead of the corpse, something unexpected happened. The corpse wrapped its arms around him. Almost immediately, another shriek was heard, in a different voice.

Kanu and Munna raced into the hall.

They discovered Amal lying unconscious, and Jiben in a pool of a blood. Jiben had conspired with Munna to remove the corpse from the table and take its place himself. And Amal had carried a knife.

Amal came to as soon as water was splashed on his face. Jiben was taken to the Emergency Room, with Kanu accompanying him.

It was past two by the time Amal returned to his room. He shrieked again as soon as he entered. That ruffianly corpse was seated on his bed! Bulbous eyes, bristly stubble on his cheeks, protruding teeth. A ghost!

The ghost spoke softly, 'Now that your fun and games are over, can you do something about me? They've lowered me on to the floor; it's freezing down there . . .'

Amal couldn't hear the rest. He had passed out again.

Light and Shade

I RECEIVED DEEPA'S LETTER.

She wrote she was coming to my place this evening. Her subject in her MA was philosophy. I was her brother's friend. My crime was coming first in philosophy in my MA exams about five years ago. Therefore I had had to take charge of Deepa's education. All these days, I used to teach her at her house. Today, she wanted to come to mine. Disaster! Was that witch thinking of snaring me? Dark as sin, teeth that stick out, sunken eyes—this multiple-rejection on the marriage market was not planning to sink me now, was she? Why did she hang around me? What *was* she planning? Visit me at home? Home was a one-room flat. My eye fell on my table-lamp—it had a discoloured, enamel shade. I don't know why, but I felt it would be a blow to my self-esteem if Deepa were to see it. I was hesitant to reveal my poverty to her. I knew she kept track of my financial situation—but still I went out and bought a fancy lampshade. The money was wasted. There was no power in our area that evening. Deepa came. I lit a candle.

'I've selected a good essay for you,' I told her. 'Copy it.'

Deepa started copying it by candlelight. I lay back in a chair in a darkened corner of the room and watched her. She copied in concentration, her eyes downcast, an unexpressed emotion trembling in her eyes, on her lips. Against that backdrop of light and shade, she seemed to cast her own glow, saying: I am not responsible for my appearance, I am responsible for my actions. I have never transgressed, never even come second in class. Gazing at this new Deepa by candlelight, I was filled with empathy. I was charmed.

Disaster!

Ten Years

AS HE SAT DOWN TO WRITE A LETTER, SOMNATH SEEMED TO discover anew that he had vitiligo on his fingers. On his face, nose and eyelids too. Lots of effort and treatment had gone into curing it, but to no avail. He sat, frowning at his fingers for some time. Then he started writing.

Pushpa,

How quickly time passes. When I looked at the calendar today I realized we parted ten years ago. We could have created an enormous family in these ten years. But none of it happened. I still live in that same room in the same mess. I have four MA degrees, even a doctorate. I've read books of all kinds. But, you know, it all seems futile. I keep walking in an arid desert, walking endlessly, endlessly, endlessly . . . I don't know if there will ever be an end to this. The final act will probably be performed only on the day I fall on my face. The most precious thing a man can get in his lifetime is not riches or honour, but love. I had got that love. I'm clinging to its memory. I still hope that this desert path will lead me to that oasis where you're waiting for me as its goddess. Shelley, Bernard Shaw—they've all argued against marriage, saying marriage kills love. But both of them got married eventually. Unless you marry, you don't seem to experience that ultimate fulfilment, you feel as though you're standing outside society, in the dock like a criminal. When romantic love dies, children come, and their touch rekindles the dead love in a new form. My life seems to be a failure, and yet I still wait for you.

191

When you got married to Mr Rajat Ray and he took you to the UK to live there, my newly-sprouted seed of love seemed to have been killed by a bolt of lightning. My heart was shattered, the flowers that I had meant to offer you had turned to ashes. That untimely bolt of lightning had darkened my sky. And then I suddenly saw a ray of hope when I heard that Mr Ray had died in the UK of a sudden heart attack. I was amazed to see new leaves sprouting on that lightning-struck seed of love. I kept hoping that you'd return. But you didn't.

You once wrote: 'The company where my husband used to work had a contract with him which stipulated that he would have to work there for five years. I told them that, if they didn't have any objections, I could do the job instead of my husband—I had an MA and a PhD too. They agreed. There's something else, too. My husband had started a publishing business with a partner, using me as a front. That business has run into huge losses. So I need money for that as well, which I'll have to earn with my labour. So I cannot return now. But once all this is done with, I will return, I will.'

I'm still relying on that assurance you gave me. As I wait I cling to all the memories—your slender frame, that beautiful smile, the slight trembling of your eyelids, the incredible look in your black eyes, the face you made by wrinkling your nose and showing me the tip of your tongue . . . Ten years have passed. I'm waiting still. I'll keep waiting till I die.

Once upon a time, you thought me beautiful too. You granted me a position higher than Apollo's. Apollo is ugly compared to you, you told me. I used to call you Urvashi. Like a flower without a stalk, you bloomed by yourself, Urvashi. By my health is no longer what it used to be. Ten years is not a small period of time—there's no artist more destructive than time. It is breaking me, making me ugly . . .

Somnath stopped here. Should he write about the vitiligo he had developed? After some thought, he decided not to.

He wrote,

I withstand the continuous whiplashes of time to count the hours for you.

Yours,
Somnath.

Somnath was in the habit of posting all his letters himself. Especially the letters written to Pushpa. Letter in hand, he went downstairs.

He saw a plump, thick-necked woman searching for a house with a specific address.

'Is this 2/2 . . .?'

'Yes, whom are you looking for?'

'I'm looking for Somnath.'

'I'm Somnath. You . . .?'

'I'm Pushu . . .'

They stared at each other in amazement.

Across the Divide

1

THE WOMAN WAS DARK. PAST HER YOUTH. BUT STILL beautiful. Grace in her eyes and face. Her eyes spoke. When we arrived, she was preparing to fry eggs for our visit. The harmonium lay close by. And next to it sat a precious little boy. Not her son, the neighbour's. We sat down too. After giving us a glance, she continued her conversation with the little boy.

'Want some eggs?'

'No.'

'Go ahead, it won't kill you.'

'Don't want.'

'All right, sing for the guests then.'

He refused. She begged and pleaded, but to no avail.

'That song I taught you yesterday—have you forgotten it already?'

The boy started fidgeting. He glanced at the door.

She looked at us. 'He's feeling shy because you're here. Or else he does everything I tell him to.'

Someone resembling a maid peeped in at the door.

'Is our Khokon here? Oh, here you are! We've been looking all over for you. Why are you here at this hour—come along now.'

'I called him over. Go home now.'

He left. She looked upset. 'He loves me a lot, you know,' she told us.

She continued frying the eggs.

Some time passed in silence.

The captain appeared with a small bottle, some mutton and bread. 'Is the ghoogni ready?' he asked.

'Yes.'

We proceeded to eat. The ghoogni was excellent. We sang its praises.

'She's a fabulous cook,' said one of us. 'I remember...'

The conversation veered round to food. Not to feasts, but to everyday food. People couldn't stop talking about things you eat for lunch and dinner every day. But we were there to listen to her ghazals.

She did sing one or two.

Then we got round to talking of her home. As soon as the subject came up, she abandoned the harmonium and started telling us about life back home in the village. Her widowed mother, sister-in-law, nephew, cow all lived there. So many tales. She seemed to bring the village alive before our eyes.

'The neighbours love me, you know. When I fell ill, everyone around literally stopped eating. The zamindar's manager came from his office every day to inquire after me, the priest came every day with flowers from the temple, and as for the doctor—he'd come around three or four times a day. So many medicines, injections... My mother has these idiosyncrasies, you know. She refused to touch foreign medicines. My sister-in-law had to put on special clothes before giving me my medicine...'

'Never mind all that. How about that song?' ordered the captain.

Her smile seemed to have been extinguished. But only for a moment. She was, after all, the famous courtesan-singer Alka. Swinging her braids and chuckling, she resumed. 'Teri nazariya...'

2

A house with a wedding under way.

The eldest daughter-in-law, Sushama, didn't have a moment to spare. She was in charge of all the cooking. Her dirty sari was blotched with spice-stains, her hair unkempt. The stove burned, neglected, while she diced the vegetables at top speed. Her little son hadn't been able to spend any time in her lap all day, and was whining next to her. The fish hadn't been sliced yet.

'Can you slice the fish please? It's already so late . . .'

Sushama's ten-year-old daughter came running.

'The car's here, Ma! You can see everything from the bedroom window. Want to see? Come along!'

Abandoning the vegetables, Sushama ran.

There was quite a crowd in her bedroom. Jomuna, Minu, Podi, Ruby and several others. The setting was clearly visible from the window. It was packed with people. There she was, getting out of the car. How beautiful she was! Dark, but what lovely features! How the sari suited her. Oh my god, her father-in-law had stepped up to welcome her personally! Mr Bhattacharya, too, greeted her reverentially. And why not! She was so talented. Many of the people present stood up. Some of them were awed; others, charmed. Radiating her fame, Alka Debi entered.

Sushama looked on in amazement.

'We're women too,' said Jomuna, 'but just look at the difference. Our lives are no better than maids'.'

'Just our luck,' said Ruby.

Sushama was thinking of her adolescence. Her father had also engaged a virtuoso for her music lessons. She used to sing beautifully. How everyone used to praise her singing! She sang all over before she got married—at functions, seminars, everywhere. She'd learnt the instruments too—the sitar, the esraj, the violin, the banjo. The district magistrate had even given her a medal after a performance. Having blossomed like a flower, that life had also wilted like a flower. Where did it go?

An electric current seemed to run through her. Alka Debi was singing. It had been a wonderful idea to bring her for a performance at her brother-in-law's wedding. What a beautiful voice. She was transported to a dream world . . .

'Bouma! The stove is getting cold. What are you doing here?'

Her mother-in-law entered.

'Yes, I'm going.'

Sushama, the perfect housewife, left with a smile.

The Tree

SOME PEELED OFF THE BARK AND BOILED IT.
Some plucked the leaves to grind them.
Some fried them in scalding oil.
To be used for skin problems.
Surefire cure for leprosy.
Some even munched on its tender leaves.
Raw.
Or, fried with eggplants.
Very good for the liver.
Many snapped off its twigs to clean their teeth with.
Doctors extolled its virtues.
Experts were pleased if it sprouted next to your home.
'It acts as a good filter, don't chop it down,' they said.
No one did. But no one took care of it either.
Garbage gathered all around.
Some paved the ground around it. That was garbage of another kind.
Suddenly a different sort of person came up to it one day.
He gazed, enraptured, at the tree. He didn't peel off its bark, didn't pluck its leaves, didn't snap its twigs. Only looked on, captivated.
'How beautiful these leaves are,' he said. 'How lovely their lines. How pretty these clumps of flowers—a constellation of stars has descended from the blue skies to this green space ... Wonderful ...'
Having gazed to his heart's content, he left.

He was a man in search of a muse, not medicine.

The neem tree wanted to run away with him. But it couldn't. Its roots had dug too deep into the earth. It stood behind the house in a heap of garbage.

In that house, the housewife, so adept at domestic chores, was in the same situation.

A Juicy Experience

RASHAMAY RAKSHIT OF THE ADVANCING YEARS CAME TO MY clinic the other day, not a little excitedly, saying, 'Pardon me, doctor, for calling your science a fraud in the heat of the argument. I've realized my mistake, I'm here to withdraw my claim. And I've come too to tell you something you don't know, or maybe you do, since you doctors are omniscient.'

'What? Tell me.'

'I've had a close shave, doctor. My wife was *that* close to becoming a widow . . .'

Rakshit picked up the newspaper to fan himself.

'Didn't you go to Hazaribagh?'

'Yes! That's where it all happened. My daughter had told me not to go, saying she'd heard there were tigers in the jungle, that it wasn't safe. But you had instructed me to walk for an hour by the clock every day, and the scenery is lovely at Hazaribagh. I used to enjoy my walks. But one day I got into trouble, doctor.'

'Are you on insulin these days?'

'It's easy for you people to prescribe it, but where's the money? Why do you suppose I took potshots at the medical sciences the other day? But now, you know, I've been made an idiot of. I may not be taking my insulin, but it's the medical sciences that have saved me.'

'How do you mean?'

'I was out on my walk the other evening, following your instructions. That evening, too, my daughter asked me not to go, and said I should be back before sundown. But as soon as I'd gone a little way, I was entranced. That song of Robi Thakur's about spring hitting the forests kept playing in my mind. The trees were on fire with Palash and Krishnachura, you know. The sun was setting, the clouds were aflame. And a bird started singing—it was the bird that drew me into the jungle. I'd never seen that particular bird before. Hoping to catch sight of it, I went in. I can't tell you how many different kinds of flowers and trees, leaves and vines, I saw in there. The bird seemed to be playing hide-and-seek with me. Sometimes it appeared to be singing to my left, sometimes to my right, sometimes in front, sometimes behind. I walked on, looking around, lost to the world. It was strangely desolate everywhere; there was a strange scent too. There were probably mahua trees nearby. I felt drunk. I moved on, practically intoxicated. That singing bird seemed to be showing me the way to a dream world with its melodious code. I began to wonder what it looked like. Was it blue? Could this be Maeterlinck's Blue Bird? I have no idea how long I kept walking, not even remotely aware that the evening darkness was getting deeper. But suddenly I got a shock. I discovered two tigers in my path! One of them was huge, wrapped in fat, while the other was lean. I must have become unconscious instantly. When I came to, I found the larger of the tigers sniffing me, his mouth wide open. I was expecting him to crunch me up any moment. But can you believe it, he didn't! Do you know what he did instead?'

'What?'

'Looking at the lean tiger he said in clear Bengali, "This fellow's breath reeks of acetone. His blood-sugar is obviously very high. Should I eat him?" The lean tiger circled me, sniffing my face a little too. Then he said, "No, don't eat him. How high is your sugar now?" "Five per cent." "Don't then. I'd better not, either—mine's three per cent today. This isn't a man, this is jelly. Let's go . . ." They didn't eat me, can you believe it! They waddled away instead. So there you are, it was the medical sciences that saved me. Oh and another thing, that proposal to reunite Bengal and Bihar seems to have had some effect, how else could a tiger from Bihar speak Bengali so clearly? They've obviously become bilingual too . . .'

What could I say? I simply smiled at Rashamay Rakshit.

Extra Fare

NOW THIS WAS WHAT YOU MIGHT CALL IRONY.

I commute to work daily. That day, after pushing my pen all day at my desk, I had just managed to arrive breathlessly at Howrah Station, and was panting in a third-class compartment. Suddenly I noticed the Bombay Mail leaving from the opposite platform—and spotted, in one of its compartments, a face that rocked my heart with joy.

Many years ago, one of my sons got lost at the fair in Tarakeshwar—he never came back. I'd looked high and low for him, but fruitlessly. It must have been God's wish, I'd consoled myself. And now, suddenly, it was that face—yes, it was that very face that I spotted in a compartment of the Bombay Mail.

How could I stay still?

I got into the train immediately. It left almost instantly. Inside the compartment, I looked again carefully—yes, it *was* him. An old man was sitting next to him.

With bated breath, stalked by fear, I asked, 'Where were you all these days? Do you recognize me?'

Oh God—he answered in Hindi. 'Are you asking for my name? Why? My name is Mahadeo Missir, I belong to Chhapra.'

I was heartbroken—I felt as though I'd lost my son a second time over.

The old man said, also in Hindi, 'He's my son, sir. What do you want?'

'Nothing,' I choked.

Surprising the father-and-son pair from Chhapra, Bihar, two teardrops rolled down my lean, dry cheeks.

I got off at Bardhaman.

And had to pay the extra fare, too.

The Debt

I WAS VISITING CHHOKU. HE KNEW AT A GLANCE WHY I WAS there. I had to visit him quite frequently, and with the same intent each time. He owed me some money, but I simply couldn't get him to pay up. Initially I had reminded him a few times, but now I was too embarrassed to even do that. But I did visit him every day. I read the newspaper in his shop, made a few comments on the current state of politics, and kept hoping that he'd bring up the subject of returning the loan himself. But he never did. When the clock struck nine, he yawned, snapped his fingers, performed the closing ceremonies before the idol of his protector, Ganesh, and made arrangements to shut shop for the day. And I came home too. Only to return to his shop the next evening. So it had been going on for quite some time now. Yet it was I who had once withdrawn a crisp five-hundred-rupee note from the bank to enable Chhoku to set up his watch-shop.

Having failed his BA exams, the poor fellow was simply whiling away his time at home, unable to find a way to make a living. 'We don't have a good watch-shop in this town, why don't you start one?' I advised him. 'Teach yourself how to repair watches, then rent a room in the market. You're bound to get business.'

'I know that only too well,' Chhoku smiled. 'But where's the capital?' Suddenly I sat down in excitement. 'I'll lend you whatever capital you need—get going.'

Chhoku got going. I knew a watchmaker in Calcutta. I sent Chhoku to him with a letter. Chhoku spent almost a year in Calcutta. He had no problems finding a place to stay in, for his uncle used to work in Kidderpore. Accepting his hospitality, he mastered the science of repairing watches. Then, one day, he told me, 'Give me the capital now. I've found a well-located room in the market. Let me book it with fifty rupees, I'll need to buy some furniture, I've managed to get hold of a few broken clocks and watches, I'm going to take that clock on your wall too, you already have a timepiece. I have to buy a few new watches too, also bands, dials, etc. . . . ' He rattled off his requirements.

I was frightened. I didn't have all that much money. Having just retired, my Provident Fund was all I had.

'I can't manage more than two hundred,' I said. 'You have to make do with that.'

'Are you mad?' asked Chhoku in consternation. 'This isn't a paan shop, it's a watch-shop. I can't even think of starting without a capital of at least a thousand, and I'll probably need more later. Here's the list . . .'

I didn't look at it.

'Look, a thousand is beyond my means,' I told him. 'I can stretch it to five hundred at best.'

Chhoku looked at me with bulging eyes and flared nostrils. Then he said, 'If I'd known you were going to betray me like this, I'd have taken that job in South Africa.'

Not that he'd been offered a job in South Africa—all he'd done was to speculate for a few days whether to respond to an advertisement in the papers. We settled at five hundred eventually. This was about five years ago. The shop must be doing well, for his lifestyle suggested a reasonable income. So many cigarettes, so many films, such an elegant life— none of it would have been possible otherwise. He had five different pairs of shoes. He never put on the same shirt on successive days. So the shop was obviously not doing too badly. But he hadn't returned a single paisa to me yet. Still I visited him every evening, spending some time at his shop. I kept hoping he'd bring it up, but he didn't. As I said earlier, I couldn't remind him verbally, though I kept doing it mentally. But after what I witnessed the other day, and after the historical analysis of the event that Chhoku provided, I gave up all hope.

Like every other day, I was wracking my brains over the conflict between Korea and Red China in a corner of the shop, newspaper in hand, when a young man entered the shop. He was holding a watch-case.

'Chhoku-babu, you have to change this watch. It has a scratch at the back, see? I didn't notice it at the time . . .'

Taking the watch out of the case, he showed it to Chhoku. There was indeed a scratch at the back.

With a smile, Chhoku said, 'Sorry, can't change it any more. You should have checked when buying it.'

The young man became defensive.

'That's true, that was my mistake. But trust me, that scratch was already there. None of us had even touched the watch. Today, suddenly, on turning it round in my hand . . .'

'It's not a matter of trust,' replied Chhoku dispassionately, 'it's a matter of principle. If you don't check something properly when buying it, both parties get into trouble. Please excuse me. Anyway, what harm can a little scratch do?'

'No real harm, except that it's a wedding gift, you can't give a gift with a scratch. Well, never mind, I'll use this one myself, give me another one . . .'

Chhoku sold him another watch. This time he examined it carefully before leaving with it.

I knew the truth. Chhoku himself had shown me the

scratch when he got the watch from Calcutta. 'I paid five rupees less because of this tiny scratch,' he had said. 'But mark my words, I'm going to palm it off at the catalogued price to someone . . .'

When the young man had left, Chhoku looked at me with shining eyes. All I said was, 'That wasn't right.'

Chhoku was a student of history. Giving the example of history, he said, 'If you accept the closeness of the relationship between business and war, then I've done nothing wrong. My biggest justification is that I've won. All's fair in love and war . . .'

'I didn't quite get the connection between business and war.'

'You would if you'd read history. All battles today have their roots in business. It was the same earlier too. The Crusaders didn't go on their crusades for the sake of their faith, but to capture the trade routes. I feel business is war. The customer is the enemy, you have to grab the money in his pocket through any strategy possible. Coax, cajole, entice, threaten—whatever works.'

I was amazed at Chhoku's academic prowess and analytical powers. Worked up by now, he kept talking. 'Take the recent situation. When the English came to India first, their business sense was good enough for them to have been able to establish an empire here. Clive fooled Umichand with tricks on red paper and white paper, Hastings had Nandakumar hanged, and much, much more. In other words, they were pure businessmen then. Hence they managed both their business and their empire. But after they had spent some time here, local conditions got to them. How can you overcome the impact of local conditions? The scoundrels turned into great men—even their businessmen became large-hearted. Let me tell you a story from three years ago—my personal experience. I haven't told anyone this story yet. You remember the wedding at the Mullicks'? They'd brought the shehnai players from Calcutta—Ghetu Mullick's daughter's wedding . . .?'

'I remember.'

'I was in Calcutta then. Ghetu Mullick wrote me a letter: "Can you please get a good watch for my son-in-law? I'm willing to pay up to five hundred for it. It has to be a gold watch." So I went to a well-known English watch-shop and bought an excellent watch. I won't tell you the name of the shop, I don't want to disclose it. I had to stay on in Calcutta for a couple of days more. I don't know what devil got hold of me, I went out with the watch on my wrist. Have you ever been to Noru's house in Shyambazar? Have you seen the ceiling-fan in their drawing room? It's so low that a tall man stretching his arms upwards is bound to hit the blades. As you know, I'm six-two. I was at Noru's place, the fan was on, as I spoke to him I raised my arms and that was it! The glass cover was smashed by the blade hitting it. One of the hands was broken too. I was at my wits' end. I certainly couldn't afford to buy another watch for five hundred rupees. Wondering what to do, I left their house.

'Suddenly I had a brainwave. Putting the smashed watch back in its case, I went to that watch-shop along with the cash memo. I met the owner. I said, "When I bought this watch I didn't take a close look at it, now I find it's smashed. If you could please change it—it's meant to be a wedding gift." The Englishman looked at me for a few moments, blinking once or twice. Then he said, "Didn't you take a close look at it? I see. Do sit down." He rang the bell on his desk, and one of the people behind the counter appeared. He told the man, "Exchange this watch please for a new one." Getting the new watch, I thanked him profusely and left, realizing that their death-knell was about to be sounded. They'd have to pack up and leave soon. And they had to, too. As soon as Mahatmaji said, quit India, they had to beat a retreat . . .'

Chhoku's business policy and ability to analyse history convinced me I'd never get my money back. But Chhoku did pay back my loan, though in a roundabout way. Visiting him at home one day, I found Badal the jeweller there. He had made a necklace for Chhoku's wife, he informed me. He showed me the necklace. It was a splendid necklace.

'How much did it cost?'

'Five hundred.'

'I hope you've got your money.'

'Oh yes I have.'

I felt some slight consolation. I may not have got my money back, but my daughter had.

Chhoku was my son-in-law.

The Exception

1

HE WAS HEALTHY, HANDSOME, WELL EDUCATED AND HAD a reasonable income. But if you asked Suren why he hadn't married, he only smiled, without saying much.

However, the significance of the small but meaningful smile remained unknown. His parents had long admitted defeat and headed heavenwards. After a few casual attempts, his friends had given up too. One or two fathers with daughters, precisely because they were fathers with daughters, had not yet given up hope, keeping up their efforts. But despite that, it didn't appear as though Suren would abandon his vow of bachelorhood. Of late he had even given up answering letters of this kind. For even a direct 'no' elicited replies replete with requests to reconsider, which then had to be answered, too. Therefore he was no longer willing to spend unnecessary time or money on this issue. A few days ago, a gentleman with a daughter of marriageable age had used an intermediary to get hold of him. The girl in question had passed her Intermediate exam, was beautiful, adept at music, social graces, cooking, housekeeping and the like. The intermediary concluded his description with the statement, 'In other words, a perfect match for you.'

Suren smiled that smile of his.

'What're you smiling at?'

Suren smiled again. 'I'm smiling at your assumptions. I can barely support myself, leave alone a wife.'

211

'With a salary of one-fifty, what do you mean you can't support yourself?'

Suren was silent, still smiling. 'I get by,' he said. 'But add one more person—and the possibility of several more—and it won't be enough. Besides, a modern, fashionable girl . . .'

He didn't finish his words, but the thought behind them was far from unfinished. He didn't have a very high opinion of the modern woman. He was old-fashioned. The news about women that was now available from the papers did not elicit his respect—they provoked fear. In the Mahabharata and the Ramayana you had the Dushshashanas and the Ravanas among men—of course, they were still visible. But the import of women-Dushshashanas and women-Ravanas was probably a contemporary phenomenon. With a monthly salary of a paltry one hundred and fifty rupees, he did not have the temerity to compete with them. Just the other day he had heard that his close friend Lalit's wife, who had a BA degree, had disappeared, taking nothing but her vanity bag with her. The rumours weren't pleasant ones. Apparently some artist . . .

Therefore he wouldn't set foot on that slippery slope. But the problem was within himself. A ravenous desire was burning inside, like an embedded arrow, which he could not deny. And yet . . .

All the thought in the world didn't provide an answer. And so the days went by . . .

2

Suren lived in a town to the west of Calcutta. His small home was by the river, at one end of town. By way of companions there was the aged retainer Hokru and a cycle.

Hokru went home every night, while the cycle spent the night leaning against the wall in the veranda. At mealtimes, twice a day, a neighbourhood dog of uncertain pedigree arrived in the courtyard, paws stretched out in eager anticipation. A cat also frequented the place in clandestine fashion at the dead of night. Sometimes one or two people with marriageable daughters or suchlike came too. Besides them, nobody else visited Suren at home. The reason probably lay in the fact that Suren was out of tune with his environment in terms of education and tastes. He couldn't quite fit in with the people around. He wasn't the kind of person to gatecrash a neighbour's drawing room and establish spurious family relations with the people there, joining in their gossip over cards. He was a little tongue-tied and, probably, proudly aloof too.

He had got his job simply on the strength of his degree.

3

It was a moonlit autumn night, three days short of full moon.

The moon was up, creating scenes of unimaginable beauty. Suren was about to leave for his evening walk, having had his tea after his return from work, when a carriage drew up before the house. Frowning as he looked in that direction, Suren's brows were furrowed even more. For the person who emerged was a young woman—and quite a modern woman at that. She had a vanity bag, dark glasses and high-heeled shoes. She asked him with a smile, 'Suren-babu, I presume?'

Returning the greeting, Suren had to admit the truth.

Noting the question in Suren's eyes, she smiled. 'I am your friend Lalit's wife.'

Stunned, Suren could only stand there in silence.

Opening her vanity bag to pay the coachman, the young woman rummaged inside before pulling out a five-rupee note. 'Oh dear, I don't have any change, is there a shop or something nearby where they can give me some change for this?'

'I'll pay the fare, I have some change,' said Suren.

The coachman left with the fare. At Suren's invitation, his friend Lalit's wife entered his drawing room and took a seat. He had to invite her in for the sake of civility. After all, she *was* Lalit's wife.

4

Needless to add, Suren had not been prepared at all for such an unexpected visit. The sudden advent of Lalit's wife—who had left her own home—without advance notice, and that too not just any old wife but a remarkably beautiful one, overwhelmed him.

Noting the state he was in, she said, 'I'm probably intruding, am I not?'

'No, no . . . intruding . . . not at all!'

With a smile, Suren brought himself under control.

'I've heard so much about you from my husband. So I thought I'd pay you a visit.'

Her earrings were lovely, the red gems glinting under the electric light to create an amazing effect. Suren was gazing at them, enraptured, when her words jolted him back to reality.

'How long have you been living here?'

'Not too long, about a year or so.'

They looked at each other in silence from their chairs.

Suren was wondering if she would ask to stay in his house. What would he say if she did?

Abha was wondering how to broach the topic, had he heard everything already? If he had, who knew which version he had heard?

After a few moments of uncomfortable silence, Suren tried to look as cheerful as possible and said, 'I've never seen you before. I simply couldn't make it to the wedding— I just didn't get leave, you see.'

The truth, of course, was that he hadn't even tried to get leave. As soon as he had heard that Lalit's would be a love marriage, he had felt a certain distaste about the whole thing. Moreover, he did not want to waste the leave he had earned in this fashion. He had plans for a holiday in Puri once he had accumulated enough leave. But you couldn't say these things. It was more polite to say you hadn't got leave.

Abha said, 'But I have heard a lot about you, which is why I came. I felt you're the only person I'd be able to trust so far away from home.'

Suren began to perspire mentally. Any moment now she would probably propose that she should stay here. These progressive women simply had no sense these days. They were capable of anything. If she could have left her husband so easily, there was nothing she wouldn't be capable of doing. Maybe she would want to move in for a few days right away. Suren would neither be able to say 'yes', nor be able to say 'no'. In desperation, he asked, 'Where are you coming from right now?'

'Oh, from my quarters. I've been appointed headmistress of the girls' school here. I'm joining tomorrow. I've heard a great deal about you, so I thought I'd make your acquaintance.' Abha smiled sweetly.

But, strangely enough, Suren was not as pleased to get this reassuring information as he should have been. On the contrary, he seemed a little crestfallen, unknown to himself, at this rather vegetarian solution to what could have been a complicated problem. Perhaps that had become evident in his expression.

Abha said, 'I really must be intruding at this hour. Were you about to go out?'

'No, nothing like that.'

The conversation proceeded along these scattered lines for some time.

Then Abha said, 'I'll take your leave now. I'll come over now and then.'

Hokru called a carriage for her, and she left.

Suren was extremely surprised. From what little he had seen of her, she didn't seem terrible at all—quite nice, in fact. Her behaviour and conversation were quite simple and natural, and yet she was the one to have left a husband like Lalit. He couldn't bring himself to believe it. There must have been . . .

Suren couldn't think of anything else all evening.

5

A few days later, Abha showed up again in the evening. She announced, 'I'm going to make demands today, ask for some tea. You looked so glum the other day I didn't dare ask for any.'

Smiling, she drew up a chair and sat down. Suren quickly asked for some tea.

'Would you like something to eat? You have to ask for everything here—as you can see, I'm a bachelor, and that ancient Hokru is my only support.'

'No, nothing to eat. A nice cup of tea is all I want. I hope your Hokru can produce that.'

'Hokru had never made tea before he came to me,' Suren smiled. 'I'm the one who's initiated him into the rites of making tea. So I can't guarantee anything.'

'Then tell him to just bring the hot water and everything else, we'll make it ourselves.'

Suren issued orders accordingly.

'Whatever you may say, there's no pleasure in life unless you can get a cup of tea just the way you want it.'

Suren smiled.

Hokru brought all the paraphernalia and laid it out on the table. Making the tea with practised proficiency, Abha both served it and drank it.

'How's the tea?'

'Excellent.'

After some conversation, Abha looked at her watch. 'I must go now, the secretary is visiting me at home.'

'Who's the secretary?'

'Don't you know anything about the world beyond your books?'

'Are you saying that the identity of your school secretary is the kind of information I should have at my fingertips?'

'Maybe not you, but that's the most important information for me right now.'

'But who *is* this secretary of yours?'

'Murarimohan Purakayastha, he's a lawyer. Very pleasant gentleman. He's gone to a lot of trouble to ensure everything goes smoothly for me here. I'd better go, he's due to visit.'

Abha left. What she had really wanted to say remained unsaid today as well. And what Suren had become impatient to hear was something he didn't manage to ask either. Both were equally eager to discuss *l'affaire* Lalit, but . . . The 'but' was what came in the way all the time. Suren wondered whether he should write Lalit a letter. But the very next moment he decided that wouldn't be right. Maybe Lalit would be very upset to know that his wife was posted in this town and that Suren had got to know of it. Why inform him unnecessarily? But who was this Purakayastha?

6

Another month passed. Lalit did not come up in their conversation. I don't know about Abha, but as far as Suren was concerned, she was now primary, Lalit secondary. It was not enough to say that Abha's influence had softened his extreme position on the modern, well-educated woman— it had completely altered his perception. He now felt that if Abha was a representative of the educated woman, then, far from panicking, society should be elated. Suren was convinced that this affair surrounding Lalit had to have some deep mystery attached to it. In sum, he liked Abha, and he had been conducting all kinds of complicated arguments with himself over the justification for liking her. Suddenly he felt . . .

But let me not write what he felt. I'm writing fiction, not poetry. He no longer went for evening walks, he stayed at home. Not that Abha visited him every day. But if she came and had to go back, that would not be right. This was Suren's thinking at the moment. Maybe you are surprised, but not more than Suren himself.

7

Two more months passed.

Three successive evenings had gone waste. Abha had not visited. On the fourth evening, as Suren waited with an ardent heart, footsteps were heard at the door. Turning his head, Suren discovered, not Abha, but Murarimohan Purakayastha entering with the gait of a crane.

'May I come in?'

'Please do.'

He came in and took a seat.

'I haven't had the good fortune of meeting you earlier. I keep hearing your praises from Abha debi. So I thought of coming to meet you—bridging the gap between the ears and the eyes, as it were.' Clearing his throat, and drawing his chair a little closer, he said, 'I've heard you're a very close friend of her husband's.'

'That's right.'

Some time passed in silence. But Purakayastha was a practical man—he wasted no time in getting to the practical issue. Frowning, he said in a low voice, 'Can you tell me what it's all about? From what I've heard, I mean . . .'

'I think it's all a lie.'

Purakayastha's expression suggested that a gigantic error had been rectified. 'Exactly, don't you think?'

Laughing a little theatrically, he said, 'These rumours, really. People are saying so many things about her concerning even someone as harmless as you.'

'Really?'

'Honestly! It's a terrible place.'

Suren was astounded. Purakayastha said, 'I'll take your leave now. There's someone else I have to visit. Don't pay any heed to those rumours—so long as we stay clean, it's fine. Why should you care for anyone? I should be going.'

Purakayastha left with the gait of a crane.

Suren sat there thunderstruck, realizing why Abha wasn't visiting him any more. Rumours were spreading in town.

8

The next evening, Suren carefully selected a letter-writing pad and envelopes at the shop, the prices being on the higher side. He was buying such expensive stationery for the first time in his life, and it gave him a lot of joy, too. Back home, he bolted the door and sat down to write a letter. He had to tear up the first few sheets, it simply wouldn't come out right. Eventually, after much thought, with a great deal of hope and anxiety, he wrote a long letter. He read the letter through several times before putting it in the envelope. Just as he was about to write the address on the envelope, he heard footsteps at the door. Familiar footsteps. Hiding the letter beneath the pad, he rose quickly to open the door.

It was Abha.

'And what are you doing all by yourself?'

Suren couldn't speak. He simply gazed at Abha.

'What's the matter with you? Are you ill?'

'No.'

'Let's go inside. I don't have much time.'

'You haven't been in a long time,' said Suren, a trifle accusingly.

'That's true, I simply couldn't make the time. I'm leaving today—so I thought I'd meet you before I leave.'

'You're leaving!'

'Yes, the job didn't work out.'

'Didn't work out! Meaning?'

'Because of Murari-babu. He became so conscientious about his duties as secretary that visiting me every evening became his daily routine. Never mind, all that is irrelevant. Let me tell you what I came to tell you. I'd been meaning to say it for a long time, but just didn't get round to it. You must have heard that I am supposed to have left your friend and walked out. It isn't untrue—I did leave him. I'll tell you why I did. I want to tell you because you're a very close friend of my husband's and I respect you. I don't want you to harbour ideas about me that aren't true.'

Suren listened in silence.

'Your friend wanted to marry a well-educated, independent woman. I don't know if I met his requirements entirely. All I know is that he liked me, and I liked him too. We got married. Shortly after marriage, he introduced me to a friend of his who was an artist, and what happened with me is just as you read in the storybooks. The artist friend wrote me a letter one day in an artistic technique. At first I thought of showing my husband what his friend was up to—and then I thought, why cause a rift between friends. I had received many such letters in my life and never made a fuss about them. I don't really feel inclined to make a fuss about such things. It was better to be silent. Without telling my husband anything, I put the letter away in a drawer. And therein lay my doom. One day that letter landed up in my husband's hands, when I wasn't home. When I returned, there was a fire raging. I will never forget the way your friend behaved that day. Without finding out the background to what was, after all, nothing but a letter, he heaped abuse on me in such filthy language that my patience snapped. I left instantly. Before leaving I told him, you are not fit to be the husband of a well-educated, beautiful woman. You should have married a little girl and locked her away in your harem.'

Abha paused.

'And then?'

'I got his letter today. He has realized his error and asked me to return. I too have realized that we have no real shelter except the shelter provided by our husbands. Wherever I go, a bunch of men is bound to chase me on one pretext or another. There's Murari-babu, of course, there are some others too whom I will not name.' Abha stopped. Then, with a smile, she continued, 'You're the only exception. Honestly, you're the only gentleman here who's behaved like a gentleman, who hasn't bothered me with letters. I really am grateful to you for this, and this is the reason I told you all this. I can see your friend was right, you really are a strict puritan. It's time you got married though. Should I look for a bride?'

Wanly, Suren pretended to smile.

Glancing at her watch, Abha said, 'Oh, there's not much time before the train leaves. I'll take your leave. Remember what I said.'

She left.

The Saving Grace

1

THE WELL-ESTABLISHED SHORT-STORY WRITER AMBUJAKSHA Bhowmick was extremely worried. All writers in the literary market were in trouble these days. There was no one to appreciate good writing, the going price for good writing wasn't high, and a group of critics was always ready with its claws sharpened to tear into good writing. But Mr Bhowmick's current cause for concern was different. He had started on a new story two days ago—started it rather pleasingly, thrilling himself several times in the course of writing—but he couldn't for the life of him decide how to end this scintillating narrative. Bringing a story to a suitable conclusion was indeed a difficult proposition—every writer knew that. Now close to the ending, Mr Bhowmick had stopped his narrative flow. Four cups of strong tea and a packet of cigarettes had been consumed since morning, but the story simply could not be ended.

Mr Bhowmick sat in the lonely second-floor room. The doors were open. Through them wafted in a slight breeze, his wife's voice, the sound of children rushing around and the cawing of two crows. The breeze wasn't unpleasant, but all the other sounds seemed to eject the plot of the story by the scruff of its neck from his mind. Frowning, he shut the door and, lighting an enormous cigar, proceeded to jiggle his knees. Some time passed this way. The knees became exhausted, but no headway was made on the story. Instead of bothering his tired knees any more, Mr Bhowmick got busy with his right ear. Inserting a matchstick gingerly into the right earhole, he screwed up his right eye and cheek. He simply had to write the ending that day, for it was the last day for submitting the story. If he missed the deadline, he wouldn't feature in next month's issue of the magazine. Not only would that mean missing out on twenty-five rupees, it would also diminish his worth—both with his editor and his wife.

He had promised the editor a long and fantastic story for a fee of twenty-five rupees, and before that he had promised his wife a sari with a price-tag of twenty-five rupees. You have to keep your second wife happy, after all.

It was only to please his wife that he had agreed to write for the magazine in the first place. Would he ever have agreed otherwise to write a sensational story for a third-rate magazine? Ambujaksha Bhowmick was a famously conservative writer. In every story of his he had depicted the victory of good and the decimation of evil. This was the kind of story he was particularly adept at. In a well-known book of his, he had proved that he was unparalleled when it came to presenting moral advice in the guise of fiction. Every young man and woman—in fact, not just young men and women, but everyone of every age—should read it. A writer such as he, having arrived at the threshold of old age, had landed himself in a pickle—by agreeing to meet a pulp magazine editor's requirements, just for his wife's pleasure. He had a nice moral story ready—how the God-fearing zamindar of Bilashpur was bankrupted in order to protect the purity of an unknown woman, how the villainous Madhablal met his death after being struck by lightning, and how that bankrupt zamindar regained his estate with the help of a holy man only because of all the good he had done. He had recounted all of this in simple, flowing language in a story named 'The Pure Woman's Blessings'. But the editor of this magazine, who probably roamed the bylanes of Continental thoughts and ideas with his minus-three-powered glasses, had not approved of that story. He had also hinted at the kind of story he would prefer. Keeping in mind his young wife's sweet but injured expression, Mr Bhowmick had muttered *que sera sera* and got down to it. But despite his determination, he wasn't getting any inspiration for the ending. Eventually he had been compelled to insert a matchstick into his earhole.

2

'Ouch!' said Mr Bhowmick as he withdrew the matchstick. Looking out of the window, he saw a monkey grimacing from the tiled roof of a nearby building, the sight of which had forced an old woman to stand guard over the food she had laid out to dry in the sun. Aware that such trivial scenes would not prove useful to the story he was spinning, he looked in a different direction. Which meant looking at the walls of his own room. But there was nothing on the walls of his rented flat, either, that could save the day for his story titled 'For Love'. Up against a brick wall, Mr Bhowmick shut his eyes and drew on his cigar. As soon as he did, he had to open his eyes—the cigar had gone out, it had to be relit. Doing just that expertly, he tried to unravel what the next steps in the story should be. The hero had just climbed over the wall of the heroine's house. It was the middle of a pitch-dark night. There was a drizzle. The hero was trying to crawl up to a guava tree and take shelter beneath it. But confronted by a cow, he was unable to proceed further.

Mr Bhowmick had written effortlessly up to this point. But he simply could not fathom what turn the storyline should take in order to preserve Art, or what intricate acts on the part of the hero would make the editor happy. He had always delineated the triumph of good and the downfall of evil—he could not work out any more what to do with this immoral hero. His personal inclination was to horsewhip the scoundrel. But that would endanger Art, and in endangering Art lay the endangering of a twenty-five-rupee fee.

'Oh God, how difficult this is!' He proceeded to call on God with all his heart. 'Oh Lord, deliver me from this dilemma. I cannot depict sin; nor can I annoy my wife. Have pity, oh merciful God.'

God seemed to hear his plea.

Everything was fixed in two minutes.

After the earthquake, the ectoplasmic Mr Bhowmick discovered that his wife would no longer need an expensive sari.

For she was now a widow.

Happenstance

1

MRS USHA SEN WAS A MODERN WOMAN.

In other words, she had a BA degree, could move around all by herself using public transport, and liked to buy things herself after extensive window-shopping. She was neither needlessly brazen nor unnecessarily shy. She was fond of literature. She had clear opinions about which writers were good and which writers mediocre. Her appearance? Not beautiful, exactly, but definitely attractive. When she walked around, immaculately dressed, most spectators looked admiringly at her. In short, Ms Sen was a brisk, refined, enlightened gentlewoman.

But there was one area in which she was traditional. She had married—and the wedding had not taken place in accordance with modern methods and tastes. The responsibility for that, however, lay with Annada Sen— Usha Sen's father. He was a fundamentalist. As soon as he heard that his daughter was attracted to a classmate named Manindramohan, belonging to a different caste, he promptly delved into horoscopes and genealogies, delivering Usha into the hands of Brajabihari Gupta and heaving a sigh of relief. Having secured his medical degree about three years earlier, Brajabihari was trying to set sail on Calcutta's sea of sickness. But there was no wind in his sails as yet. Usha had been unable to object to the wedding, not having the determination required for it. Hers was a rather soft, gentle heart. That was why the intention of committing suicide also remained secret, without being converted into action. But Usha Sen had made one vow—'I will never dress in a georgette sari.' Manindramohan was extremely fond of georgette saris and was supposed to buy Usha one in the future—but Brajabihari's advent made that impossible. Everything in her life shattered, Usha Sen vowed at least never to dress in a georgette sari.

But as I said before, she lacked determination. This vow was broken too. This story explains how that happened.

2

Parul was visiting Usha and Brajabihari.

Parul Maitra had been a year senior to Usha in college, but she wasn't married yet. She was far from indifferent to clothes and cosmetics, thanks to both of which she actually looked younger than Usha. After some gossip, she said, 'I'll be off now, I need to go shopping.'

'What for?'

With a demure smile, Parul said, 'I want to buy a sari. I believe the georgettes are lovely this year.'

'Really?'

Parul left.

The conversation about georgette saris reminded Usha of Manindramohan. She felt some sadness too—especially at the fact that the intensity of her sadness at not having got Mani seemed to have dissipated. Why, she didn't even think of Mani all that much any more. Two years had passed, and she no longer had any information about him. She was now Mrs Gupta, and there was no denying that she had entwined herself entirely with Brajabihari's joys and sorrows. Her heart no longer paid homage to the memory of the past. It was busy with the pulsating present. Brajabihari was not a bad person, he left no stone unturned trying to make Usha happy, and he was, moreover, her husband. Bit by bit he had conquered Usha's heart.

Realizing this, Usha found her mind drifting. For no particular reason, she recited to herself, 'I love him. I love him still. I will never dress in a georgette sari in my life—I will *not* break my vow.'

The second bomb on this avowed fortress was dropped by her sister Sandhya Sen, who had now become Sandhya Das. Her husband was a Deputy Magistrate. Needless to say, the Deputy was more capable than the freshly-minted doctor when it came to earning an income. For this reason, and because of the closeness of their ages, Usha was a little envious of Sandhya. Now that both of them were adults, catfights were no longer permissible. On the contrary, each tried to outdo the other in verbally expressing generosity towards each other. But silently, they still competed through the weapons of jewellery and clothes. If Usha bought a pair of delicate earrings to adorn her ears, Sandhya would immediately dangle an even more delicate pair, provoking Usha to look for the most delicate of them all. If Sandhya were to somehow let it slip that her sandals had cost five rupees, Usha immediately had to inform her, 'Yes, very nice sandals, personally I love them. But he just hates the straps. See, this is what he chose for me—six-and-a-half rupees, can you believe it! And it's horrible how they squeeze my toes!'

Therefore, when the very same Sandhya appeared before her sister on two successive evenings in two different kinds of georgette saris, Usha was in trouble. But she still would not dress in a georgette sari. 'They're not that expensive,' she told herself. 'If not for my vow I would have bought some ages ago.'

The third bomb was hurled by her friend Chhaya.

Chhaya had come to fetch Usha on their way to the cinema. She was dressed in a georgette sari too. A lovely white georgette with beautiful embroidery. As soon as Usha appeared in her carefully arranged silk sari, Chhaya said, 'Silk in this weather! Don't you have a georgette?'

'No.'

'They're very popular these days—why don't you buy one? They're not very expensive either. This one I have on cost just eleven rupees . . .'

'Is that all?' The words escaped Usha's lips.

The appearance of several georgette saris in different shades between her and Manindramohan's image in her memory dimmed that image not a little. Usha watched the film somewhat distractedly. Its story, too, was a tragic tale of unsuccessful love. The heroine in this story too had not got the man she had loved when young, and was now learning to love the man she had been married to instead. This was the strange tragedy of life. During the interval, Usha noticed that one or two of the women among the audience were also dressed in georgette saris. At this point she finally told herself, 'If I could actually marry someone else, then why get worked up about the georgette? All those vows I made—how many have I actually managed to keep anyway? How many are even possible to keep! But still, I'm not buying a georgette . . .'

Despite the onslaught of several devastating bombs, Usha's avowed fortress had not collapsed as yet. It still stood upright, somehow. But that evening, at a performance of *Chitrangada*, she was completely overcome. A fusillade of bombs seemed to be hurled continuously at her fortress. Georgette saris everywhere! She felt as though she was the only one there in a sari from Kashmir, and that everyone was laughing at her georgette-less appearance.

The final bomb was hurled from a car.

Later that evening, a car drew up before the house. A young woman in a georgette sari sat inside. Very pretty. Standing at a first-floor window, Usha saw her husband emerge from his dispensary with a big smile as soon as the car drew up and get in beside the young woman. Who was she? A patient? She didn't look sick. Usha was not to be blamed—curiosity was bound to peak in such a situation.

As soon as her husband returned, she asked, 'Who was that girl who came to fetch you?'

'A nurse at the hospital. Dr Biswas hosted a tea party for us today, you see. That was Susie.'

'Very pretty girl. She looked lovely in a georgette. Buy me one, won't you?'

'Why not? How much is it, though?'

'How expensive can it be? They're quite cheap these days, I believe. Maybe ten or fifteen rupees. Chhaya was dressed in one the other day—eleven rupees, she said. No hurry . . .'

'All right, let me see. One of my patients owes me sixteen rupees. I'll send a bill tomorrow. If he pays up I'll buy you the sari.'

3

The very next day her friend Chhaya appeared. She had a secret to share. Conjuring up a mysterious expression, she whispered into Usha's ear, 'Mani-babu is in Calcutta for a few days. I didn't know. Malati got to know from a friend of hers. Do you want to meet him? I've got hold of the address—here you are. I have to go now. Go on, meet him— no harm meeting, is there?'

Usha just sat there, holding the address. Mani—so close

by. The half-forgotten days from college crowded her mind. The madness of those days long gone seemed to take hold of her all over again. That same gentle, timid man— quiet, peaceable, modest. She could see Manindramohan's face clearly in her mind's eye. No, she simply wasn't going to get herself a georgette sari—she would tell her husband not to get one as soon as he came home . . . Of course, she would meet Mani-babu—Harish Mukherjee Road was quite close by, in any case.

Usha went out as soon as evening fell. Locating the house didn't prove much of a problem. But what happened inside was completely unexpected.

'Why didn't you let me know?'

'I didn't have your address. You didn't keep in touch ever since you left college. I heard from someone you'd got married. Where, to whom—I knew nothing.' Mani-babu smiled. At that moment—with the words 'And how are we today?'—Dr Brajabihari entered the room, only to be immensely surprised.

'You here!'

Usha was no less astonished.

'We were in college together. Is he your patient?'

A little later, in their car, Brajabihari showed Usha a packet. 'Here's your sari. He was the one who owed me the money. Luckily he paid up today, which let me save face with you. Do you like the colour?' Brajabihari proceeded to unwrap the packet himself.

Usha couldn't speak.

Penance

1

THE TRAIN ROLLED ON.

Chandra-babu was alone in his compartment. But although at first sight there was no one else in there, the thoughts of countless people were piled up all around him. A thousand viewpoints of a thousand people, depicted on different kinds of paper in different words, different ways, different shades of ink. Silent and yet eloquent. It was drizzling—the dead of night, dark—the perfect time for a visit to dream land. In a reverie, Chandra-babu popped a paan into his mouth. Taking his little tin of zarda from the pocket of his shirt, he tapped on the lid a couple of times before opening it, and then took a generous pinch, half-closed his eyes, and placed it luxuriously in his mouth before opening the window and spitting. He had to shut the window instantly because of a strong gust of wind. Still lost in his reverie, Chandra-babu returned slowly to his seat. He was a man deliberate in his actions—not the kind to rush into things impulsively or behave restlessly. Whatever he did was after detailed consideration. He had already shortlisted five letters. There was no time to read each and every letter—he had a job to do, after all. Had he the time, he would surely have read many more—if not all—of the letters. His curious mind was never fatigued where such things were concerned. He had mastered different techniques for opening envelopes secretly, always carrying the necessary equipment with him.

Chandra-babu turned the envelopes over in his hand before proceeding to read the letters one by one with great concentration.

2

Chandra-babu was neither a young man, nor an immobile old man. As a matter of fact, in appearance he resembled a ripened coconut. He was middle-aged, but it was difficult to say just which zone of middle age he occupied. His employment records showed him as forty-eight, but that was a lie. It was difficult to say how many years he had snipped off his age, for none of those who did know were alive any more. Nor could you make out his age from his features. He had taken refuge in the razor and hair-dye as soon as his hair, moustache and beard started greying. He was not someone who would be caught unprepared before his young—and third—wife Madhuri. But no matter how old he was, Chandra-babu hadn't dried up within. Even the ripe coconut secretes sweet juice, after all. The lifeless look in his glazed eyes, typical of the addict, actually reflected the reveries he was perpetually sunk in. He had been on a quest for sensual pleasures since adolescence. It's true that he had never written poetry—such trivial pursuits never satisfied him. What use was writing poetry? *Being* the poetry or *feeling* the poetry—in other words, tasting it through real life—was the true purpose of existence. Which he had done many times over. Had his cousin Tena been alive, he could have recounted with what eagerness—and ignoring what kind of hardship—Chandra the adolescent boy used to eavesdrop near the wedding chambers of newly married brides and grooms. There was no count of the number of windows he had tried to listen through, the number of holes he had peeped through. He had been very lusty as a young man too. That history was known by the doctors who knew him then, as well as his two departed wives. Wish—and it shall be granted. God had secured for him the perfect job: he was a mail sorter on the Royal Mail Service.

He'd had—and would continue to have—the opportunity to feel a great deal of poetry.

Oh, the things he had seen in all those letters! Such amazing things. Take the letterhead of that man with formidable degrees—but just such a man of letters had written to his wife (though God alone knew whether she was his wife or not) in the kind of obscene language that could not possibly be repeated. However, it had been a pleasure to read.

Earlier, Chandra-babu used to open letters written in a feminine hand only—he still opened a few of them—but experience had shown him that women could not write salacious letters. Theirs were mostly replete with sentiments like 'I am fine' and 'How are you?' At the most, 'I miss you' and 'When will you come?' And, at the end, the same tried and tested words, 'Do write back. Yours respectfully . . .' Plenty of spelling mistakes, too. He had got a few 'My kisses', but most of them were tripe. It wasn't as though he had never encountered a woman with romance in her words—and it was in that expectation that he still deigned to open one or two letters written in a feminine hand—but that was very seldom indeed. Most of them were useless. The other day he had got a long list of things to be purchased. Women simply did not write entertaining letters—such was Chandra-babu's experience.

When he saw a woman's name on the envelope, written in a male hand, Chandra-babu was delighted. Only men's letters had any body to them. Of course, he had sometimes been disappointed there as well. He was not familiar with any language other than Bengali or English. Sometimes he would open a letter addressed to a woman in a male hand, only to find the letter within written in Hindi or some other language. Or perhaps it was a letter from a father to his daughter, or from a son to his mother. Sometimes he also opened pedestrian letters where the relationship between the man writing them and the woman receiving them wasn't clear at all. But even discounting all of these, it was on the whole letters from men that Chandra-babu had enjoyed the most. He had even copied portions of the best letters. Men had no reservations—they let their pens run riot. Moreover, they were reckless. It was in a letter written by a man that he had once found a hundred-rupee note. Someone had sent it secretly to his sweetheart. Of course, he had found a currency note just that one time, but he had found photographs many times. An entire album of his had been filled up. All kinds and all manner of photographs, representing many different nationalities and peoples— French, German, Jew, Japanese, Bengali, Oriya . . .

Women's letters did astonish him sometimes, though. One of the letters had the imprint of a pair of lips. They even spoke ardently sometimes. But still, Chandra-babu was more inclined towards men's letters.

3

He was disappointed with the first letter in a woman's hand that he opened. But still he read it.

Didi

We got your reply card yesterday. It may not be a matter of shame for you to write to us on a reply card, but it is for us. You should realize I have to take care of everything here all by myself. Baba doesn't look after anything at all. On top of that I have my job. I don't get a moment to spare. Even so, two days before getting your letter I had sent Gadadhar to the jeweller's. Your ornaments are ready. When I had checked a week ago they hadn't got beyond the earrings. I was supposed to have checked again on Saturday. But I simply don't have the time. I'm very busy with the prize distribution ceremony at school, and I'm in charge of the Girl Guides too. I'm sending your receipt to Talukdar-babu rightaway, you can write to him to have your ornaments delivered. The earrings are marvellous. I can't tell about the others, as there's no time to go and see them. I beg of you not to write such cruel letters. They upset me.

Yours
Namita

Chandra-babu sniffed at the letter. It had a faint fragrance. Shutting his eyes, he tried to conjure up the image of a sharp-tongued, incensed young woman. But the picture that inevitably swam up in his mind's eye every time was of a teacher whom he knew—distended veins in her neck, the appearance of a witch, her bones sticking out, a hooked nose . . .

'To hell with it!'

Chandra-babu opened the second letter.

Dearest

I have received your letter. If all of you don't exercise a little control in these difficult times, how do you expect me to cope? The price of rice has crossed forty rupees, dal is incredibly expensive, vegetables and fuel are following suit. Nilambar said flour with soapstone in it is seventy-five paise. Mustard oil has hit two rupees. I didn't even dare ask the price of ghee. Still I have purchased as much as I could of the month's supplies. I couldn't pay for everything. A lot of it is on credit. I had no choice but to borrow some money, Navin needed twenty rupees. How much can I manage on my own? Do you *have* to wear a petticoat in such bad times? Why did you have to go and buy that one-rupee-a-yard fabric suddenly? That too on credit? Do you think I'm a font of money? They wear me out to the bone, but these people give me, not a thousand, not five hundred, but a mere seventy-five rupees. How many times do I have to remind you of that? I'm at the end of my tether. Why do you need to buy such expensive zarda? That shop next door is going to make me bankrupt . . .

'What a pain . . .'

Frowning, Chandra-babu returned the letter to its envelope. In four pages of minuscule handwriting, the entire letter was in the same vein.

The third letter was also in a man's hand.

The name on the envelope said Nilima Basu. The envelope was pink. This letter disappointed Chandra-babu too. Nilima was a man's name!

Nilima-babu

You left a couple of things behind: your hockey-stick and your cigar case. I'm enclosing your urine test report, which has just arrived. Four per cent sugar—that's terrible . . .

'Oh damn!'

He opened the fourth letter. This was a nice thick one, also written in a male hand. As soon as he opened it, a photograph fell out. An amazing photograph. He had seen all kinds of photos on all kinds of postcards, but never one of this kind. Beautiful! Chandra-babu gazed at it, enraptured. His lifeless eyes suddenly came to life. Putting the photo aside, he began reading the letter breathlessly. Wonderful! At last, the pot of gold at the end of the ranbow. Now *this* was a letter. Quite a lad, the writer. From Vatsyayana to Freud via Havelock Ellis, he'd left no one untouched. What phrases! What descriptions! Chandra-babu's nostrils flared, his lips quivered. Once . . . twice . . . He read the letter thrice over. Still he wasn't satisfied. He had an impulse to keep the letter—but no, that would be unethical. No need to keep it, all he had to do was to copy the best parts. There was pleasure even in copying such material. He must read it out to Madhuri. Of course, he wasn't going to meet her for three days—but he would after three days, wouldn't he? He had read out such letters to Madhuri many times in the past. Suddenly her face swam up before his eyes. Madhuri was a queer sort. Nothing seemed to please her; she always had a glum expression when he went near her. And yet how lovely she was, a dimple appeared when she smiled—but she just wouldn't smile. Be that as it may, he had to read out parts of this letter to her. He'd see whether she smiled or not once she had heard those lines.

He copied them eagerly.

Once he had finished, he read it from start to finish once more before putting it back in the envelope. The photo stayed outside, however.

Now for the fifth letter.

The address was typewritten in English on a blue envelope.

This kind of letter often held unexpected pleasures. Many husbands left typed envelopes with their wives. Those typist girls also wrote saucy letters to their boyfriends sometimes. He had struck gold several times in typewritten envelopes.

Transferring some more paan and zarda into his mouth, Chandra-babu moved his jaws slowly, eyes half-shut. His mouth filled with juice. Opening the window once more, he spat. God, how loud the thunder was. He shut the window. The fourth letter seemed to have intoxicated him. What stupendous details. Once he read it to her, Madhuri would surely . . .

He opened the fifth letter.

Ananga

I'm so happy to hear you're coming. I've been waiting for you so long. I can't take it any more. Take me away, I beg of you, take me away wherever you can. I'll go wherever, however you want me to go with you. Just rescue me from this hell. The fossil will be away on duty from tomorrow morning. He'll be back in three days. I do hope you'll be here by tomorrow morning or evening. I'll be ready. A thousand kisses.

Yours and yours alone,
Madhuri

There was a violent crack of thunder.

Ramshebak the Devotee

RAMSHEBAK ROY EVENTUALLY DID SOMETHING EXTRAORDINARY, though he was not an extraordinary man. Born into a middle-class Bengali family, he had been brought up in the traditions and practices—good as well as bad—of such families. The brass idol of the god Narayan, complete with all his accessories, used to be worshipped ritually every day in his home, and he used to be part of the process too. As an adult, he continued reposing his faith in the god, performing his daily worship twice a day before the idol. Only once in his youth had he strayed marginally, falling in love with Montu before his marriage. But she was a girl from the neighbourhood, compatible in terms of family and caste, which meant there was no particular obstacle.

Ramshebak had been a good student at school.

Those were the days of British rule. He applied for a prized position that had fallen vacant, but didn't get it. Not even vows made to the gods and goddesses helped. The Englishman appointed the son of an acolyte.

Struggling as a clerk all his life, he had managed to earn a salary of only two hundred rupees close to the end of his life. Not even the most ardent of pleas and prayers to the deity installed at home had led to any improvement in his finances. He'd had eight children, three of whom had died. He had left no stone unturned for their treatment, praying to the gods with all his might. But still they had not survived. One died of tetanus, one of cholera, one of

241

typhoid. The doctors' treatment failed, the gods were not kind either.

After retiring from his job, Ramshebak had had one more desire. He had stood in the elections for the post of commissioner of the local municipality. Plenty of money was spent, a priest was engaged to step up the level of rituals for the family deity. But he did not win the war. Golok-babu, well known for being a drunkard and a scoundrel, was elected.

Eventually his hour of death arrived. As per tradition, his children surrounded him, chanting the names of the gods and goddesses.

Suddenly Ramshebak shouted, 'Shut up!'

The eldest son said, 'Baba, shall I bring the idol of Narayan for you?'

'Shut up!'

The offspring were dumbfounded.

Montu was seated near his head, sobbing. Ramshebak said, 'Come here before me, before me.'

As soon as she did, he took her hand and, looking into her eyes, breathed his last.

The local newspaper, however, said Rameshebak Roy died with the names of the gods on his lips.

A Tagore Tale

ONE SUMMER I HAD BEEN TO VISIT HIM. IT WAS VERY HOT that day. Seeing me perspiring profusely, he asked, 'Feeling very hot? Come closer to the fan.'

He smiled. 'We have electricity here at last. After years spent here at the height of summer . . .'

'It must have been very hard . . .' I said.

'No, it wasn't,' he smiled in reply. 'I know an excellent way to dispel the heat.'

I looked at him, a question in my eyes.

'Writing poetry,' he said. 'I'd start on a poem at noon— who knew where the afternoon went. Suddenly I'd discover it was evening.'

When I visited him another day, he was hunched over his desk, writing.

'Sit down,' he told me. I thought it must be very painful, writing in that hunched pose.

'They have all these different kinds of desks these days,' I said. 'You can write even when you're leaning back in your chair.'

'I have all of those,' he said, 'but still I have to write this way at this desk. The water's running low in the pitcher, nothing comes out unless you turn it upside down.'

The Next Day

EVENTUALLY HE MET THE ALMIGHTY HIMSELF.

'Who are you?' asked the Almighty.

'I am Dibakar.'

'Dibakar? My creation, Dibakar the sun, emits a million rays, he's unbounded energy. But you're so scrawny. Who named you?'

'My grandfather . . .'

'What do you want?'

'A job.'

'Any degrees?'

'BA.'

'What do you know?'

Dibakar was caught short. He realized he couldn't hoodwink the Almighty. He was omniscient.

'I know nothing, sir. I copied to pass all my exams.'

'Why did you do that?'

'Sir, they don't need knowledge in the job market, they need jobs, so that's where my inclination lay. I've spent a lot of money for a degree. But I haven't got a job. If you could get me one . . .?'

'But I have no portfolio. You can't get anyone a job if you don't have a portfolio.'

Dibakar lost his head suddenly.

He forgot whom he was talking to.

Brandishing the homemade pipe-gun in his hand, he said, 'I'll murder you if you don't get me a job.'

A gentle smile appeared on the Almighty's face.

244

'Why waste a bullet on me?' he said. 'I am immortal. I have been living since the beginning, I will live for eternity. I came to you because you were crying out for me so desperately. But you are asking me for something that is not in my power to provide. You can't get anyone a job if you don't have a portfolio.'

'Then you have to do something for me.'

'What can I do? Since you're ignorant, you must live like a beast—eat, drink, roam.'

'But what shall I eat? I'm starving. I haven't eaten for two days.'

The Almighty had a small pot with a nozzle.

'All right, open your mouth. I will give you food.'

'What's in there?'

'Nectar. It satiates the hunger of the gods, makes them immortal.'

Dibakar opened his mouth, and the Almighty poured nectar into it. But Dibakar wasn't satisfied. 'I felt nothing,' he said. 'No taste, no smell. I don't even feel as though I've had anything.'

'That's what nectar is like.'

The Almighty disappeared.

The next day it was clear Dibakar was a man, not a god. For the nectar neither satiated his hunger, nor made him immortal. His corpse was found in the garden, with a bullet wound in his temple.

The Will

1

'LOVE, LOVE, LOVE! NO CONCERN ABOUT THE INHERITANCE going to the dogs . . .'

Alone in his room, Binoy-babu uttered these words quite loudly, and proceeded to stare at the wall before him with bulging, reddened eyes. On the wall hung a photograph of a smiling young man. The smile did not pale an iota under Binoy-babu's angry glare. Binoy-babu went on staring at the photograph for some time more. Then he took a sheet of paper from a drawer of his desk, inserted it in a large envelope and wrote the address. 'Jagadish! Jagadish!' he called.

Jagadish, the servant, entered.

'This letter needs to be sent by registered post. Registered with acknowledgement due. Got it? Very important letter. What happened to the coffee that Sukhan was bringing?'

'Let me check.'

Jagadish left with the letter.

Sukhan entered a little later with the coffee tray. Not only did the tray have the coffee paraphernalia, it also held a plate of grapes. Warm grapes soaked in brandy. A doctor with a degree acquired in the UK had taught him this technique for consuming grapes. It was an expensive affair, but ever since he had adopted it, the debilitation of his nerves had diminished a lot. They were delicious, too. So he had been continuing this regimen for the past six months.

Finishing his coffee, along with the grapes, he told Sukhan, 'Send Jeetu in now.'

About ten minutes later, the dark servant-boy named Jeetu entered. Some time ago, he used to play the role of Krishna in the local theatre troupe. Now, attracted by a higher salary, he had become Binoy-babu's masseur. Binoy-babu bathed only after his body had been massaged with three different kinds of oil. He started with piping hot water, gradually reducing the temperature till he ended with ice-cold water. It took him almost two-and-a-half hours to finish the whole thing. The rice in his meals was of the best variety, imported from Peshawar. His indulgences over his meals were by no means minimal. A fish curry, fried fish, and a sweetened sauce at the end were compulsory, besides two kinds of dal and vegetables. Dinner consisted of a small quantity of pulao, an entire roasted chicken and steamed apple. He was very particular about his beverages, using nothing but the best tea and coffee. No sooner did summer arrive than he had to hotfoot it to Darjeeling or Shimla or Mussoorie or Ranikhet. He simply couldn't bear to remain in Calcutta after April.

In short, his lifestyle was quite an expensive affair. He didn't have to work at a job, for he owned a large business, being the joint owner of the enterprise named Chatto–Gango. But still he was worried. He had become extremely alarmed about the future. And at the root of it all was love.

You will find it difficult to understand unless I explain everything from the beginning. So let me start where it all began.

2

Long ago, Binoykumar Chattopadhyay and Manindrakumar

Gangopadhyay used to study together in the same college. They were very close friends. They occupied the same room in the same mess, doing everything—studies, sports, daily activities—together. Neither of them could spend much time away from the other. During vacations, they spent their time together, dividing it equally between their respective homes.

After spending their college life this way, when it was time to start earning a living, separation seemed imminent. Binoykumar left Calcutta with a job as a college professor. Not having got himself a job yet, Manindrakumar accompanied him. A couple of months later, Acharya Prafulla Chandra Roy came to the Annual Day celebrations of the college. The essence of his lecture was that Bengalis were doomed unless they set up their own business ventures. He said that rather than take up a poorly-paid college teacher's job after getting an MA degree, or haunting the trees around the court precincts after securing a BL degree, it would be preferable even to set up a paan shop. 'Bengali young men are intelligent,' he said, 'and if they could add firmness of character to that quality, they would be unbeatable as businessmen.' He even gave an indication of how many different types of businesses could be started with low investments. He concluded by saying that the real capital needed for business was not money but character.

Shortly afterwards, a childless uncle of Manindrakumar's died. As his heir, Manindrakumar received about five thousand rupees. The two friends then decided after a discussion that it would be better to get into business than to remain in slavery. They would be able to stay together, and earn together. Even if Binoy could not contribute money to the capital it didn't matter. If he could invest the capital of his character in its entirety, Manindrakumar had no problems in sharing the profits equally with him. That was how Chatto–Gango Enterprise was born. After his father's death, Binoykumar had also contributed five thousand rupees to the capital.

They started with a textile business. Acharya Roy's prophecy proved true, and the business made rapid strides.

Both the friends got married after their business enterprise took wing. Binoykumar was the first to get married, Manindrakumar following suit after four years. He took his time because of frail health.

Binoykumar had a son and Manindrakumar a daughter. Because of this happy situation, which was a matter of chance, another possibility occurred to them. Manindrakumar expressed the wish that in future he hoped to see his daughter Debi marry Binoykumar's son Unmesh. Binoykumar agreed eagerly. As they discussed this, their emotions ran so high that they decided to lock this wish into law. Because they were opposed to child-marriage they didn't get them married to each other right away, but they decided mutually to write wills that would ensure that even in their absence their children would be compelled to honour this special wish of theirs. It was decided that the wills would state that only if Debi and Unmesh were legally married to each other would they inherit their respective shares of Chatto-Gango Enterprise. If either of them was not willing to marry the other, he or she would be deprived of his or her share of the inheritance. If neither was willing, both of them would be deprived. In that case ownership of the business would pass to the Ramakrishna Mission, with the profits being used for the Mission's work. Their lawyer Rajanibhushan Kanungo was a far-sighted, wise man. He said, 'It wouldn't be right to impose so many conditions on the likes and dislikes of your children. They should be given some freedom. What are your fathers' names?'

'The late Motilal Chattopadhyay.'

'The late Srinath Gangopadhyay.'

'I'm drafting what I think would be appropriate and logical, take a look . . .'

Mr Kanungo scribbled on a piece of paper. 'If Miss Debi Ganguly refuses to marry a direct descendant of the late Motilal Chattopadhyay, she will be deprived of her inheritance. If Mr Unmesh Chatterjee, too, refuses to marry a direct descendant of the late Srinath Gangopadhyay, he will be deprived of his inheritance. In that case, Chatto–Gango Enterprise will be handed over to the Ramkrishna Mission.'

Binoy and Manindra saw nothing to object to in this, for they were the only children of their fathers, who in turn were the only children of their fathers. So this will would effectively meet their requirements for their children.

Mr Kanungo proceeded to draw up a will in legal parlance, and had it registered in due course. A year after the will was made, Manindrakumar died suddenly. Debi was five at the time. Manindra had not had any other children. Nor had Binoykumar, for Unmesh's mother died shortly after he was born. Binoykumar had not opted to marry again, devoting himself to bringing up his own son Unmesh and his friend's daughter Debi properly.

3

Here's where things stood sixteen years later.

Debi was reading for her MA, while Unmesh, having completed his studies in the country, was in London. Enjoying the easy and assured profits from the business, Binoykumar had become very self-indulgent. Not just indulgences, he had also lost his head over some vices, wasting a lot of money in speculation and investment in dud shares. His son Unmesh, too, was recklessly extravagant. The outcome was dire. The auditor of Chatto–Gango Enterprise had informed Binoykumar a few days ago that for several years he had been taking more money out of the company than his share of the profits. His debts were so large that his partner Manindrakumar's widow, Niharbala, was now for all intents and purposes the sole owner of the company. What Binoykumar had been spending had been given to him as a loan out of Niharbala's profits. Binoykumar was astounded. That was normal, for you never realize anything when spending money, you are astonished only after you do the calculations.

Binoykumar was a self-respecting man. That he was in debt to his friend's widow every single day was a blow to his self-esteem. He couldn't sleep for two nights wondering what Niharbala must be thinking. Finally he decided to talk to her directly about the situation. He would tell her about the will too. He had not told anyone about the will all this time. But he kept postponing the visit—and meanwhile, Niharbala suddenly died. Her only daughter Debi should by rights have become the inheritor.

Binoykumar tried to bring up the subject of the will with her one day.

Debi said, 'Kaka-babu, I'm very busy with my studies. I can't rack my brains over a will now. I simply have to get a first class . . .'

'One minute. Do you have any objections to marrying Unmesh?'

'Unu-da?'

She giggled suddenly.

'Why such a question?'

'There's a reason. If you're not willing to marry Unu, according to Mani's will you won't get your share of Chatto–Gango Enterprise.'

'Then who will?'

'Unu. Provided of course he's willing to marry you.'

'And what if he isn't? There's no guarantee he will, see how dark I am. Do you know Unu-da's nickname for me? Witch! He probably won't agree. What then?'

'He won't get anything either. After my death everything will go to the Ramakrishna Mission.'

'Never mind. Why worry about all that now?'

'I'm worrying because I have already spent my share of the profits. I'm having to borrow from what should be your share. It's going against my conscience. If you'd agree to be my daughter-in-law, it wouldn't. And that's what Mani had wanted . . .'

'All right, I have no objection. What about Unu-da?'

'I don't know yet. I have written to him.'

4

Binoykumar was crushed at Unmesh's response.

Unmesh had written . . .

Respected father,

I've received your letter. I cannot marry Debi out of greed for my inheritance. I have decided to marry a girl named Lucy. She's a wonderful girl, I'm sure you'll like her. But the wedding is some way off. She is already married to someone else, but she's estranged from her husband. They have filed for divorce. The divorce will go through. After that I will marry her. My exams will be over in a month. I will return home after that. Lucy will join me once the divorce is sorted out. We will get married in India. I await your approval and blessings.

Your son,
Unmesh

Binoykumar remained flabbergasted for some time at this letter. Just one thought kept recurring in his mind— would he have to remain indebted to that girl all his life? Unmesh was in the UK to learn more about textile engineering, the business might prosper more after his return, but unless he married Debi the business wouldn't even stay with him. Of course, he was taking some exam at Oxford University which might get him a job on his return. But would he, Binoykumar, be able to live in a household with Lucy? Impossible. After much thought, he wrote a long letter to his lawyer Rajanibhushan Kanungo, asking for advice. He put down everything in detail, but was then assailed by doubts over whether it was right to reveal family matters to an outsider. Unable to make up his mind for the next few days, he put the letter away in a drawer. But finally he did have to make up his mind, realizing after plenty of thought that when it came to the law he had no option but to seek Kanungo's help. Dispatching the letter through registered post, Jagadish brought him the receipt. He awaited Kanungo's reply impatiently.

5

Debi was done with her exams. They had gone off very well. Unexpectedly well. She had decided to go on a long holiday. She had become preoccupied with plans for a trip to Kashmir, when she suddenly heard about Unmesh one day. Unmesh had apparently returned to India and Binoykumar had apparently thrown him out of his house. The reason, it seemed, was that Unmesh had decided to marry a foreigner. She chuckled at the news. So she would soon be the sole owner of Chatto–Gango Enterprise. Suddenly Unmesh's face swam up before her eyes. Strikingly fair, a thin moustache, an arrogant expression. Quite full of himself. He thought the world of himself because he had secured a first class in his MSc Physics. She would get a first class too and show him she was not inferior. Not just a first class, she might also come first. Where was Unu-da now? Couldn't he have paid her a visit? Someone knocked on the door loudly. She suddenly wondered whether it was Unu-da. Opening the door, she saw it wasn't Unu-da, but the peon. He had brought a letter, a registered letter, with acknowledgment due. A letter from Binoykumar. She was surprised. What could Kaka-babu have to say to her through a registered letter? She opened the letter quickly.

My dear,

You will be amazed by this letter. But even after a great deal of thought, I am unable to find another way out. Unmesh is back from the UK. He has decided to marry a foreigner. He will not marry you. I have thrown him out of my house. I am enclosing a copy of the will that your father and I had made jointly. As you will realize when you read it, if you marry anyone from the family of my father, the late Motilal Chattopadhyay, the property will not have to be handed over to the Ramakrishna Mission. I do not want the institution that my friend and I built together to go into the hands of outsiders. It would have been wonderful had Unmesh and you been married. But he is a traitor, who does not care for the honour of the family. I do not know how much longer I have to live. It is clear from the auditor's report that, considering the amount I have spent, I will effectively have to throw myself on your mercy for the rest of my life. If I live a very austere life, I may just be able to pay back my debt before I die. But at this age, it will not be possible for me to change the way I live. It is very difficult for me to forego the luxuries that I have been used to all these years. Keeping all this in mind, I wrote a letter to our lawyer, Mr Kanungo, for his advice. He has written that all problems will be solved if I marry you. Hence I am proposing marriage to you through this letter. Even if it appears a laughable proposition, it is not illegal. If you agree, we can still save our enterprise. Keep in mind, too, that if you don't, you will have no rights over your inheritance.

Think it over carefully and let me know your reply as soon as possible. My best wishes.

Yours . . .

About a week later Binoykumar received her reply. Debi wrote . . .

Respected Kaka-babu,
I cannot possibly accept your proposal. I am solving the problem you have referred to in another way. I am gifting my inheritance to you. The deed of gift is being sent through registered post. I was ready to marry Unu-da, I still am. Therefore I am indeed the inheritor according to the will. But I am gifting you all my rights to the inheritance.

Yours sincerely,
Pronota Debi

6

Two years later, Binoykumar received another letter from Debi.

Respected Kaka-babu,
I hope you are in good health. I am writing to you with some good news. I had moved to this town as a professor in the local college. A few days later, Unu-da also turned up here as a professor of physics. He did not marry Lucy, who had reconciled with her husband instead of divorcing him. Do you know what Unu-da said to me about six months

ago? 'Debi, I would definitely have married you, but the thought that I would have to marry you in order to claim my inheritance was not acceptable to me. I met Lucy around the same time and came to like her. That's why I didn't agree to marry you. Now I dare not propose to you anymore. But I do think I would have been happy if you'd been mine.' Can you imagine! I didn't agree at first. But you know how adamant he can be. He kept bringing it up day after day. Eventually I agreed. We got married three months ago. We've rented a lovely bungalow by the river. Why don't you pay us a visit? If we know you're coming we'll prepare the first-floor flat for you.

Yours,
Pronota Debi

The Proof

THE VETERAN DOCTOR GHANYASHAM SEN LIMPED HIS WAY
to the throat specialist Dr Hazra's clinic. Dr Hazra was an
old-time friend of his. Their conversation was as follows.

SEN: A fish-bone seems to have lodged in my throat
during lunch. Can you pull it out? Seems to be stuck in the
tonsils. I *told* that fishwife not to give me small fish, but
she wouldn't listen, would she?

HAZRA: But you normally buy your own fish, don't
you? I don't remember you ever buying those small fish.
Then why all of a sudden . . .?

SEN: At the insistence of that hag of a fishwife. The rest
didn't have the large varieties today, except her—she had
some splendid chital and aar. So I asked her for a portion,
and she refused. 'Doctor, you've got gout, you're limping.
How can I give you aar? It's not allowed when you have
gout.' I said, 'Then give me some of that chital.' 'That's not
allowed either,' she said. I said, 'You think you know more
than me, when I'm the doctor here?' Rolling her eyes, she
said, 'I know very well which kinds of fish you're not
allowed with gout. You may be treating others, but not
yourself. You're a patient now, and you're as stubborn as
a baby.' Then she went and got me some small rohu from
someone else. Each of them a fountain of pointed bones.
One of which lodged in my throat barely as I'd begun my
lunch. Can you get it out?

HAZRA: Open wide . . .

257

Sitting in a chair, Dr Sen opened his mouth very wide. Using a tongue depressor to prevent the tongue from coming in the way, Dr Hazra shone a light into his throat.

HAZRA: Oh yes, you're right. The bone is in the tonsils all right. I'll get it out right away, keep your mouth open. Here . . . we . . . are. It's out. A very small bone . . .

Dr Hazra showed Dr Sen the bone at the tip of his forceps.

SEN: Naturally it's small, given the size of the fish . . .

HAZRA: You need to gargle.

Having finished gargling, Sen pulled a cigar out of his pocket and, lighting it perfectly, smiled at Hazra. 'What a mess.'

HAZRA: How cunning that fishwife is. I suspect both the aar and the chital had gone bad. She knows you're on good terms with the health officer, so she didn't dare palm off rotted fish on you. Pretending to be a well-wisher she got you fish from another shop. Clever witch . . .

SEN: You may be right. They're no less sharp than we are. But there's something else . . .

HAZRA: What . . .

SEN: That same fishwife had herself got gout once. I treated her. I was the one who told her not to have those kinds of fish. I'd told her to eat nothing but small fish.

HAZRA: But does it say anywhere in medicine that you must avoid aar, chital and bowaal when you have gout?

SEN: There's nothing in our medical sciences that links certain kinds of food to certain illnesses—at least, I haven't read any such thing. All this business about a specific kind of dal causing colds, or eggs causing gout, doesn't exist in our books. But ordinary people have a lot of faith in this kind of thing. And I try never to shake their faith.

HAZRA: So you think she's genuinely a well-wisher?

I don't think so. It's hard to believe that those who cheat you on weights whenever they can, sell fish that's gone bad, frequent the black market, will suddenly turn into generous well-wishers.

SEN: I can't prove it, but I think . . .

He smoked his cigar in silence.

But the proof became available the very next minute.

'Is Ghanyasham-babu the doctor here?' was heard in the local dialect.

Opening the swing doors to his clinic, Hazra discovered an ugly crone standing outside. Dr Sen, who had followed him, recognized the fishwife instantly.

'What is it? '

The essence of what the hag said in her dialect was:

'I know you haven't eaten today. We got large rohu in the evening at the market. Very fresh. So I got some for you. They said at your clinic you were here, so I came here to give it to you . . .'

'How much is it?'

'We can talk about the price later . . .'

The Second Bird

1

THIS STORY IS NOT BEING WRITTEN TO PROVE A SUPERSTITION. The objective is not to attribute authenticity to superstitions. It is just a recounting of what happened.

Educated in a convent school, Nandini Shome believed in a particular Western superstition. Spotting a single mynah led to sorrow, spotting a pair led to joy. One for sorrow, two for joy—it was a formula she had learnt from a classmate, the Anglo-Indian girl Alice. She had verified several times that it was true. When a single magpie kept strutting around the day of the mathematics exam, and she just couldn't spot a second one, all the questions proved so difficult that she failed. Another time, she saw the power of a pair of mynahs. The exams were just a week away, but she was completely unprepared for the history test. Every day, though, two mynahs appeared on the terrace of the house across the road. Whenever Nandini raised her eyes, she saw them, sitting side by side. Then, suddenly, a political wave swept over the city. The exams were postponed by three months. And Nandini Shome passed with honours in history. Since then, her faith in the mynah-theory had been unshakable.

2

Then she got to know Bhupen Rakshit. Back from the UK, Bhupen Rakshit was the zoology professor at their college. He was deeply interested in birds. They visited the bird-market in Calcutta frequently. He had bought Nandini a Paradise Flycatcher, but Nandini simply could not make it survive in her hostel room. It refused to eat, and one day she found it dead in its cage. Heartbroken, she had told Bhupen Rakshit, 'Don't buy me any more birds, I'll never have birds as pets again.'

Bhupen Rakshit had smiled. 'There's this one bird, though, that you will *have* to have. He won't starve to death. He will eat anything you offer. He won't fly away even if you keep the cage door open.'

A smile had appeared on Nandini's lips, a dream in her eyes.

'Agreed?' Bhupen Rakshit had asked.

'I have no objection. You have to write to Baba. I can't do anything without his approval.'

Nandini hadn't said anything more. What more *could* she have said?

3

Nandini Shome belonged to a town in Bihar. After completing her college education in Calcutta, she went back home. And was immediately plunged into the world of mynahs. As soon as she reached, she saw a pair of them strutting around in the yard. She cheered up immediately, looking at the pair of birds with smiling eyes. Mynahs couldn't bear to be gazed at for too long, they flew off. But they gave an audience to Nandini every day. A seed of hope had already been planted in the secret recesses of Nandini's heart. Thanks to the pair of mynahs, a few green leaves now began to sprout from it. About ten days later, a letter arrived from Bhupen Rakshit's maternal uncle. He was Bhupen's guardian. He had written to Nandini's father:

My nephew Bhupen Rakshit wishes to marry your daughter Nandini. I am not opposed to the proposition. If you agree, too, we can proceed to finalize dates according to mutual convenience.

Needless to add, Nandini's father had no objection either. Nandini noticed with joy that the pair of mynahs was putting in an appearance every single day. Sometimes on the parapet, sometimes on the terrace, sometimes in the field, sometimes in the yard.

Then it was time for Holi. Nandini's father had a job in a paint shop. He brought Nandini some durable German colours. The blue, in particular, was excellent—once a dab of it was applied anywhere, it never came off. Nandini had just filled her festive syringe with the blue shade when the mynahs appeared on the wall. Nandini sprayed them. They fled immediately. But they returned the next day. Nandini saw one of them had a splash of blue—the white feather beneath its wing had turned blue. Like the feather of a bluebird. They kept coming for several days after that, the blue not having faded yet. In fact, it looked increasingly beautiful. Bhupen's letters arrived regularly, too, lovely poetic letters.

Then, one day, the blue mynah didn't appear. Nandini's heart skipped a beat. The other mynah walked around, forlorn, alone. Nandini looked everywhere, but couldn't see the blue mynah anywhere. She visited other neighbourhoods in search of the bird but it was nowhere to be found. Bhupen's letters stopped, too. He used to write almost every day, but now there was no letter for almost a month. The solitary mynah still walked around.

A month later a letter from Bhupen finally arrived.

How fortunate the wedding didn't take place. When I got back from college the other day I started bleeding from the mouth. The doctors suggested an X-ray. Now they're suspecting tuberculosis. So I have to go to the sanatorium instead of the wedding venue. Your life would have been ruined if you'd married a sick man like me. You're a wonderful woman. I love you. That's why I hope with all my heart that you will be happy.

4

Several months passed.

Nandini had got a job as a schoolteacher. She still saw mynahs, but seldom in pairs. Sometimes a bunch of them, sometimes three, sometimes just one. It's not as though she had not seen a pair at all, but very rarely. Bhupen wrote sometimes. He said he would never marry. He knew her father wouldn't be willing to have his daughter marry a tuberculosis patient. Not even if he recovered. An uncrossable ocean appeared between Nandini and Bhupen. And on that same ocean, in sailed someone else—Nabin Ghosh. A handsome income-tax officer who had just passed his exam. Nandini liked him. Nabin Ghosh liked her a great deal too. Nandini's father wrote to Nabin's father, and the usual trite discussions went on for some time. Finally the wedding date was fixed. Nandini wrote a letter to Bhupen. 'I am getting married in March. I need your good wishes.'

Bhupen arrived on the morning of the wedding. He had a cage in his hand, a mynah in it.

'What's that . . .?' Nandini asked in surprise.

'I saw this fellow at Sultanganj station peddling birds. He had this mynah. There's something special about it. The white feather beneath its wing has a blue tinge. That's why I bought it. He threw in the cage. Isn't the blue lovely?'

Somebody drew a blue line of memory on the horizon of Nandini's heart.

'Let it go . . .'

The bird flew off as soon as the door was opened.

Flowers and People

BIKASH WAITED AFTER BANGING ON THE CLOSED DOOR. HE lingered for quite some time before the door to Alo's room. But while he waited, another piece of drama was unfolding in the veranda around the corner. There was a rajnigandha plant in a pot, the flowers blooming. A bee buzzed near the flowers.

'You're beautiful, you're beautiful, you're so very beautiful. But . . .'

The rajnigandha looked at the bee in silent inquiry. Her gaze contained her unspoken questions—'But what . . .?'

'If you weren't white but pink like the lotus, you'd have been even more beautiful. You'd have been unique . . .'

'But can I be anything but what I am?'

'Of course you can. Is there anything you cannot do? The creator himself awaits your orders eagerly. He will rebuild you just the way you want. All you need to do is wish for pink petals instead of white, and it will happen. Will you?'

After a silence, the rajnigandha said, 'I will. Since you ask.'

The bee flew away.

But he left in the rajnigandha's heart an unsaid statement—I prefer the colour of the lotus petal to yours.

Alo opened the door.

Her face lit up when she saw Bikash.

'Bikash! You were supposed to have been here in the morning. Why didn't you come? Where were you?'

'I'd gone to meet Tanima. I'm the secretary of their tennis

club. We had a meeting in the morning. We're sending Tanima this time too—she'll be the champion again.'

'Tanima's very versatile, isn't she?'

'For sure. She acts beautifully too. And have you ever heard her speak in public?'

'No . . .'

'She's wonderful!'

A shadow descended on Alo's face.

'You're very old-fashioned, aren't you?'

'I am who I am.'

'But you can change yourself if you want to. You're so fit and supple, you could set the tennis courts on fire. It's not difficult at all. And with a little practice you could sing, give speeches, anything you want . . .'

'I could?'

'Of course you could!'

'Would you be happy if I did?'

'Of course!'

The bee returned to the rajnigandha.

The rajanigandha couldn't become the lotus.

She tried, but couldn't.

The bee saw she had dried up.

He called her, kept calling her. But there was no response.

But Alo did.

She did become a well-known sportswoman, a well-known singer, a well-known public speaker. Her photographs were published in the papers. Enraptured crowds cheered her everywhere.

She and Bikash were married, too.

But though he got her, Bikash didn't get her. He felt that the light of his life—Alo, whom he had loved—had been put out, had changed, had been lost.

The Reunion

1

I WAS A GUEST AT A FRIEND'S HOUSE LONG AGO. CHHOBI WAS a former classmate of mine. We had studied together up to our matriculation examinations, but hadn't met since. Life had taken us our separate ways. I had become a clerk and he, a doctor. I suddenly ran into him at the railway station one day. I hadn't recognized him at first, not realizing that my childhood friend was hidden within the man with the salt-and-pepper beard, glasses and loose kurta-pyjamas. But he had spotted me all right. My emaciated appearance, sunken cheeks and lustreless deep-set eyes had not succeeded in fooling him. Suddenly he appeared before me, saying, 'Shotu, isn't it?'

I looked at him in surprise.

'I'm Chhobi.'

We embraced.

'Where are you going?'

'Liluah.'

'Is that where you live?'

'No, a brother-in-law of mine stays there. He works with the Railways.'

'Come, let's sit on this bench. The train won't leave for some time yet. Let's chat awhile. You look in pretty bad shape.'

We sat down side by side on the bench. 'For ten years now I've been ill with one thing or the other,' I said. 'I need

266

a change of air. My brother-in-law is going to Puri on holiday, so I decided to visit him, in case I can tag along. I'm not equipped to go on my own, physically or economically.'

I was embarrassed by my sudden confession. What was the point of telling someone else about one's poverty?

Chhobi looked at me with a frown. What he said after that was unexpected.

'I have a house in Madhupur. That's where I'm going. Come with me.'

I was surprised.

'I don't think so. I don't want to stay with a family whom I don't know. You may be my friend, but they're not. They'll consider me a burden.'

Chhobi laughed at the top of his voice. I had no idea he could laugh like that. The platform seemed to reverberate.

'You can rest assured on that front. I have no family. I'm not married. Tukra is all I have at Madhupur.'

'Who's Tukra?'

'A Santhal servant of mine. Come with me, there's no problem.'

Sincerity rang through his invitation. I went off with him.

2

I was charmed by what I saw at Madhupur. A huge house in the middle of an enormous, empty field. Gardens all round. It was winter. There was a carnival of roses.

I asked Chhobi, 'How far is the doctor? I have this stomach-ache at night sometimes . . .'

'I am the doctor. You'll be just fine here. Have some chicken every day. Tukra is a very good cook.'

I was walking round his garden. I sensed he was not only wealthy but also a man of fine tastes. He had so many different varieties of flowers in his garden. A small plant in one corner entranced me. It was covered with flowers, each of them streaked with white and violet. It looked, for all the world, like a girl in a sari with a floral print, laughing.

'What plant is this, Chhobi? How lovely it is.'

'I don't know what it's called. Tukra had planted the seed. Some wild plant.'

'I'd love to take some seeds home.'

'I'll tell Tukra . . .'

I stayed in Madhupur for a month. I'd have stayed longer, but I ran out of my leave of absence. However, there was a remarkable improvement in my health during that month. Chhobi didn't prescribe medicines. He only arranged for good food. I didn't get the stomach-ache either. The day I was leaving he said, 'The lack of good food is your real illness. At home you must eat what you were eating here.'

'How will I afford it?'

'I'll pay for it. I'll send you fifty rupees every month.'

'But why . . .?'

'I have the money. Spending it on other things would only mean wasting it. I don't want to do that. You're my childhood friend. What I got from you during this month is something I haven't got anywhere else. It's rare, it's priceless. You must come here whenever you can take some time off.'

Forcing a bundle of notes into my hand, he said, 'You must eat well. If you're alive, one of the problems in my life will be solved. I have no one, I'm all alone.'

He seemed to be crying in pain.

Just before my departure Tukra gave me a black seed.

'The seed you wanted, sir. Plant it anywhere and see it grow.'

Putting the seed in an envelope, I placed it in my pocket.

3

Back home, there was one crisis after another. Both my sons were ill, my wife had a pain in her side, the milkman went missing, we were out of sugar, the cycle had a puncture—all these disasters seemed to have been lying in wait for me, attacking me on my return. I had forgotten about the seed, remembering only about a fortnight later. I couldn't find it in my pocket anywhere. I searched everywhere, but it was no good.

4

A year went by. I hadn't had a chance to visit Madhupur again. A clerk doesn't get leave more than once a year. But Chhobi did send me fifty rupees every month without fail. I didn't hesitate in accepting it. The self-respect of a poor clerk is never perfect. But the money was almost never put to the use for which it was sent. I couldn't use it to buy fruit and milk, eggs and fish and meat for myself. The money just made things a little easier for my family, that was all. It's not as though I never managed to buy some good food. But all of us shared it. This was deception in a way. But could an impoverished clerk lead a life free of deception all the time? Sometimes he had to accept alms, sometimes he had to resort to deception too.

Then the bombshell came. I was told Chhobi had committed suicide. I rushed to Madhupur. He had been cremated by the time I reached. Apparently he had written a last note:

No one is responsible for my death. I'm leaving because I wasn't happy.

I heard the note was with the police.

5

A couple of months later I got a letter from a lawyer. It seemed Chhobi had bequeathed ten thousand rupees to me in his will. He had left a letter for me too with his lawyer, with instructions for sending it to me after his death. The sealed letter was included in the envelope in which the lawyer's letter came. It was a short letter.

> Dear Shotu,
>
>   It's no good. I'm off now. I'm leaving ten thousand rupees for you—you must eat well.
>
> Yours,
> Chhobi

I hadn't been able to get my eldest daughter married because of the lack of money. It became possible now.

My second son ran up to me suddenly one day, saying, 'Baba, come see what a beautiful flowering plant has grown in that rubbish heap over there.'

I saw that same exquisite plant that I had seen in Chhobi's garden, the one whose seed Tukra had given me, now chuckling at me with flowers blooming all over it.

The Wall

THE PHONE RANG.

THE PHONE RANG. Shovonlal was surprised. He had been under the impression the phone was out of order. He had been sitting outside in the garden, from where he heard the phone ring. Who was telephoning at this hour? He didn't feel like getting up to answer. He was in fact afraid to enter his room. Who could possibly be telephoning him now? Was there anyone here in this town who might want to? He had got a phone only because of his urge to speak to Sujata. It was through the phone that he had some contact with Sujata once in a while—and that too, never at Sujata's initiative. Only if Shovonlal phoned her did she pick up the receiver to speak to him.

Apparently her mother stood beside her all the time. But at least he got to hear her voice.

This was enough for Shovonlal's satisfaction. It was for Sujata that he had moved to Bihar. The only consolation was that he was near her.

The phone kept ringing.

Suddenly Shovonlal wondered whether it might be Sujata who was calling. But Sujata never telephoned. Besides, she wasn't even here—she had gone to Munger the day before. Was she back already? She had said she would be away for seven or eight days. Maybe she was back.

Shovonlal went in. The phone stopped ringing as soon as he entered. Still, he picked the receiver up.

271

'Hello . . . who is it?'

No response.

'Hello . . . hello . . .?'

No response.

Putting the receiver back in its cradle, he returned to the garden.

He thought about Sujata. He had known her since childhood. They had gone to the same school, passing their matriculation exams together. Then he had gone away to college in Calcutta. He used to write to Sujata from there. Had Sujata kept those letters? She had told him on the phone that she had burnt them. He had some of her letters too. Simple, restrained letters, but even in them, within those unassuming words, Shovonlal used to seek deeper significance. She would never write, 'I am well.' She would write, 'I am in good health.' Shovonlal used to imagine hidden meaning in there. 'I am in good health' meant she wasn't cheerful, she was miserable. Things like that couldn't be written openly. She wrote, 'You must be happy with new friends at college in Calcutta.' She never added, 'You must have forgotten me.' That part remained unsaid, but Shovonlal had no trouble reading between the lines. It was her unarticulated statements that held deeper meaning for him. He felt that what she had not said in so many words had actually been conveyed in a far better manner. To say them would have meant being done with them. Not saying them had placed them in the category of the infinite. They could never end. There was no count of the number of times Shovonlal had read Sujata's short letters, discovering new meaning in them each time. In one of them she had written, 'I hope your studies are going well.' Shovonlal had savoured the silent mockery in it.

He was rapt in his thoughts of Sujata. The incessant

chirping of crickets, the black clouds in the sky with a few stars in the gaps between them, that huge banyan tree amidst the mass of darkness—all of them seemed to be imbued with Sujata. Shovonlal felt that this darkness was just like the darkness that shrouded Sujata's life. This indefatigable call of the cricket—we hear it every day, but do we ever hear the entreaty it holds within? Do we ever try to understand the essence of the message that gives the darkness its heartbeat? Had we understood Sujata? Had we succeeded in honouring her rare displays of joy, just like the handful of stars amidst the clouds? Had we come to know that banyan tree subtly ensconced in the darkness—so alive, its life-force flowing in its arteries and veins, its joy expressed in its leaves and buds, its festive identity camouflaged in its silence? We had not. Just like we had not come to know Sujata either. She had once said, 'Our freedom is on paper only. The insurmountable wall all around us has only changed its colour from time to time, it has not been dismantled. It remains as insurmountable as before.'

After her mother's death, the wall had become still more insurmountable. Sujata's mother liked Shovonlal. She might even have agreed if the subject had been broached. Inter-caste marriages were taking place, after all. But Shovonlal didn't get the opportunity to talk to her. She died of a heart-attack before that. Then Sujata's father was transferred to Bihar. Shovonlal followed him there. It was impossible for him to stay far away from Sujata. He'd had to rent a house in Calcutta too, just like he was doing here. In fact, rents were lower in this town. Shovonlal would have come even if they'd been higher. There was nothing to prevent him, for he had no ties anywhere. Not only did he not have parents or siblings to worry about, he was also not fettered by a job or a profession. He was a poet, a writer. Had it not been for his father's bank balance, he would have been in serious trouble. But he was not. He had moved to this Bihar town six months after Sujata's father.

He had visited them as soon as he arrived, discovering that Sujata's father had married again. And he had married, of all persons, Amita, who was Shovonlal's classmate in college. Not just his classmate, but someone who had fallen in love with him and had wanted to marry him. He had kept her numerous letters for a long time, planning to show them to Sujata. But he hadn't got the chance. And he had burnt the letters. Who would have imagined that the same Amita would end up as Sujata's stepmother and guardian. The first time that he had visited Sujata here at home, he was startled to see Amita. She must have been surprised, too, though she didn't show it. She had simply disappeared inside the house, half-covering her head. As though she didn't know him, had never seen him. Shovonlal hadn't been able to stay there much longer either. He had made the proposal of marriage through a letter to Sujata's father. He still remembered the reply . . .

Dear Shovonlal,

You are highly educated. I did not expect a letter like this from you. I love you like a son, and had expected you to think of Sujata like a sister. Moreover, Sujata is the daughter of a Brahmin, while you're a Vaidya. Vaidyas are trying to establish themselves as Brahmins these days, but society at large has not yet acknowledged that. Sujata's mother—although she is her stepmother, she is a genuine well-wisher—will never agree to this wedding. When I showed her your letter, she said: if you go ahead with this wedding, I will leave home. Sujata's mother said something else too— that given your proclivities, it would be best for you not to visit our house any more. My best wishes are with you. May God give you good sense.

Yours sincerely,
Harananda Chatterjee

The wall was insurmountable indeed. Amita's advent had made it even more so. It did not take Shovonlal long to fathom why Amita had become so concerned about Sujata's well-being. If she had not been there, he would have been able to persuade Harananda. He had met Harananda one day in the field near Jhau Kuthi. Shovonlal used to visit that desolate spot for a walk every day. It was a huge bungalow set in huge grounds, with a tiled roof. There were long verandas and steps all around the house. And enormous grounds. Shovonlal loved the place. He went there for a walk every evening. He had told Sujata on the phone, 'I have no way of visiting you at home. Can't you come to Jhau Kuthi on some pretext? I haven't seen you in so very long a time.' Sujata hadn't agreed. A couple of days later he met Harananda in the field near Jhau Kuthi. Apparently the government wanted to buy the house, and he was there to inspect it on behalf of the government.

'Still here, Shovon?'

'That's right . . .'

'How long are you planning to stay?'

'Permanently.'

Harananda was taken aback by his answer.

'Have you returned to your senses?' he asked.

'I had never lost them,' Shovonlal answered courteously. 'What I had written to you was not in jest. I will wait for Sujata all my life. If you had considered the whole thing more rationally, you would not have been angry with me.'

Harananda looked at him for a while. Then he said, 'I

had asked Sujata, she isn't unwilling. Given the way the wind is blowing in society these days, I would probably have agreed too. But the problem is with Sujata's mother. The letter I wrote you was dictated by her. She has threatened to either leave us or to hang herself if this wedding takes place. What can I do? Let's see if she changes her mind.'

Shovonlal knew she wouldn't. He also knew that at this age Harananda would not go against his young wife's wishes.

Shovonlal kept thinking of Sujata. Suddenly he felt someone standing behind him. He rose to his feet quickly—but no, there was no one there. He sat down again. A cold wind whistled. But still he remained sitting. A little later a dog barked. Shovonlal rose to his feet again, flashing his torch all around. The dog stopped after barking for some time. Then the owls began hooting. They were trying to say something in their rasping voices, which Shovonlal could not understand. He thought they were saying: can't you see, can't you see, can't you see . . .?

What was it that he should see? There was nothing but darkness. He let his tired body slump into his chair. But he couldn't help feeling someone was moving around—he could sense a presence circulating silently, a gentle smell of hair in the wind. Then everything stopped. Shovonlal lay there like an inanimate object.

The phone rang again.

Shovonlal ran into his room quickly.

'Hello, is that Sujata? Sujata, yes, how are you?'

'Come over. We can meet this time . . .'

Sujata's voice seemed to be coming from a very long distance.

'Shall I come to your house?'

'No, come to Jhau Kuthi. You had asked me earlier, I couldn't go then. Now I have. Come . . .'

'How did you get to Jhau Kuthi at this hour of the night?'

'I'll tell you when you come.'

At Jhau Kuthi, Shovon found Sujata sitting on the steps, alone. He hadn't spotted her at first, seeing her only after he lit his torch.

'Sujata?'

'Yes. The walls around me have been broken, I am free—there are no more impediments.'

In the torchlight Shovonlal could see the joy in Sujata's eyes.

'What do you mean, free?'

'I was in Munger. I died a short while ago, buried under a house. Didn't you feel the earthquake here?'

'I did . . .'

'What about you, then . . .?'

'No, I am alive.'

'Then your walls haven't been broken. How shall we be together then?'

Sujata stretched her arms out. Shovonlal tried to take her hand, but couldn't. He only touched air, Sujata was flesh and blood no more.

'How shall we be together then? All my walls have crumbled. But yours haven't. How shall we be together . . .?'

Sujata sobbed.

'Tell me how we can be together. You must tell me, Sujata . . .'

'There. Jump in. Break the walls . . .'

Sujata pointed at the old-fashioned well. Shovonlal was transfixed.

'Come with me . . .'

Sujata advanced slowly towards the well. Shovonlal followed her mechanically.

At the edge, Sujata said, 'Jump in. Break the walls, get rid of the obstacles . . .'

After a few moments, Shovonlal jumped.

Tuni and the VIPs

I'D BEEN VERY BUSY SINCE MORNING. WE HAD HAD SEVERAL VIP visitors at home, and several rounds of discussions—why the country's administration wasn't running properly; how to solve the unemployment problem; whether it was wise to construct a bridge over the Ganges at such high cost; where the flaw in the education system lay; what the use was of raising demands for using Bengali everywhere in a state where the names of most shops and business establishments were in English and where most people could not speak in Bengali without uttering a few expletives in English, and so on. We held serious deliberations on all of these. Everyone consumed their tea and snacks, leaving me gratified. Till ten in the morning, there wasn't even time to draw a breath. The road in front of the house was overrun with cars.

After ten, I let myself down with a sigh of relief into the easy-chair on the veranda, opening the day's Bengali newspaper. But that too was full of news about the country—what projects were being undertaken; who the members of different committees and sub-committees were; what steps the government was taking against corruption, to eradicate poverty and to rid the country of unemployment. Interspersed between these was other news about the country's administrators—whose dog had caught a cold, whose garden had blossoming flowers, whose blood-pressure was fluctuating, who was getting married to whom. Along with these, there was also news and photos of people who were the staple diet of journalists, but then all this was national news too. The newspaper was full of national news. I felt proud of the fact that we kept thinking of our country all the time, working with all our might for its betterment. Suddenly there came the sweetest of calls from the road.

'Dadu . . .'

Turning my head, I saw it was Tuni, dressed in a dirty frock. Its back was in tatters. Her mother worked as a maid, and had worked for some time at our house too. Tuni had addressed me as Dadu ever since. She could frequently be seen dancing down this road. The girl never sauntered. She gathered cow dung from the street, sometimes she accompanied her mother with a basket balanced on her head, sometimes she danced by with a shopping bag. But always smiling, always on the move. Dark-skinned, with hair that cascaded to her shoulders, she had eyes that always shone with laughter. Sometimes she came up to our house and called, 'Dadu!' Sometimes my wife gave her a few titbits to eat.

Tuni waited expectantly. Possibly hoping to get something to nibble on.

I said, 'Wait, have something to eat before you go.'

As soon as I went inside, my wife said, 'What titbits? Your VIPs have eaten up every morsel. There isn't even a biscuit left.'

Going back outside, I told Tuni, 'Come back in the evening, all right?'

Tuni danced off.

She didn't come back in the evening.

It was a trivial incident. But it brought home to me an enormous truth.

Sulekha's Tears

SULEKHA WAS CRYING.

It was late at night, the moonlight spilling outside. In these fantasy surroundings, on a milk-white bed, Sulekha, the alluring sixteen-year-old, lay face down, weeping her heart out. All by herself—there was no one else in the room. A sliver of moonlight had stolen into the room. And after breaking in, it seemed to have stopped short at the sight of the forlorn, tearful beauty. Why these tears?

Love? It certainly could be. On this moonlit night, the flow of tears on the lovely sixteen-year-old's eyelashes could definitely have been caused by love. Love had, after all, knocked on Sulekha's doors once. That was before her marriage. She used to hold the young man she referred to as Arun-da in the highest esteem—in absolute privacy, in her heart. This esteem could have culminated in love in other circumstances, but social mores came in the way. And those mores ensured that it was not Arun-da, but a man named Bipin around whose hairy neck Sulekha had placed her wedding garland.

Maybe at this midnight hour, under the touch of moonlight, it was that Arun-da whom she kept thinking of. Perhaps this offering of tears to her lonely bed was in his memory. But it was also true that she had never conveyed the timid message in the recesses of her heart to Arun-da. The fervour and the desire that had risen in her heart had dwindled gradually after marriage, under the relentless onslaught of time.

Though Bipin wasn't Arun-da, he was Bipin—unadulterated Bipin. And, strange but true, Sulekha had come to love Bipin's Bipin-ness too. She had been happy as well. Was Sulekha's heart so frozen in the past that her eyelashes would suddenly become wet in memory of the near-forgotten Arun-da?

Maybe. The mind of a woman is inscrutable. Her psychology is unfathomable, too. It would not be proper to comment casually on it. As a matter of fact, any observation on the female of the species is a difficult affair. A woman who looks nineteen or twenty turns out after investigation to be thirty-five. Wiser after this error, when one assumes another woman's age to be twenty-five, it is proved that she is not a minute older than fifteen.

Therefore, when it comes to women, it would be idiotic to make snap judgements. It is far more circumspect to hesitate politely. Having drawn this conclusion, I will make no rash statement about Sulekha's tears. I do not claim to know the reason. All I'm doing is to enumerate all the decorous and logically possible causes.

A young woman weeping continuously on her bed in the dead of night—this could also be the first chapter of a detective novel. But we know through reliable sources that it is not the case here. Readers can rest assured on this issue, at least. From what little I know of Bipin and Sulekha, I don't think they have the qualifications to be the hero and heroine of a detective novel.

Leaving aside Arun-da, I can think of another reason for Sulekha's tears. She had had a child some time ago. Her first child. But the child had died a couple of months later of diphtheria. The memory of his face could have elicited tears from the mother in Sulekha. She'd had fits for two days after the incident—we do know that from reliable sources.

Even the sternest of males yearn for getting back, be it momentarily, what has been lost forever. For a soft-hearted woman to feel that way was not surprising in the least. Grieving for one's son could well be the reason for the tears.

But yes, there could be another reason too. Pardon me for raising this immediately after talking of grieving for one's child, but I cannot ignore this admittedly facetious possibility behind Sulekha's tears. A well-known film was being screened at the neighbourhood cinema for the past few days. Local men and women had been going to watch the film in droves, singing its praises in lavish terms. But Bipin was so dour of character that despite repeated requests from Sulekha, he had not taken her to see the film, rejecting her overtures in plain terms. Whatever Sulekha enjoyed frequently turned out to be things that made Bipin angry. This Bipin was certainly a strange man. The last show had ended a short while ago. The road to the cinema went past Sulekha's window. The audience had returned this way in a joyous chorus only a short while earlier. That may have made Sulekha's grief over missing the film boil over. But why was she alone? Where was Bipin? Sensing that matters had reached a head, had he gone off to book seats for the morrow?

Maybe. A man can do anything to mollify his young wife. So what if Bipin was hirsute, he was a human being, after all. Besides, Bipin did love Sulekha from his heart— we have been informed as much by reliable sources. You see, we writers are informed of many things by reliable sources. Therefore it was not impossible for these tears to be related to the film.

Anything was possible. As a matter of fact, the more I thought about it, the more I was convinced that any of these could be the reason for Sulekha's tears. Why, that very evening Sulekha had had an enormous disagreement with Bipin over the colour of a sari's border. Bipin had done exactly what rude males normally do. He had won on the strength of his vocal chords, shouting at the top of his voice. The strategy that soft-spoken women normally used for victory may have been just what Sulekha had adopted—tears.

Whatever the reason, it was all undoubtedly tragic. The lateness of the hour and the captivating power of the moonlight made the tragedy seem even greater. If some sympathetic reader—man or woman—were to term it the greatest tragedy of all, I would not protest. For Sulekha was a young woman. No matter how bewitching the hour was, no matter how flooded the sky was with moonlight, we are probably unanimous that had it been a boy or an old woman weeping, we would not have been as sensitive. On the contrary, we would have been annoyed.

But Sulekha was a young woman. The heart melts accordingly, and it cannot be denied, either, that there is no comfort to be had until the reason for Sulekha's tears has been identified. In fact, the heart is even desirous of penning some cheap verse concerning Arun-da. It keeps saying, 'Why not? On a moonlit night such as this, could not the bud of that adolescent love have bloomed fully? There's the bird singing indefatigably in the distance. The flowers in the garden are dream-laden. There is an ocean of moonlight all around. At such a rare moment, is the thought of Arun-da either impossible or a crime?'

Stopping the speech being delivered by the heart, the door opened suddenly. Bipin entered busily, a shadow of apprehension on his face. He probably hadn't been able to get the tickets. But what was this he was saying!

'Is the toothache better?' Bipin asked.

'No, it's aching very badly.'

'Take this tablet, then. The doctor said he'd come by in the morning, don't cry now. This will make it better, darling.'

The sliver of moonlight chuckled.

See? Didn't I say anything was possible?

A Moment of Greatness

1

WE'LL SEE WHAT SHE DOES NOW.

Standing before the mirror, Gurgan Khan flexed the muscles of his left arm. His real name was not Gurgan Khan, though, it was Kalikanta. But he was well known as Gurgan Khan because, a long time ago, he had played the role of Gurgan Khan in the stage version of *Chandrashekhar*, quickening the heartbeat of many a woman.

At the moment Gurgan Khan was a little over twenty-five years old.

A pointed French-cut beard adorned his face.

A matching moustache, too. Brown in colour.

Sharp eyes.

Hairy chest.

But all this was only an external description.

A zamindar.

A bachelor.

A meat-eater.

2

Gurgan had been attracted to a woman named Srimati.

But Srimati's love flowed in a different direction.

She loved a skeletal young man with no money.

This had become intolerable to Gurgan.

That lily-livered boy instead of him!

All his muscles puckered in hatred.

One slap would send that boy reeling to the floor. But

Gurgan had not tried to send him reeling to the floor. Instead, he had tried various means, in a civilized manner.

In other words, he had serenaded her with his hoarse, deep voice.

Put on dainty shoes.

Used cream on his face.

Even grown sideburns.

But the unmoved Srimati had eyes only for that skeletal stripling.

Gurgan burnt with rage.

3

Srimati had come that evening.

She had stayed a long while, too. But she wasn't really there.

Gurgan could clearly make out that her heart was with that skeletal young man. She had come only because Gurgan had sent for her. You couldn't disobey Gurgan and still survive in this village.

Suddenly, Gurgan lost control.

Pulling a revolver out of a drawer in his desk, he shouted melodramatically . . .

'I want you! Want you today! Want you now! Or else, the revolver . . .'

He was bursting with rage.

Srimati looked at Gurgan, her eyes bright with laughter.

Then she spoke softly. 'Don't shout so. I want to ask you something. What will you do if you can't have me?'

'I will kill Tinu!' Gurgan roared.

Tinu—that skeletal young man.

'All right, give me some time to think it over,' said Srimati. 'I need to be alone. Please go into the other room. Shut the door after you.'

'How long do you need?' asked Gurgan in a voice throbbing with emotion.

'Ten minutes.'

'Fine.'

Gurgan left with faltering steps.

4

We'll see what she does now, Gurgan mused as he stood before the mirror with flexed muscles.

After ten minutes of thought, Srimati had said she would come tonight. A carriage should be sent for her at ten o'clock precisely.

Glancing at the clock, Gurgan saw it was only 9 p.m. There was still an hour to go.

'Ouch!'

It wasn't a mosquito bite.

It was the impatient Gurgan's lovesick groan.

Suddenly, Gurgan found something funny—very funny.

What would happen to that skeletal chap now? Poor fellow!

Poor fellow?

Gurgan gnashed his teeth in rage.

The impudence of that ape!

Gurgan looked at his muscular body in the mirror again.

A gentle smile played on his lips.

5

It was past ten.

The carriage had been dispatched.

Gurgan waited eagerly, pouring cologne on his clean handkerchief.

His state of mind?

To use a metaphor, like a kettle on the boil.

Suddenly a carriage was heard up the road.

The eight hooves of the pair of horses seemed to be dancing a thunderous beat on his heart as they cantered.

The carriage stopped.

She could now be heard climbing up the stairs.

She paused near the curtains, then parted them to enter.

'Srimati!'

Srimati's expression halted Gurgan's surging amour in its tracks.

'I trusted your word and came,' said Srimati tearfully.

'What word have I given you?'

'That you won't hurt Tinu. You won't, will you?'

'No.'

They stood face to face for a few moments.

A few tense moments.

Who knew what happened during those moments?

Suddenly shattering the silence, Gurgan said, 'Go.'

Srimati was astonished.

Then she left.

As soon as she did, Gurgan thought: what have I done? I had her and I let her go.

Who was it that spoke with his voice? Who?

Amazing!

In utter surprise, he listened to the fading sound of hoofbeats.

Moving Pictures

A BEAUTIFUL, WELL-DECORATED ROOM. A YOUNG WOMAN was sewing.

Sewing bored her. She moved to the piano to sing a song. That didn't work either. Eventually she began to arrange flowers in a vase on the table, humming all the while. I was charmed. I wondered whether what lay in my heart would ever get to her.

I learnt that she was particularly bothered right now over two of her numerous suitors. One of them was the son of a rich man, a plump aristocrat. He courted her every day with an array of gifts and a display of teeth. He took her for drives in his car. The young woman's father saw nothing reprehensible in this. For he wanted this plump man as his son-in-law. His departed wife had wanted it too—it was to honour her last wish that this slender beauty had agreed to marry the roly-poly fellow. Who wouldn't want to fulfil their mother's dying wish?

The roly-poly man was a gentleman, quite wealthy, far from ugly and in the pink of health. But . . .

The young woman considered the situation from different perspectives. The 'but' could not be pushed away. Her roly-poly suitor was nothing like the dashing young man who had rescued her the other day just as she was about to be trampled by a horse.

She wanted that nameless young man with all her womanly heart.

But Roly-poly was relentless.

The young woman couldn't tell him off either. Her mother's last wish, after all. She kept recalling her mother's wan expression with the shadow of death looming over it. So she simply could not say anything to Roly-poly.

But that young man. She had found out who he was. He looked after and rode horses for a zamindar. But working with horses or not, he was well educated. From Shakespeare to Galsworthy, he was well versed in literature. He even kept track of Arlene. A star student at the university, he could have been the jewel in the country's crown, but fate had pushed him into looking after horses.

He was both beautiful and handsome. A lively and powerful rebel. Despite his humble profession, he had a dazzling smile on his face, a glittering spark in his eyes.

I was relegated to the back burner.

Between Roly-poly and the brilliant, handsome young man, what room was there for insignificant me? I reflected on the situation, running my fingers over my only asset— my moustache.

Suddenly, things took a turn. The young woman and the young man who looked after horses had already met a few times in secret on the bridge outside town. They had even exchanged kisses one evening. But what happened that day was truly exciting.

It was late at night. The young man arrived on an enormous horse, the brown stallion galloping up, snorting.

As soon as he whistled outside the young woman's house, she came out. For a brief moment, her mother's face swam up before her eyes—but only for a brief moment. The young man pulled her onto his horse effortlessly. And then, they galloped off.

My blood boiled along with the sound of the hoofbeats.

A little later, Roly-poly got wind of affairs. When he realized that the object of his affections had indeed cut through the chains of their courtship and escaped, his expression was a sight to behold. Rejected Roly-poly, desolate Roly-poly, maddened Roly-poly. He was a vision. As soon as he drove out in his car, an old woman showed him the direction in which they had escaped. His huge Rolls-Royce headed down that road. A distraught Roly-poly gripped the steering wheel. Thirty, forty, fifty, he kept accelerating. His hair blew in the wind.

What an edge-of-the-seat chase it was! The horse covered fields, forests, mountains like a comet, Roly-poly chased them at the speed of light. He was about to catch up, when a river appeared in front of them. The horse crossed the river easily with a leap; Roly-poly's Rolls-Royce could not. Letting go of the steering wheel, Roly-poly clutched his head in frustration.

Splash!

Roly-poly had jumped into the water. But he couldn't swim. It was a swift mountain stream. He tried in desperation, not ready to give up easily. Water entered his eyes, his nose, his ears. He was tossed around by the current, almost drowning, but still he wouldn't give up. What superhuman, incredible effort—now this was love. With all his soul, all his might, Roly-poly wanted to get to the other side.

His beloved had been abducted by the assassin, after all.

Roly-poly fought a losing battle. He had lost all sensation, his limbs were exhausted, almost paralysed. He grew limp. Was Roly-poly going to drown?

At that precise moment the young man and the young woman stood on a mountain range on the other side, gazing at the sky as the moon rose through a layer of clouds.

Suddenly the young man noticed someone drowning in

the river below. 'Look, someone's drowning!' he said. 'I must save him.'

'But that's Roly-poly,' said the young woman. The young man was not an ordinary mortal—he was a superman. Smiling, he said, 'I know. Roly-poly it may be, but he's a human being, after all. How can I stand by and watch him drown?' He rode his horse swiftly down the mountain to the river.

A little later, the young man could be seen walking back up the mountain, bearing Roly-poly on his shoulders. Imagine climbing a mountain with that heavy, unconscious man on your shoulders! What torture it was. The young man had the glow of a god on his face, the strength of a giant in his body.

The horse followed them, hypnotized.

Then how the two of them tended to Roly-poly! The young man covered him with the only blanket he had, braving the cold himself.

The young woman said, 'Darling, you are not a man who looks after horses, you are a god.'

'Right you are,' said Roly-poly under his blanket. 'But go to sleep now.'

The young woman dreamt as she slept. Her mother seemed to be saying, 'Marry the most befitting man, my daughter. This is the post-script to my wish.'

Awaking, she spotted a pair of lovebirds kissing on the boughs of a tree. By her side, Roly-poly was already awake. 'You deserve the young man,' he said in a burst of emotion. 'Just help me cross the river. May you be eternally happy.'

'Thank you,' said the young woman. 'I am sure he will help you cross the river. Please wake him up.'

Roly-poly saw the young man close by, asleep. He called but there was no response. He nudged him, but still there was no response. The young man had a high fever, and wasn't conscious any more.

He had no choice but to climb down the mountain by himself. His clothes were still soaked, he was covered in mud, and his expression was crestfallen.

How tragic that downward journey of Roly-poly, the disappointed lover.

The film ended. As I walked back, the strangest feelings assailed my heart. What could I do? I lit the half-smoked cigarette I had tucked behind my ears.

Spot the Fiction

1

RAMLOCHAN SIGHED DEEPLY WHEN HE HEARD IT.

This was the final event of this tale. The series of incidents before this, which had made this last act possible, spanned the history of Ramlochan's entire life. Not only is a meticulous description extremely exhausting, it is also irrelevant. Therefore, let me be as brief as I can.

Although Ramlochan Mitra is of advancing years now, it can indeed be accepted that the spirit of youth had ruled him once. And not merely ruled, but ruled with force. All kinds of artistic fancies used to flower in his mind, thrilling his heart. He used to look upon music, painting, poetry, gastronomy, fashion and so on through the eyes of an artist, and lived his life accordingly. Those who know Ramlochan-babu may be smiling derisively at this claim. That the young man with a headful of curly, flowing locks who, in the Calcutta of the 1880s, spent all his time discussing with friends the thumri, Raphael, the pilaff from Kashmir or the subtlety of silk could have metamorphosed into today's bald, dhoti-clad, emaciated old man was something that had to be seen to be believed. I don't blame those who are laughing at the idea. I will only entreat them to believe that the ugly, foul-mouthed Ramlochan of today was indeed handsome and had the sweetest of tongues once upon a time.

2

The young man that he was back then, Ramlochan-babu
had even sworn to marry the kind of woman who would be
able to satisfy his artistic sensibilities. In short, his bride
would have to be a virtuoso cook, a proficient painter and,
of course, beautiful. Dance was not popular in those days
as an art form. Or else, Ramlochan would undoubtedly
have wanted his bride to be a magnificent danseuse too. Of
course, it could also be stated unequivocally that had he
harboured such a desire, it would have been in vain. For it
was proving difficult enough to find a paragon of the original
qualities that he had been looking for. There weren't all that
many young women who combined the qualities of a
musical genius, an outstanding painter, a superb cook
and an extraordinary beauty. Even if there were, either
Ramlochan could not track them down, or they could
not snare him. In brief, the match desired for just did not
materialize. After some time, left with no options, Ramlochan
had to prune his ambition. He decided that he would marry
any attractive girl who could cook reasonably well. Never
mind if she did not know how to paint—she could always
be taught. But alas, sad as it was, one must acknowledge in
the interests of truth that such a bride was not forthcoming
either. After a prolonged search, Khemankari was finally
unearthed. It was rumoured that the girl could sing
songs from plays, accompanying herself on the harmonium,
and that she was adept in the kitchen too. Khemankari's
relatives and neighbours were unanimous about this
claim. Ramlochan supported this view too, after sampling
her singing as well as her cooking one day. She was not
attractive, however. Ramlochan reflected once more,
and arrived at the conclusion that if he were to refuse to

compromise on his ideals, he would never be able to marry. But since that eventuality was completely ruled out, it would be best to take the plunge with this one in his arms. So he did.

3

I do not know exactly how Ramlochan and Khemankari spent the first few years of their married life together. When, several years later, I did have the opportunity to inquire after him, I discovered that the intervening time had not been unproductive. Six sons and five daughters had lit up the household and given Khemankari arthritis of the hips. One day, Ramlochan disclosed regretfully that all the passions of his youth had now disappeared. Soon after their marriage, he had noticed that the knobs in Khemankari's frame were rickety. Whenever she caught a cold or worked too hard, she developed excruciating pain in her joints, having to take to her bed. Initially he had blamed intangible fate for this. But as Khemankari became more and more afflicted with each child she gave birth to, the reason no longer remained intangible, becoming very tangible indeed. Following the doctor's advice, he blamed himself for this and began behaving with Khemankari accordingly. As long as he was in her presence, he used to behave as guiltily as a thief. In the grips of this disaster, not only did Ramlochan not have the occasion to encounter a suitable demonstration of Khemankari's musical prowess, he also lost his bearings because of a crisis of cooking. As a matter of fact, the latter was now the principal problem of his life. Although she was an invalid, Khemankari was an exponent of the culinary arts. Therefore she could not approve of a mediocre cook. Ramlochan would get hold of a new

cook after much effort, and in a couple of days his
shortcomings would become palpable to Khemankari.
Ramlochan had to acccept the impossibility of overlooking
those shortcomings, promptly dispense with the cook's
services, and go hunting for another. The truth that he
had only surmised while hunting for a wife in his youth was
now something that he was able to believe wholeheartedly—
it was impossible to find perfection in this country.

4

The latest cook was a native of Mithila. Dressed in saffron
robes, with a vermilion mark on his forehead, he had
closely cropped black hair, a very fair complexion and lotus-
shaped eyes that stretched from ear to ear. His appearance
was a sight for sore eyes. But nobody engages a cook for
viewing pleasure. The skill for which they do was one that
was truly unique in this man of pleasing appearance from
Mithila. Sitting down to his meal, Ramlochan was served
rice that resembled mounds of earth, along with inedible
vegetables. One of them had been bruised by the flames,
one by the salt, and the third remained quite uncooked.
Perhaps because he was very hungry, Ramlochan managed
only a few mouthfuls to assuage his hunger. He did not
say anything to Mr Mithila. Having come into contact
with several cooks by now, Ramlochan had concluded that
he would only get himself into trouble by losing his temper.
He rose from his meal with a display of extreme restraint
and told Khemankari in a very controlled voice, 'This cook
isn't much good, you know. He hardly knows how to
cook.' Possibly because she had studied singing, Khemankari
could not speak without jangling. Now, too, she jangled,
'How do you expect to find a new cook every day? You

have to make do with this one. At least he isn't dirty. The last one was a prince of filth. This one keeps things clean and tidy.'

'I see. Never mind, then.'

Ramlochan left fearfully, his anxiety mounted. He fell asleep wondering how he could be delivered from the cooking of this man from Mithila.

5

As soon as he woke up, Ramlochan felt a surge of happiness. A beautiful melody floated into his ears. Someone was humming an alaap in the Bhairavi Raagini in the sweetest of tones. How wonderful! Within Ramlochan's age-beleaguered heart, the music-lover of his younger days woke up too. That self sat up eagerly, compelling Ramlochan to leave his bed forthwith. Stepping outside his room, he saw that the newly hired cook from Mithila was seated at the other end of the corridor, singing the alaap, lost to the world. Thrilled to the core, Ramlochan instantly started an intensely respectful discussion with him. He discovered that the cook was not only a music-lover, but had also devoted himself to taking music lessons. 'That's wonderful,' Ramlochan said, 'you must stay on here with me.' Never mind the quality of the cooking, he thought, how much pleasure the cook's singing would bring. He encouraged the singer.

6

The next day, Khemankari jangled, 'Get rid of that cook instantly. He won't do.'

'Why?' asked Ramlochan, stammering.

'Not only can he not cook, the useless fellow was singing in the kitchen. Get him out of here—right now.'

Ramlochan never opposed Khemankari's decisions. That day, too, he didn't.

He only sighed.

7

His story completed, the writer looked at his wife with a smile. Her eyes danced in merriment. 'As if you've ever had to eat a single meal made by a cook,' she said. 'Didn't you like the mutton tonight?'

Her husband smiled. 'People imagine only what they do not have. It's nice to imagine the exact opposite of one's situation. Will you play that new Behaag Raag you've learnt?'

'Not tonight, it's very late,' she said and suddenly switched off the light.

Foreign Exchange

GOBORDHON WAS A DECENT SORT. PRAMATHA WAS HIS friend. Pramatha's stars were luckier, he had more resources to bank on. He had got a job. Gobordhon had not. Compounding his problems was the fact that he was married, and that his beautiful wife made demands of her husband.

One day, Gobordhon told Pramatha, 'I couldn't even meet a simple wish of hers today. "I haven't had lobster in such a long time," she told me, "get some lobster." I borrowed ten rupees from Jogen to get some. But there was no lobster in the market. Apparently all of it is being sent abroad to earn foreign exchange. Anything of high quality we produce in this country is earning foreign exchange abroad. The best fabric, the best rice, the best fruit—it's all being sold in foreign markets. Our mines have been depleted. Even large frogs are being exported. The best young men and women are going abroad to earn foreign exchange. I had to buy some nondescript fish and explain the mysteries of foreign exchange to my wife. "I can't manage such tiny fish," she said, "the bones stick in my throat." So difficult . . .'

About a month later, Gobordhon came running to Pramatha again, his hair dishevelled, a wild look in his eyes.

'What's wrong?'

'Found my wife missing when I went home. She's left this letter.'

The letter said, 'I'm leaving to earn some foreign exchange too . . .'

'What should I do? Tell the police? Your uncle knows the home minister, doesn't he? Will you ask him for help?'

The Meta-scientist's Story

'AS YOU KNOW I DON'T POSSESS A WATCH OR ANYTHING, ALL I have to depend on is the shadow of the palm tree behind my house. When the shadow moves out of the terrace I can tell the sun has set, it's time to meet friends for the evening. But an amazing thing happened the other day. The shadow simply stood still. Going outside, I discovered the sun was stuck in the sky, not moving . . .'

'Stuck? Not moving?'

'Yes. It simply wouldn't set, it just stayed put in one place. There was a huge commotion everywhere. There are many lotuses in the pond behind our house. Their expressions suggested that they thought the sun was so charmed by them that he was refusing to move on. There were many planes in the sky—the scientists were up there trying to discern the reason. They said on the radio that a team of scientists had apparently spotted the sun's eyes. Another scientist had claimed that this was the outcome of experiments with the gravitational and nuclear forces conducted by some other scientists. Meanwhile, it just wouldn't get dark—all the nightbirds, unable to emerge from their holes, started screaming in protest. People began to blow on their conch shells. The military threatened the sun with their guns and cannons. But the sun remained unmoving. I decided to consult our guru. He was in his personal haze, completely unaware of what the sun was up to. I told him everything. He said, "Why bother with guesswork, why don't you just visit the sun and find out

301

for yourself?" "How will I go?" I said. "Open your mouth," he said and popped in some kind of pill. I swallowed it. "Off you go," he said. And then, it was amazing— you just won't believe it—I did fly into the sky! In a short while, I reached the sun. "What's the matter? Why don't you set?" I asked.

'"I want to watch a film," the sun chuckled. He really had grown a pair of eyes. "You can't watch a film from this distance," I said. "Disguise yourself as a human being and come with me. You'll have to buy a ticket to get in. I'll organize everything, just come with me." As soon as the sun took on the appearance of a human, darkness fell. I bought him a first-class ticket to a very successful film. And then something else happened. In a few minutes the sun started laughing at the top of his voice. Still laughing, he ran out into the street, and was instantly run over by a double-decker bus. There was an uproar, but the body simply couldn't be found. It had been completely pulverized. The next morning, however, the sun rose again. But it wasn't the real sun. The real sun had died. Brahma, the king of the gods, had cobbled together an imitation sun from odds and ends. Don't you see? This sunlight is not warm at all . . . The cold's killing—'

At this point, the friend patted him on the shoulder, saying, 'What a yarn! Come on, roll another joint . . .'

Surama

'YOU? HERE! THIS IS BEYOND MY WILDEST EXPECTATIONS!'

It was indeed Surama who got off a rickshaw. Someone else was with her—in soiled clothes, shrinking into the seat, clearly ill at ease. Surama came up to me with a bag in her hand.

'It's wonderful to have you here! Let's go inside.'

'No, I haven't come to stay. I've come to give this back to you.'

'What is it?'

Surama didn't reply. The fire in her eyes frightened me.

'What's in the bag?'

'The jewellery and money you'd sent me. You're so unscrupulous and shameless, you want to buy me. And only because my husband is a harmless, decent man, has he not given you a thrashing. Here are your things . . .'

Tossing the bag at me, Surama left. She climbed back into the rickshaw. The man in the soiled clothes had a smile on his face.

That Girl

SHE WAS STANDING THERE WHEN I GOT OFF THE TRAM, leaning against a pillar. She greeted me with a smile. I returned the greeting, though I couldn't recognize her. I assumed she was a student of mine. She was quite beautiful. She walked some distance along the pavement. My house was in the lane to the right. Walking in that direction, I looked back after a bit. She was following me. It appeared she wanted to tell me something. I stopped at the entrance to my lane. She smiled at me again, standing by my side. She really was beautiful.

'Is this where you live?'

'Yes.'

'Would you mind if I came home with you?'

I was both surprised and bothered by the question. Still, I was forced to say, 'No, why should I mind? . . . But I don't think I quite know who you are.'

'I know you, though. Don't be so formal with me, please. I am much younger than you are. When you were reading for your BA at Presidency College, I was reading for my Intermediate degree. You were a famous student, everyone knew you, including me.'

'Why do you want to come home with me?'

'Just curiosity, that's all.'

'All right, come along.'

I was unmarried. I lived in a small ground-floor flat. Unlocking the front door, I entered, the girl behind me.

'You can sit on that chair. I need to change . . . A cup of tea?'

'No, thank you.'

I went into the next room. When I came back after having changed my clothes, I saw the girl looking round my room.

'I must commend your taste. Everything here is so beautiful . . . Would you believe me if I told you something?' she asked, turning her head to look at me.

'If it's believable, why shouldn't I?' I said.

'A match had been arranged between us.'

I wasn't prepared for this. 'Really!' I said.

'Yes. My father had sent you a photo of mine. You didn't return it, though. Do you still have it?'

'I had to go abroad suddenly. I'd lost some of my letters then. Maybe yours was among them. I didn't notice.'

'I see. I should go. I just wasted your time, I'm sorry.'

'What are you doing now?'

She was silent for a while. Then she smiled and changed the subject.

'I have a request to make. If you do find the photo, please burn it.'

'Burn it? Why?'

She was silent again.

'We'll see when the time comes,' I said. 'Do have something to eat, I have some excellent biscuits, just a minute . . .'

I went inside to fetch the biscuits. When I came back, she was gone. I was surprised. I hadn't expected such behaviour. The doors were open. I peeped outside, but couldn't see anyone.

But despite her strange behaviour, or perhaps because of it, I rather liked her. I started thinking of her all the time. She wasn't just beautiful, she was mysterious too.

One day, rummaging through some old letters, I did find her photo and her father's letter. I realized I hadn't even opened the envelope. But when I looked at the photo, she didn't seem all that beautiful. Someone seemed to whisper to me, 'Burn that photo. The photographer did a bad job. Burn it.' There was no one there, of course. Just my imagination.

But she took over my mind. I had the photo enlarged and put up on the wall. I expected her to return, if only to collect her photo, but she did not.

I wrote her father a letter too. 'I had had to go abroad suddenly. Hence this delayed response. I like your daughter. May I request you for a visit?'

I expected a response every day. But there was none.

One day, back from college, I found the enlarged photo lying face down on the ground. Splinters of glass were littered on the floor. The original photo was gone.

Her father's letter came a few days later.

Thank you for your letter. I am sorry to inform you that my daughter has died in a bus accident. She used to think a lot about you. She would have been very fortunate to have had you as her husband. But that was not God's will. It's all fate.

Yours sincerely . . .

Female Prototype

1

VERY LATE AT NIGHT.

Under the mosquito net, Sunanda had surrendered herself to a monthly magazine. Next to her, Tamalkanti snored, his arms around a bolster. Although unnecessary, I will mention it nevertheless—they were husband and wife. They had been married for a year, and hadn't had children yet.

This was what Sunanda did every night—that is, take a book to bed and, switching on the bedside lamp, read with sleepless eyes. Tamalkanti, too, did the same thing every night—that is, go to sleep uncomplainingly.

As she flipped through the magazine, Sunanda's eye was caught by a story titled 'Not a Story'. What a strange name. The author's name was missing. Sunanda started reading it. As she read, her heart began to bleed for the woman named Nirmala. Initially she was angry with the young man named Biswanath, but that didn't last long. When Biswanath grabbed Nirmala's hands at the hour of his departure and burst into tears, Sunanda's anger dissipated completely. Biswanath didn't get Nirmala—he got Kadambini. The story in brief:

The young man named Biswanath was visiting his maternal uncle's house during the summer holidays. Having little else to do there, he camped by the nearby pond with the objective of fishing. One day, when he was about to go blind staring fixedly at the float on his fishing rod,

307

something happened. The float sank and, pulling out the hook with a jerk, Biswanath was mightily disconcerted.

'Oh my god!'

Startled, he looked back to see the hook caught on a young woman's dress. Needless to add, the young woman was no one but Nirmala.

That was the beginning.

Thereafter, they exchanged amorous feelings in as many ways as was possible within the bounds of decency, and would have continued to exchange them had Biswanath's uncle not appeared on stage. Smiling indulgently behind his considerable moustache, the uncle dismissed the whole affair as adolescent madness and applied Kadambini as an antidote.

Biswanath stood his ground at first. But what could he do alone? At most he could keep his uncle at bay, but it was beyond him to keep all of society at bay. For Biswanath was a Brahmin while Nirmala was not. Accordingly, he could do nothing but hold Nirmala's hands and sob.

It was a lovely story. Sunanda felt very sad for Nirmala. When she switched off the light to go to sleep, a tear for Nirmala still trembled in her eye. How cruel society was!

2

The next evening, Tamalkanti returned home from the office to discover all hell had broken loose. The poor fellow was a long-distance commuter. Every morning he could barely wake up, have his bath and breakfast and rush to catch the 8.57 local, returning by the 7.42 local at night.

He had never noticed such a transformation in Sunanda before. Her face was long enough to sweep the floor with. As soon as Tamal entered she stood up and, without wasting words, handed him his bucket and towel and headed into the kitchen to get him his tea.

Not a word had been spoken. As he took off his shoes and clothes, Tamal wondered what the matter was.

Sunanda re-entered about five minutes later with a cup of hot tea. Her face was still as long as before.

Sipping his tea, Tamal said, 'You know, they were hawking a hair oil named Tryst with Flowers on the train. They do every day. I'm planning to get a bottle tomorrow. Nice scent, and Mr Mullick was saying it's nice and cooling too.'

Sunanda left the room in silence.

Tamal realized the wind wasn't favourable. But what *was* it! Draining his cup of tea, Tamal went outside to discover Sunanda knitting a half-finished woollen muffler. Smiling, he asked, 'Why so serious tonight! Why such a face? What's the matter?'

Sunanda could contain herself no more. She exploded.

'Why this display of love with me? Go off to your Nirmala, the one whose hand you'd held before getting married and cried, "My heart stays with you Nirmala. Only my body's going to get married. I am going to be sacrificed at the altar of society's heartlessness."'

'Who's Nirmala?' asked Tamal in surprise. 'Have you gone mad?'

Without another word, Sunanda handed the stunned Tamal a copy of the magazine she had been reading and the letter from its editor.

The editor had written:

Dear sir,

Your story titled 'Not a Story' has been published this month. I'm enclosing a copy of the magazine. Please excuse us for the delay in publishing it. We'll be happy to publish more of your stories.

Yours faithfully,
Nrisinghaprasad Talukdar

In a flash, Tamal remembered he had indeed sent the aforementioned story to that magazine two years ago. Since then he had got married, got a job, and got out of literature. He had completely forgotten about the story. What unexpected danger it had plunged him into!

'I did write that story a long time ago,' Tamal stammered. 'So what?'

'Story! But you yourself titled it "Not a Story"!'

Forcing a smile, Tamal said, 'That's just a . . . matter of style . . . don't you see? . . .'

Sunanda did not. She didn't want to, either. If she had Nirmala's address, she'd have checked for herself how beautiful Nirmala was. Whether she was as beautiful as Sunanda's husband had said she was.

Her entire being burned with jealousy. And just a few hours earlier, she had had tears in her eyes at Nirmala's grief.

You and I

I'VE GOT YOUR LETTER. A VERY ANGRY LETTER.

> You'd promised. That you'd give me one—that you'd definitely give me one. I never expected you to break your promise . . .

You'd asked for a short story. But I just couldn't think one up. Big trouble. I was hoping a plot would pop into my head. It didn't. My faithful retainer Arjun turned up. 'Should I clean the old trunk now?' he asked.

'Go ahead,' I said.

There were lots of old letters in there. I'd asked Arjun to throw them away and clear the trunk out.

Arjun brought the trunk and pulled out bundles of letters. I suddenly spotted an old letter from you. That same light blue envelope and violet ink—I couldn't possibly be wrong. Opening it, I read it. This letter, too, was quite an angry one.

> I made the cutlets myself—just for you. I waited till ten o'clock—just for you. But you didn't come. I promise not to invite you again, or to write to you again.

The letter was about three years old.

You've invited me several times since then. Written many letters. In other words, you couldn't keep your promise either. Promises can't always be kept. I'm noting the whole thing down and sending it to you. I don't know if this works as a short story. Or whether you're still angry.

Late One Night

LATE ONE NIGHT, I WOKE UP SUDDENLY.

The silence of the night, the moonlit indigo night sky partly visible through the open window, the slow meandering of a small slice of white cloud through the stars towards Venus. The murmur of leaves.

Suddenly, I felt she hadn't come. She could have, but she hadn't.

I sat up in bed. The distant circular mountain range looked mysterious under the spell of the city of dreams—the as-yet-unstated seemed to be peeping from the other side of the line of sight.

I walked up to the window with slow footsteps.

What!

The two palm trees that daylight had shown as standing at either end of the vast expanse had moved close together—one of them was whispering a secret into the ear of the other.

Suddenly they realized I was staring at them. Instantly they returned to their original positions, at either end of the expanse, like naughty boys. A bird whose name I did not know cried out—it seemed to be laughing. I waited in silence.

Let It Be

ENTERING HER ROOM ON A WHIM, I FOUND RIBBONS OF different colours in a box. Another box next to it, with a plastic lid, held all kinds of beads. Three thick exercise books lay on the shelf. Opening them, I found all of them filled with pictures. One of them had pictures from Walt Disney's toy adventures. Another held colourful pictures of butterflies and birds. And some of dogs. Lovely pictures, all of them. The third had stamps . . .

Calendars hung on two walls. One had a picture of a child in tears, the other, of the Taj Mahal. Books were arranged neatly on the shelf to the left. Most of them were college textbooks, but there were volumes of poetry too—Tagore's *Sanchayita* and *Gitabitan*. The blue table was placed next to the shelf, with the fancy table-lamp on it. The lamp resembled the street lights put up by the municipality in olden days. There was another lamp on the wall. Its paper shade was beautifully decorated with floral patterns. A white switch was suspended by the bedside.

The tiny bed was still covered by a dainty bedspread. There was a shelf next to it. On it stood a small timepiece which had stopped, not having been wound. There was other bric-a-brac next to it—an unusual, squat bottle of perfume, besides hairpins, ribbons and a paperweight made with small seashells. There was another paperweight of glass—dark brown, egg-shaped. Over in the cupboard was a display of dolls. Earthen figures of deities. Bronze-hued figures of young women with pitchers. A farmer couple, the wife carrying a basket on her head; the husband, their son. On the other side, a crane and a bust of Rabindranath, a stylish tray behind it. A lizard and a cockroach near the tray—looking for all the world as though they were alive, but actually earthen figures. A Buddha, a shivalinga, an incense-stand, a photo frame, a bald grinning man with a protruding belly, a wooden dragon, an owl. Directly above that, exquisite figurines of three milkmaids, proudly making their way with their pitchers of milk, swinging their arms.

So many flower vases—of stone, of clay, of glass, of brass, of china. Lacquer artefacts from Rangoon next to them, more flower vases, tins, tea trays. Figures of Buddha in the Chinese style, also in stone from Gaya. A trophy next to it, won in a recitation competition. A couple of photographs of Sri Ramakrishna and Sri Sri Ma. Arrangements of stones from Kanyakumari and of pebbles of different kinds. All kinds of shells and seashells. A multicoloured paper fan folded away in a corner. Lots of other things—small cups, small birds, earthen fruit, a wooden flower vase from Nepal. A figure of Ganesh behind them . . .

Bhutan and Jumbu, the two dogs, lay glumly, their heads on their paws. Where was she?

Just married, my daughter had left them all and gone off with her husband. She didn't need a single one of these any more. She would get new things in her new house for her new household.

Her memories lay everywhere. I was desolate. And yet, let these things be as they were. It hurt, but it was a sweet pain. That sweet pain was all I had left for myself.

The Artist's Indignation

ALTHOUGH MADAN GHOSHAL HAD NEVER WRITTEN A POEM or painted a picture in his life, it wouldn't be wrong to say he was a first-class artist, for he had savoured every moment of life with the joy of an artist. He was unique, too.

He had gambled at the races, not for the money, but to experience the drama and the madness. He had revelled in the company of dancing girls more than once, but had never touched the girls. He had had his daughter married into a very wealthy family. It wasn't the bank-balance that had captivated him, but the son-in-law's shooting skills. The lad had amazing aim with a gun.

It's said that when he had to send a special gift to the groom's family at the time of the marriage, he had told the groom's father, 'I'm a poor man, I cannot offer a gift worthy enough. I am unable to send you anything extraordinary—I am only sending a single item, a sweet. I will be much obliged if you accept it.'

The letter enraged the groom's father, but he had no choice but to be astounded when he beheld the gift—a gigantic paantua, floating in a sea of syrup in an enormous pot. Sixteen men had brought it on their shoulders, using bamboo sticks slipped through hoops attached to the rim.

Inquiries revealed the paantua was 40 kilograms in weight.

Mr Ghoshal had always been a generous donor. The more dramatic the offering, the more the joy he got out of it.

A neighbour burdened with a daughter awaiting marriage

had asked him for some money. The girl was dark, which meant providing additional dowry.

Mr Ghoshal didn't offer any money—he got his son to marry the girl instead.

When he was young, he was said to have had multicoloured pigeons as pets to despatch letters to his new bride. Attaching his letter to the pigeon's throat, he would turn it loose, gazing at the sky as it flew away, his heart oscillating between hope and expectation.

Many such stories were aired about Mr Ghoshal. He had launched all his fancies like multicoloured hot-air balloons on the streams of his whims.

That day Mr Ghoshal was looking in dismay at his neighbour Haren-babu. He didn't know what to say. How could he claim he had no money, and why would Haren believe him if he did? Haren had always got some cash whenever he had asked. But he really had no money today, it was all gone. He maintained an appearance of luxury, but it was all hollow inside. He truly was bankrupt today. And yet Haren had approached him in blind faith.

The artist in Madan Ghoshal was savouring the inherent drama. He was sad for the needy Haren Chakraborty, but he was even sadder for the destitute Madan Ghoshal.

Uncertainty written in his eyes, Haren-babu said again, 'I've come to you with a lot of hope. I'm sure you of all people will not disappoint me. I really am in dire straits, Mr Ghoshal. There's nothing to eat at home, nothing to wear, my son's ill, I don't even have the money to buy medicine for him. The school's disqualified my elder son because I haven't been able to pay the fees. I am at my wits' end. I'm not asking for much, if you could see your way to let me have just fifty rupees . . .'

The penniless Madan Ghoshal hesitated, looking out

through the window in embarrassment. It was indeed unbelievable that he did not have fifty rupees to spare. Still looking out of the window, he fingered the ends of his moustache. The artist Madan Ghoshal waited with bated breath.

Let's see what the bankrupt Madan does.

After an uncomfortable silence, just as the penniless Madan Ghoshal was about to break the news gently, the drama took an unexpected turn.

A clearly poor man in dirty clothes entered, greeting Madan Ghoshal reverently.

'I am your tenant,' he said. 'I'm here to pay the fifty rupees I owe you in tax.'

The bankrupted Madan seemed to have received manna from heaven. Handing the money over to Haren-babu at once, he breathed a sigh of relief.

His mission successful, Haren left with misty eyes and a muffled thank you.

But the artist in Madan was rather disappointed by the problem being resolved in such a prosaic way. 'What is your name?' he asked the subject.

'Janardan Goswami.'

'I've never heard your name before, where do you live?'

'In your kingdom.'

He might have asked a few more questions, but the family priest rushed in, looking shattered.

'Something terrible has happened, sir—the idol has disappeared!'

'What! Are you sure it hasn't fallen or something?'

'No, I've checked carefully.'

'Please check once more.'

The priest left. It was a golden idol of Janardan made by one of his forefathers . . .

The artist in Madan Ghoshal was suddenly electrified by a thought that had occurred to him. The family deity Janardan was not to be found on his throne; the tenant's name was Janardan Goswami. Had Janardan decided to come to the aid of the destitute Madan Ghoshal? . . . He found himself unable to think any more.

His eyes glittered, his lower lip trembled uncontrollably.

Turning, he discovered that Janardan the tenant had left. Running out into the veranda, he looked up and down, but no—he had indeed left.

The priest returned.

He was smiling.

The idol was back. He had discovered the deity seated in his rightful place when he returned.

'I suspect Master Montu must have taken away the idol,' he chuckled. 'He's been hankering after Janardan, he had even asked me for the idol once . . .'

Montu was Madan Ghoshal's grandson, about five years old. The artist in Madan Ghoshal was at the peak of his excitement.

'Send for Madhob the book-keeper,' he ordered.

The book-keeper appeared shortly.

'Madhob, can you check whether we have a tenant named Janardan Goswami? We don't, as far as I recall.'

'Let me check.'

Madhob left.

Madan waited anxiously for the next scene. The drama has been heightened, he kept saying to himself. Now for the climax . . .

Madhob returned. 'Yes sir, we do have a tenant named Janardan Goswami.'

'We do? You're sure?'

'Yes sir. He owes fifty rupees in tax.'

'Did I ask you to check whether there are outstanding payments?' Madan berated him angrily. 'All I asked you to check was whether there *is* someone by that name.'

'There is.'

'You're sure?'

'I am.'

'All right, you may leave now.'

Madan Ghoshal sat down indignantly. The drama's falling flat these days. Inevitably strikes a false note. It's all become so insipid.

The Ghost

1

PEOPLE SAY IT IS ZEUS WHO WIELDS THE THUNDERBOLT. BUT THAT day it became obvious that even the feeble old peon was capable of hurling a thunderbolt. He hurled one at Sushama's head with practised ease, disappearing nonchalantly.

Sushama sat holding the letter in a state of shock.

Prashanta had written . . .

I know my letter will hurt you—but I have no choice but to write. I have tried my best, believe me, but my parents refuse to agree to an inter-caste marriage. It is impossible for me in these circumstances to hurt them by marrying you. I cannot be the cause of such unhappiness to the two people who have made many sacrifices to bring me up. Would my married life be happy without their blessings? What can I do? We are not destined to be together in this life. If there is such a thing as rebirth, and if we are reborn as members of the same caste, and if our memories persist after we're reborn, perhaps we will be together then.

Don't be angry. I cannot explain how I feel. I have no words to express how miserable I am. My only consolation is that this misery is for your sake. Unhappiness takes love to greater heights. If I can, I will meet you in a few days.

Could Zeus's thunderbolt be more lethal?

2

But a thunderbolt even more lethal was being prepared.

It fell two days later.

It was the same feeble, emaciated peon who delivered it.

The letter was brief, but the news was tragic.

Prashanta had committed suicide.

The sky, with the sun in it, began to sway before Sushama's eyes.

3

Sushama was a teacher in a country school.

Her living quarters, available free, were located in one corner of the sprawling school compound. Sushama shared it with another middle-aged schoolteacher, Mrs Bose. They slept in adjoining rooms, a curtained door separating them.

It was late at night.

Suddenly Sushama screamed horribly.

Mrs Bose ran in from the next room in dishevelled condition.

'What's the matter?'

'There was someone at the window!'

Her corpulent chin quivering, Mrs Bose expressed the suspicion that it must be the school secretary's wayward nephew. His behaviour and demeanour had long been a source of annoyance for her. But there was no way to catch him in the act. He was remarkably cunning.

Sushama did not say anything to Mrs Bose.

But she had seen the figure clearly.

It was Prashanta's figure.

Identical!

She couldn't speak.

4

Sushama dragged her bed into Mrs Bose's room to protect herself.

But still there was no respite.

The banyan tree behind the school was clearly visible from Mrs Bose's bedroom. It looked menacingly shaggy at night. Waking up in the middle of the night, Sushama was petrified to see someone perched on a low branch of the tree, swinging his legs. He could be seen clearly in the fading rays of the setting moon.

Prashanta!

Shivering, Sushama shut her eyes.

Another time, it seemed to her that someone was leaning against the railing of the veranda, staring at her.

How hungry the look in his eyes was!

There was dense darkness everywhere.

Mrs Bose was snoring in the next bed. Prashanta's ghostly gaze seemed to penetrate the darkness—like a beam from a torch—to pierce her soul.

Terrified, she closed her eyes and muttered a prayer.

Another evening, she was on her way back after a walk.

As she was about to enter through the gate, he seemed to flash past her, vanishing in the bush beside the gate.

She had loved him so much when he was alive, now she was terrified of him in death.

Every evening, as soon as the sun set, Sushama felt her skin prickle.

5

It was a holiday.

Mrs Bose wasn't in—she had gone home. At night, Sushama considered asking Karuna-didi, another teacher who lived next door, to spend the night with her. But she discovered that while Karuna-didi had no objection, Mentu-didi was vehemently opposed to the idea. She couldn't stay alone.

Helpless, Sushama went to bed with the servant being the only other person in the house.

She woke up in the middle of the night at the touch of someone's hand on her brow.

The touch was ice-cold.

Turning, she discovered him sitting by her side.

Screaming, she fainted.

After some time Sushama opened her eyes.

The ghost himself was splashing water on her face to awaken her.

There was a rattling in Sushama's throat. Something coiled up within her stomach. But the ghost wouldn't relent.

He kept splashing water on her face.

6

Sushama resigned the very next day.

She had no choice.

When she had packed and got into the taxi waiting for her, her face was red with mortification.

'I'm so embarrassed . . .'

'Now that my parents have agreed, do you suppose I'm scared of anyone? I just hope we don't miss the train. I was only testing you, that's all.'

The taxi began to move.

Inspiration

1

THAT DAY, TOO, WHEN HARIRANJAN-BABU DISCOVERED ON his return from the courts that his son Gopal had been flying kites instead of studying, he couldn't control himself any longer, lunging at the boy with his umbrella. Gopal was about to escape, dodging the umbrella thrust at him, when Hariranjan-babu grabbed him. But in a couple of minutes, the new act in their domestic drama—featuring a dishevelled Hariranjan-babu and a tearful Gopal— was interrupted unexpectedly.

A car sounded its horn at the gate. Peeping out, Hariranjan-babu discovered it was his recently appointed boss, the young judge, who had arrived in his car. He worked as a clerk in the office of the judge, who had of late been transferred to this town. Although he was young, he was supposed to be brilliant—he had apparently stood first in his examination. A stern, distant personality, he did not venture out of his home too often, but he had made Hariranjan-babu's acquaintance on his own initiative. This was the judge's third visit to his house.

'Good evening. Is that Gopal I hear crying? What's the matter?'

'Nothing, sir, nothing at all . . .'

'Discipline time?'

The judge climbed on to the veranda.

'He's not at all interested in studies, sir. All he does is fly

324

his kites. Our maid has a son too—the two of them just roam around all day. Not a moment with his books.'

'Indeed.'

His head lowered, Gopal was furiously rubbing his eyes with both his hands. Ruffling his hair, the judge said affectionately, 'And what do you use to give your kite string the sharpest edge?'

Still rubbing his eyes, Gopal answered in a voice tremulous with tears, 'Glue and ground glass.'

'I'm going to teach you another trick . . .'

After a quick glance at the judge from the corner of his eyes, Gopal chuckled and disappeared inside the house in a flash.

'Ma! The judge is here in his car, Ma. What a lovely car, Ma . . .'

'I saw.'

'Will you do me the honour of having a cup of tea, sir?' Hariranjan-babu inquired deferentially. 'May I ask for a cup of tea to be made for you?'

'I've had some tea already. But all right, I don't mind another cup . . .'

Hariranjan-babu quickly offered him a chair with a broken armrest. 'Please take a seat, sir. I'll have the tea ready in a minute.'

Bustling busily, he disappeared inside the house. 'Minu, a cup of tea for the judge! Can you make him a cup quickly? Serve it in the new teapot I bought the other day, all right? Gopal, go borrow a tea-cup from Goju-babu. Use the back door, he mustn't see you.'

2

Tea was over.

The discussion veered round to Gopal's reluctance to

study. Hariranjan-babu said he would have engaged a private tutor for Gopal if he could afford it. That may have helped.

'You can't assume anything,' said the judge with a smile. 'Let me tell you a story. It's a true story, actually. There was a man with two sons. They seemed to have vowed never to study. Their father kept engaging new tutors, kept putting them into new schools, but to no avail. They used to skip classes every day. They'd vanish from sight the moment the subject of private tutors came up. Since their mother spoilt them, their tutors were not allowed to spank them either. Even so, one particular tutor, having reached the end of his tether, had done just that, but without any effect. Their father didn't lack for money. Eventually, he advertised in the newspapers, offering a reward of a hundred rupees—over and above the salary—to anyone who could persuade his sons to study. A young tutor applied. He didn't even bring up the subject of studies at first, keeping the boys occupied with marbles, kites, paper boats and so on. Some time went by. Then the tutor took the boys out for a walk. Evening had just set in. There were one or two stars in the sky. Pointing to one of them, the tutor said, "There's a star."

'"There's another . . ." said the elder of the two boys.

'"How many is that?"

'"Two . . ."

'"And look, there's another. How many now?"

'"Three. Another one over there, sir."

'"How many in all?"

'"Four . . ."

'"There's another one above the tree. So that's four plus one equal to five, right?"

'"Yes sir."

'The younger one hadn't said a word all this while.

'"Dada, he's teaching us sums . . ." he finally alerted his brother.

'He raced off homewards at once. His brother followed him. The tutor left straight away. He was convinced these boys would never amount to anything.'

The judge paused.

'And then?'

'And then the elder son died of cholera a few days later. The younger son became even more spoilt as a result. He didn't even bother to think of studies.'

The judge paused again.

'How will a spoilt child study, sir?' Hariranjan-babu observed, assuming the judge was giving an example of the ill effects of over-indulgence.

'But the spoilt child did start studying seriously one fine day. And began to breeze through his examinations one by one.'

'Really!'

'Yes! You never can tell.'

'Oh yes sir, you're right, of course.'

'All right, I'd better be going now. I was just passing by. All well at home, I hope?'

'Yes sir, thank you.'

The judge left. He had deliberately left his story incomplete. In the rest of the story, the boy had become friends with the nine-year-old girl next door. 'It would be wonderful if you married me, Minu,' he had said to her, away from prying eyes. 'Will you?'

'Why on earth should I marry an ignorant boy like you?' Minu had answered. 'My husband will be a very well-educated man.'

Apparently the boy started studying at once.

The judge hadn't revealed the identity of the boy either.

DAYS AND NIGHTS IN THE FOREST

Sunil Gangopadhyay

Translated by Rani Ray

'He lay flat against the bed of wet earth and fallen leaves and stared at the sky. He felt euphoric, lying totally naked inside the forest. Baring the body had achieved baring of the soul.'

Set in the turbulent 1960s *Days and Nights in the Forest (Aranyer Dinratri)* was the second novel that a young Sunil Gangopadhyay wrote. Largely autobiographical, it is the story of a whimsical, impromptu journey that four city youths— Ashim, Sanjoy, Shekhar and Robi—take into the forests of Palamau.

The four friends blithely imagine that their escapade into the wilderness will distance them from 'civilization' and take them closer to pristine nature. In reality, the solitude and austere majesty of the forest force them to look deeply into themselves and confront their all-too-human follies and 'civilized' foibles in new, unexpected and frightening ways. As they hear the ominous sound of one tree after another being felled, encounter mercenary traders bent on milking the forest for all it is worth, and see the simmering unrest flickering in the eyes of the tribal inhabitants, they are compelled to look well beyond their own time to a plundered and violated world where the forest can never be a pastoral utopia—a world that is, inexorably and inescapably, our own. They return to Calcutta ineffably changed— sadder, older, more introspective.

Days and Nights in the Forest was made into a celebrated film by Satyajit Ray very soon after its publication. Now translated for the first time from the original Bengali into English this prescient and sophisticated novel remains as sharply relevant more than forty years after it was first written.

Fiction
Rs 250

ILLICIT

Dibyendu Palit

Translated by Arunava Sinha

Ashim didn't attract her anymore. She had not realized that she had lost interest in this wooden, mechanical and tedious relationship. Until she met Partha.

Eight years into her marriage to Ashim, responsible and conscientious to a fault, Jeena, an attractive housewife, finds herself drawn to Partha Mukherjee. Stolen glances and clandestine meetings lead to a weekend trip to Puri while Ashim is away on business. At Puri, however, after a night of passion turns violent, Jeena is besieged with doubts about her illicit relationship.

This first-ever translation of Dibyendu Palit's intimate novel explores Jeena's turmoil and brilliantly captures the subtle.

Fiction
Rs 150

Read more in Penguin

THERE WAS NO ONE AT THE BUS STOP

Sirshendu Mukhopadhyay

Translated by Arunava Sinha

'Love was one thing, sin was another—and although it was difficult to tell love from sin, Trina had learnt to identify some of the signs.'

Set in Calcutta in the 1970s, *There Was No One at the Bus Stop* is a powerful exploration of adultery and its overwhelming consequences.

Trina, a married woman, impulsively decides one day to stop living a lie and walks out on her husband, daughter and son, in whose lives she no longer plays a role. But will she be able to sever the bonds and join the man she loves in his home? The man, Debashish, is haunted by his wife's recent suicide and is tormented by the possibility that his young son would rather live away from him.

Through spare prose and searing dialogue, this novel unfolds over twelve hours on a single day. It reveals the often complex reasons that hold human relationships together and the motives that break them apart.

Fiction
Rs 150

Read more in Penguin

IT RAINED ALL NIGHT

Buddhdeva Bose

Translated by Clinton B. Seely

'It's over—it happened—there's nothing more to say. I, Maloti Mukherji, someone's wife, someone else's mother. I did it. Did it with Jayanto. Jayanto wanted me, and I him . . . How did it happen? Easy. In fact I don't know why it didn't happen before—I'm surprised, at my self-restraint, at Jayanto's patience.'

Banned when it was first published in the Bengali in 1967 on charges of obscenity, *It Rained All Night* went on to become a best-seller.

Maloti, an attractive middle-class Bengali girl, marries the bookish college lecturer Nayonangshu only to find him insecure, sexually timid and unable to satisfy her. She discovers passion in the arms of the confident, earthy journalist Jayanto whose love provides her solace from the demands of her wifely duties. Maloti and Jayanto's growing intimacy does not go unnoticed by Nayonangshu, but his pride restrains him from reaching out to his wife.

Bold, explicit and shockingly candid, *It Rained All Night* is an unforgettable tale of desire, adultery, jealousy and love.

Fiction
Rs 150

Read more in Penguin

THE MIDDLEMAN

Sankar

Translated by Arunava Sinha

'A veil had descended on the city. It wasn't very late, but Somnath felt as though the sun had suddenly set on an impenetrable forest, giving way to a dangerous darkness.'

1970s Calcutta. The city is teeming with thousands of young men in search of work. Somnath Banerjee spends his days queuing up at the employment exchange. Unable to find a job despite his qualifications, Somnath decides to go into the order–supply business as a middleman. His ambition drives him to prostitute an innocent girl for a contract that will secure the future of Somnath Enterprises. As Somnath grows from an idealistic young man into a corrupt businessman, the novel becomes a terrifying portrait of the price the city extracts from its youth.

Sankar's *The Middleman* is the moving story of a man torn between who he is and what he wants to be. Stark and disquieting, the novel deftly exposes the decaying values and rampant corruption of a metropolis that is built on broken dreams and morbid reality. The evocative prose and vivid imagery in this first-ever translation successfully capture the textures of the Bengali original.

Satyajit Ray's award winning film *Jana Aranya* (The Middleman) was based on this novel. Ray described it as the only bleak film he ever made.

Fiction
Rs 200

Read more in Penguin

CHOWRINGHEE

Sankar

Translated by Arunava Sinha

'Here, day and night were interchangeable. The immaculately dressed Chowringhee, radiant in her youth, had just stepped on to the floor at the nightclub.'

Set in 1950s Calcutta, Chowringhee is a sprawling saga of the intimate lives of managers, employees and guests at one of Calcutta's largest hotels, the Shahjahan. Shankar, the newest recruit, recounts the stories of several people whose lives come together in the suites, restaurants, bar and backrooms of the hotel. As both observer and participant in the events, he inadvertently peels off the layers of everyday existence to expose the seamy underbelly of unfulfilled desires, broken dreams, callous manipulation and unbidden tragedy. What unfolds is not just the story of individual lives but also the incredible chronicle of a metropolis.

Written by best-selling Bengali author Sankar, Chowringhee was published as a novel in 1962. Predating Arthur Hailey's Hotel by three years, it became an instant hit, spawning translations in major Indian languages, a film and a play. Its larger-than-life characters—the enigmatic manager Marco Polo, the debonair receptionist Sata Bose, the tragic hostess Karabi Guha, among others—soon attained cult status. With its thinly veiled accounts of the private lives of real-life celebrities, and its sympathetic narrative seamlessly weaving the past and the present, it immediately established itself as a popular classic. Available for the first time in English, Chowringhee is as much a dirge as it is a homage to a city and its people.

Fiction
Rs 325